John Adams Vinton, Herman Mann

The Female Review

Life of Deborah Sampson

John Adams Vinton, Herman Mann

The Female Review
Life of Deborah Sampson

ISBN/EAN: 9783337307431

Printed in Europe, USA, Canada, Australia, Japan

Cover: Foto ©Raphael Reischuk / pixelio.de

More available books at **www.hansebooks.com**

THE FEMALE REVIEW

LIFE OF

DEBORAH SAMPSON

THE FEMALE SOLDIER

IN THE

War of the Revolution

WITH

AN INTRODUCTION AND NOTES

BY

JOHN ADAMS VINTON

Boston

J. K. WIGGIN & WM. PARSONS LUNT

M DCCC LXVI

EDITION:

Two hundred and fifty Copies, Small Quarto.
Thirty-five Copies, Royal Quarto.

INTRODUCTION.

THE American Revolution was a great event. Thirteen feeble colonies, scattered along more than a thousand miles of seacoast, and vulnerable at every point, dared to resist the colossal power of one of the oldest and strongest monarchies of the world. Without adequate preparation, without a general government, without a revenue, without a navy, and almost without an army, or the means of keeping an army together, they entered the fearful struggle, and, by the help of God, prevailed. All well-authenticated facts, even the most minute, connected with this great struggle, possess a deep and an enduring interest. Every individual history included in that great drama serves to help out and enlarge our idea of what was then transacted.

Viewed in this light, the story of Deborah Sampson will be found worthy of attentive consideration. It is sufficiently romantic in itself; but, considered as a tale of Revolutionary times, it is entitled to special regard. It affords, to some extent, a picture of those times, and opens before us scenes of trial and hardship, of patriotism and fortitude, that enable us better to conceive of that great conflict.

The general credit of the facts recorded in this volume cannot be shaken. It is sustained by tradition yet freshly existing in

Middleborough and the vicinity; by the Records of the First Baptist Church in that town; by the Resolve of the Legislature of Massachusetts, in 1792; by the Records of the Pension Office of the United States; by the act of Congress, granting her pension to the heirs of Deborah Gannett; by the obituary notice published in the papers after her death; and, lastly, by the list of subscribers to "The Female Review." Many of these subscribers were highly respectable gentlemen, resident in Middleborough, Sharon, Stoughton, Dedham, Walpole, Wrentham, Providence, and other towns in the vicinity. Clergymen, physicians, lawyers, merchants, and other intelligent men, would not have subscribed for such a work, but for its substantial verity.

The story of our heroine has found a place, more or less enlarged, in "Allen's Biographical Dictionary," third edition; in Mrs. Sarah Josepha Hale's "Biography of Distinguished Women;" in Mrs. Elizabeth F. Ellet's "Women of the American Revolution;" and in some other publications.* In several of these volumes, minor inaccuracies may be found; but the main facts have never been called in question.

The editor remembers to have heard of this remarkable case full fifty years ago, in his childhood, when living in Braintree, midway between Boston and Middleborough. He has since made it a subject of careful and prolonged investigation.

The story, concisely told, is as follows: Deborah Sampson left her home in Middleborough, Mass., in May, 1782, being then in her twenty-second year. She assumed the masculine garb; enlisted as a Continental soldier; was mustered into the

---

* Some years ago, as the editor has been informed, a volume made its appearance, professing to give memoirs of eminent colored women, and Deborah Sampson was claimed as one of the number!

service at Worcester ; joined the army at West Point ; performed the duties of a soldier with more than ordinary alertness,
gallantry, and fortitude ; participated in several engagements,
in one of which she was wounded ; though mingling constantly
with men, preserved her purity unsullied ; suffered severe illness in a hospital in Philadelphia, where her sex was discov-
ered ; received an honorable discharge from the army at the
close of the war, and returned to her relatives in Massachusetts.

These facts, and others connected with them, are set forth,
with no inconsiderable amount of what was meant for embellish-
ment, in "The Female Review," a small volume of 258 pages,
12mo., compiled by Herman Mann, and printed for him at Dedham, in 1797. This book has long been out of print, and is now
rarely to be met with. Considered merely as a composition,
this volume does not rank high. The style is pompous and affected, the manner prolix and verbose. Throughout the volume,
there is an evident straining after *effect.* Instead of presenting
a simple narrative, "a round, unvarnished tale," the writer made
a kind of novel, founded, .indeed, on fact, but with additions of
his own. He aimed at weaving a web of gaudy colors, which
should strike strongly on the fancy of his readers. He introduces a great deal of extraneous matter, which serves only to
fill out his pages, without at all helping forward the story. He
proceeds with too little caution in his statements of fact, following, sometimes, the practice of Voltaire, who, when asked at
the table of Frederick II. how he could allow himself in statements so variant from the truth, replied, " I write history to be
read, not to be believed." This volume, however, has furnished,
in great part, the material which has been used by most of the

writers who have hitherto attempted to give an account of Deborah Sampson; and there can be no doubt that the well-authenticated facts of the case will repay a thoughtful consideration.

To disengage what is true from what is of doubtful authority; to separate the real from the fictitious; to disentangle the facts from the fancies with which they have been mingled, — is the design of the present edition. But to draw the line accurately between the two has been found no easy matter.

It appears that the heroine, ten or twelve years after her return from the army, became acquainted with Mr. Mann, the original author; and some materials for the narrative were gathered, principally from her own lips, but in part also from some scattered memoranda of hers, from conversation with her relatives, from officers who knew her in the army, and from other sources. A journal, which she had constantly kept while in the service, was unfortunately lost with her trunk, in the passage by water, which she attempted to make, from Elizabethtown, N.J., to New York, in a heavy gale, as she states, while on her return from a Western tour to the headquarters of the American army, in October, 1783. It was necessary, therefore, to rely chiefly on her memory; and, in regard to all important facts, this could hardly fail.

It seems, however, that both the writer and the heroine of "The Female Review," after the issue of that volume, became dissatisfied therewith: it seemed, even to them, a crude and imperfect sketch. Many marks of carelessness, and of a want of due preparation, were too clearly seen; some things were untruly stated, and a general looseness of style and of sentiment was apparent. The resolution was formed, therefore, to prepare

a worthier and more comely volume. The writer had now become better acquainted with his subject, and possessed of an
ampler stock of materials. The book was therefore rewritten,
with much enlargement in respect to facts, obtained from the
heroine herself. The memoir, thus revised, is said to have been
carefully examined and fully approved by Mrs. Gannett, who
exacted the promise, however, that it should not be printed
till after her decease. She died in 1827, and the author was
thus relieved of the obligation. But a severe and protracted
illness, which resulted in the author's own death in 1833, prevented his fully completing the work.

The manuscript, after the author's death, fell into the hands of
his son, to whom it appeared capable of still further improvement. The younger Mann, therefore, took pains to remodel it
thoroughly, omitting much of the extraneous matter, and making the heroine throughout to speak in the first person ; thus
giving more animation and directness to the narrative. The
dramatic style is employed wherever there is room for it. We
cannot avoid the impression that the MS. is dramatic throughout, — quite as much so as the historical plays of Shakspeare,
while there can be no comparison in respect to artistic merit.
The manuscript memoir, or novel, — whichever the reader
pleases, — was completed in 1850. It is a decided advance
on "The Female Review," in style and manner, though still
abounding in superfluous phrases, and containing much irrelevant matter. It exists only in a manuscript of 336 pages, and
will probably never appear in print. All that is valuable in it
has been incorporated in the present volume. The constant use
of this document by the editor is an advantage which has not
been enjoyed hitherto by any one who has given to the public

an account of Deborah Sampson. He has thus been enabled to present a more full and, he trusts, a better history of this remarkable woman.

As the language of the manuscript memoir is susceptible of much improvement, I have not confined myself to the exact words. Though Deborah is ostensibly the speaker, the words are Mr. Mann's. He speaks in her behalf, as her representative and interpreter. From the language employed by him, I have felt at liberty to depart whenever I thought the form of expression could be improved; dropping expletives, throwing off superfluous phrases, and changing one word for a better; new modelling whole sentences and paragraphs for the sake of clearer and fuller expression; but never changing the idea. Even if I had Deborah's own words before me, the practice of good writers, in similar cases, would have warranted a careful and thorough revision.

The original work, however, — "The Female Review," — is, in the following pages, literally and fully reprinted, that subscribers may possess the text as first printed in 1797. Copious notes are added wherever it seemed necessary, for the purpose of correcting erroneous statements, or presenting additional information.

From the nature of the case, there could be no other evidence in regard to most of the facts herein reported, but the statements of the heroine herself. Whether these statements can always be trusted, or whether, indeed, she ever made some of them, the reader must judge. The main thread of the story will undoubtedly hold true, confirmed as it is by so many concurring testimonies. But for some of the details of "The Female Review," and of the MS. memoir, an easy faith is required.

Some years ago, my friend, Rev. Stillman Pratt of Middle-borough, became interested in the story of Deborah Sampson, and collected in that vicinity some facts not before published, which, with other matter copied, without material alteration, from " The Female Review," he gave to the world in his paper, " The Middleborough Gazette." The additional information thus obtained will be found in the ensuing pages. In several in-stances, it is at variance with statements purporting to have been received from the heroine.

The time when Deborah Sampson enlisted into the army has been untruly stated. Mrs. Ellet, in her " Women of the Revo-lution," says she enlisted in October, 1778, when eighteen years of age. This statement is copied by Dr. Allen, in his " Bio-graphical Dictionary," third edition. It is manifestly erroneous, for reasons which will soon appear. " The Female Review," and Rev. Mr. Pratt, who here copies from it, state that she enlisted in April, 1781. The MS. memoir, of which mention has already been made, repeats the same statement. It is sustained by the following document, which has just been obtained from the Pen-sion Office in Washington. It is a declaration made by Mrs. Gannett, under oath, at the time when she relinquished her in-valid pension, and received the benefit of the Act of Congress, passed March 18, 1818.

" UNITED STATES :
    " *Massachusetts District.*
            " Deborah Gannett of Sharon, in the county of Norfolk, and district of Massachusetts, a resident and native of the United States, and applicant for a pension from the United States, under an act of Congress entitled, ' An Act to provide for certain persons engaged

in the land and naval service of the United States in the Revolutionary War,' maketh oath that she served as a private soldier, under the name of Robert Shurtleff, in the war of the Revolution, upwards of two years, in manner following, viz.: Enlisted in April, 1781, in the company commanded by Captain George Webb, in the Massachusetts regiment commanded by Colonel Shepherd, and afterwards by Colonel Henry Jackson, and served in said corps in Massachusetts and New York until November, 1783, when she was honorably discharged in writing, which discharge is lost. During the time of her service, she was at the capture of Lord Cornwallis, was wounded at Tarrytown, and now receives a pension from the United States, which pension she hereby relinquishes. She is in such reduced circumstances as to require the aid of her country for her support.

"DEBORAH GANNETT.

"MASSACHUSETTS DISTRICT, Sept. 14, 1818."

The foregoing was copied, Feb. 21, 1866, from the original, in the Pension Office in Washington.

At a later period, Mrs. Gannett applied to Congress for further aid, in a petition of which the following is a copy : —

" *To the Hon. Senate and House of Representatives*
in Congress assembled.

" The petition of Deborah Gannett of Sharon, in the county of Norfolk, and Commonwealth of Massachusetts, Humbly shews, That she served as a soldier in the Army of the United States, during the Revolutionary War ; that she was wounded while in the service ; and that while others were on the list of pensioners, and received their pensions soon after the termination of the war, she was not on the list of pensioners until the first of January, 1803, owing to the great disadvantage she was under to procure sufficient credentials which were necessary to lay before Congress. She therefore prays that Congress would allow her at the rate of four dollars per month from the time that others in similar situations received their pensions, up to the first day of January, 1803. And as in duty bound will ever pray.

"DEBORAH GANNETT.

"SHARON, January 25, 1820."

This petition was forwarded to Washington, to the care of Hon. Marcus Morton, then a representative in Congress from Massachusetts. As appears by an indorsement thereon, it was referred, March 28, 1820, to the Committee on Pensions and Revolutionary Claims. March 31, 1820, it was considered, but not allowed. The original petition is now before me.

The following document was furnished on application from the editor : —

"DEPARTMENT OF THE INTERIOR,

Pension Office, February 13, 1866.

"SIR, — In the matter of Deborah Gannett, about which you make certain inquiries, I have to state, that, on the 11th of March, 1805, she was allowed a pension of four dollars per month, as an invalid soldier of the war of the Revolution. Her pension commenced January 1, 1803. The name of the pensioner was inscribed upon the Massachusetts Invalid Pension Roll. In 1816, her pension was increased to six dollars and forty cents per month. On the 18th of March, 1818, Congress passed an Act, granting pensions of eight dollars per month to those soldiers who served, continuously, nine months and longer in the Continental line, and who were in need of the assistance of the country for support by reason of reduced circumstances. No person who was in the receipt of a pension could receive the benefit of this Act, unless he relinquished the pension he was receiving under former acts. In 1819, Deborah Gannett relinquished her Invalid Pension, and was pensioner under said Act of the 18th of March, 1818, at the rate of

3

eight dollars per month, and drew said pension of eight dollars per month until March 4, 1827. She died in 1827. The papers upon which she was allowed her Invalid Pension were burned in 1814, when the War Office was burned by the British troops. The nature of her disability is not known, further than that she was severely wounded at Tarrytown. The soldier enlisted under the name of Robert Shertliff, in April, 1781, under Captain George Webb, in a regiment of the Massachusetts Continental line, commanded by Colonel Shepherd, and afterwards by Colonel Henry Jackson, and served until November, 1783, when she was honorably discharged. She was at the capture of Cornwallis.

"Benjamin Gannett, the husband of the soldier, survived her as a widower, until 1837, when he died. On the 7th of July, 1838, Congress passed an Act, a Special Act (see Statutes at Large, vol. 6, page 735), directing the Secretary of the Treasury to pay to the heirs of the soldier the sum of four hundred and sixty-six dollars and sixty-six cents, being at the rate of a pension of eighty dollars per annum from the 4th of March, 1831, to the 4th of January, 1837.

"As this amount of four hundred and sixty-six dollars and sixty-six cents was paid at the Treasury, I am unable to state to whom, or when, it was paid. The foregoing embraces the information afforded by the files of this office, and, it is believed, every allowance made by law to Deborah Gannett, or her heirs.

"I am yours, very respectfully,

"JOSEPH H. BARRETT, *Commissioner.*"

Subjoined is a letter from the Secretary of War, in 1805, at the time of placing her name on the Invalid Pension Roll. The original, and also the original of the document which will immediately follow, are now in the possession of Mr. Jeremiah Colburn, of this city, who has kindly permitted the use of them by the editor: —

"WAR DEPARTMENT, 11 March, 1805.

"SIR, — You are hereby apprised that Deborah Gannett, who served as a soldier in the Army of the United States, during the late Revolutionary War, and who was severely wounded therein, has this day been placed on the Pension List of the United States, at the rate of four dollars per month, to commence on the first day of January, 1803. You will be pleased to enter her name on your books, and pay her, or her legally authorized attorney, on application, accordingly.

"I am, sir, very respectfully,

"Your ob't servant,

"H. DEARBORN.

"BENJAMIN AUSTIN, JUN., ESQ., *Boston.*"

Here is the first receipt given by Mrs. Gannett for her pension : —

"COMMISSIONER'S OFFICE, April 10, 1805.

"No. 12.

"Received of Benjamin Austin, jun., Agent for paying Invalid Pensioners belonging to the State of Massachusetts, One hundred and four dollars, 53½ cents, being for 26 months' and 4 days' Pension due to Deborah Gannett, from the first day of January, 1803, to the fourth day of March, 1805 ; for which I have signed duplicate Receipts.

"DEBORAH GANNETT.

"*Dollars* 104.53½."

The following is the Special Act of Congress referred to in the foregoing communication from the Pension Office : —

"An Act for the relief of the heirs of Deborah Gannett, a soldier of the Revolution, deceased :

"Be it enacted, &c., That the Secretary of the Treasury be, and he is hereby, directed to pay, out of any money not otherwise appropriated, to the heirs of Deborah Gannett, a revolutionary soldier, and late the wife of Benjamin Gannett of Sharon, in the State of Massachusetts, now deceased, the sum of four hundred and sixty-six dollars and sixty-six cents, being an equivalent for a full pension of eighty dollars per annum, from the fourth day of March, 1831, to the decease of Benjamin Gannett, in January, 1837, as granted in certain cases to the widows of revolutionary soldiers by the Act passed the fourth day of July, 1836, entitled an Act granting half pay to widows or orphans where their husbands or fathers have died of wounds received in the military service of the United States, and for other purposes.

"Approved July 7, 1838."

The subjoined Report of the Committee on Revolutionary Pensions, taken from Reports of Committees, Twenty-fifth Congress, 2d Session, Vol. I., No. 172, January 31, 1837, adds some facts not elsewhere stated.

Mr. Wardwell, from the Committee on Revolutionary Pensions, made the following Report:—

"The Committee on Revolutionary Pensions, to which was referred the petition of Benjamin Gannett of Sharon, State of Massachusetts, report:—

"That the petitioner represents that he is the surviving husband of Deborah Gannett, to whom he was lawfully married on the 7th day of April, 1784; that she died on the 29th of April, 1827. He also states, that, in the early part of her life, the said Deborah enlisted as a soldier in the army of the Revolution, under the assumed name of Robert Shurtleff, where she faithfully served her country three years, and was honorably discharged in November, 1783; that, on account of a wound received in the service, she received a pension as an invalid, until the passage of the Act of 18th March, 1818; and that she received a full pension under the Act until her decease. The petitioner further states, that the effects of the wound which she received followed her through life, and probably hastened her death. The petitioner represents himself to be eighty-three years of age, infirm in health, and in indigent circumstances. He states also that he has two daughters dependent on charity for support. The petitioner prays that he may receive the amount of the pension of his wife, from the time of her decease, and that it may be continued to him till his death.

"It appears, from a letter received from the Commissioner of Pensions, that Deborah Gannett, deceased, was placed on the Massachusetts roll of invalid pensioners, at $48 per annum, which was afterwards increased to $76.80 per annum. This she relinquished, in 1818, for the benefit of the Act of March 18, 1818. She was placed, under that law, at the rate of eight dollars per month, from the 14th September, 1818, which she received up to the 4th March, 1827. It further appears, from said letter, that the papers containing evidence upon which the original pension was granted were burned in 1814, when the British troops invaded Washington, and destroyed the War Office, with its contents.

"On the 14th September, 1818, the said Deborah made her declaration, under oath, that she served as a private soldier, under the name of Robert Shurtleff, in the war of the Revolution, upwards of two years, in manner following: Enlisted, in April, 1781, in a company commanded by Captain George Webb, in the Massachusetts regiment commanded by Colonel Shepherd, and afterwards by Colonel Henry Jackson; that she served in Massachusetts and New York until November, 1783, when she was honorably discharged in writing, which discharge she had lost. She was at the capture of Cornwallis, was wounded at Tarrytown, and, up to the date of her declaration, she received a pension therefor.

"P. Parson testifies, under oath, that she lived in the family of Benjamin Gannett more than forty-six years after he married Deborah Sampson; that she well knew that said Deborah was unable to perform any labor a great part of the time, in consequence of a wound she received, while in the American army, from a musket-ball lodged in her body, which was never extracted. She also states that she saw Benjamin Gannett married to Deborah Sampson at his father's house in Sharon.

"Benjamin Rhoad and Jeremiah Gould, the selectmen of the town of
Sharon, in the State of Massachusetts, certify that they are acquainted
with Benjamin Gannett, now living in said Sharon; that he is a man of
upwards of eighty years of age; that he is destitute of property; that he
has been an industrious man; that he was the husband of the late Deborah Gannett, deceased, who for a time received a pension from the
United States for her military services during the Revolutionary War.

"William Ellis, formerly a Senator in Congress, in a letter to the
Hon. William Jackson, now a Representative in Congress, states that
said Gannett has been a very upright, hard-laboring man; has brought
up a large family, and is a poor man. He further states, that he has
long since been credibly informed that said Gannett had been subjected
to heavy expenses for medical aid for his wife, the said Deborah, for
twenty years or more, and before she received a pension under the Act
of 1818, on account of wounds she received in the United States service.

"There are other certificates among the papers in this case, showing
the physician's bill alone, for attendance on the said Deborah, to be
more than six hundred dollars.

"The Committee are aware that there is no Act of Congress which
provides for any case like the present. The said Gannett was married
after the termination of the war of the Revolution, and therefore does
not come within the spirit of the third section of the Act of 4th July,
1836, granting pensions to widows in certain cases; and, were there
nothing peculiar in this application which distinguishes it from all other
applications for pensions, the Committee would at once reject the claim.
But they believe they are warranted in saying that the whole history of
the American Revolution records no case like this, and 'furnishes no
other similar example of female heroism, fidelity, and courage.' The
petitioner does not allege that he served in the war of the Revolution,
and it does not appear by any evidence in the case that such was the
fact. It is not, however, to be presumed that a female who took up
arms in defence of her country, who served as a common soldier for

nearly three years, and fought and bled for human liberty, would, immediately after the termination of the war, connect herself for life with a
tory or a traitor. He, indeed, was honored much by being the husband
of such a wife ; and as he has proved himself worthy of her, as he has
sustained her through a long life of sickness and suffering, and as that
sickness and suffering were occasioned by the wounds she received, and
the hardships she endured in defence of the country ; and as there cannot be a parallel case in all time to come, the Committee do not hesi-
tate to grant relief.

"They report a bill granting to the petitioner a pension of $80 per
year from the 4th day of March, 1831, for and during his natural life."

The foregoing documents seem to prove conclusively that
Deborah Sampson enlisted in the army in the month of April,
1781. The following documents prove as conclusively that she
did not enlist till May, 1782. The reader will take notice that
the preceding papers are all of a much later date than those that
follow ; and he will naturally be induced to ask why the statement that the enlistment was in April, 1781, was not inserted in
so important a document as that which we shall now copy, and
which was made when the facts of the case were so recent.

In January, 1792, Deborah Gannett, formerly Deborah Sampson, signed a petition to the Legislature of Massachusetts, of
which the following is an exact copy : —

"*To His Excellency the Governor, the Honourable Senate, and the Honourable Houſe of Repreſentatives, in General Court aſſembled, this Eleventh
day of January* 1792.

"The Memorial of Deborah Gannet
Humbly Sheweth, that your Memorialiſt from Zeal for the good of her
Country was induc'd, and by the name of Robert Shirtliff did, on May
20, 1782, Inliſt as a Soldier in the Continental Service, for Three Years,

into the 4th Regiment, Col? Shepard's, (afterwards Col? Jackfon's) in Capt George Webbs Compy. & was mufter'd at Worcefter, by Capt Eliphalet Thorp of Dedham, the 23^d of the fame Month, & went to the Camp, under the Command of Sergeant Gambel, & was conftant & faithful in doing Duty, with other Soldiers, & was engag'd with the Enemy at Tarry Town New York, & was wounded there by the Enemy, & continued in Service untill difcharg'd, by General Knox at Weft Point October 25, 1783. – – – – – Your Memorialift has made fome Application to receive pay for her fervices in the Army, but being a Female, & not knowing the proper fteps to be taken to get pay for her fervices, has hitherto not receiv'd one farthing for her fervices: whether it has been occafion'd by the fault of Officers in making up the Rolls, or whether Effrican Hamlin paymafter to the 4th regiment, has carried off the papers, &c. your Memorialift cannot fay: but your Memorialift prays this Honourable Court to confider the Juftnefs of her Claim, & Grant· her pay as a good foldier; and your Memorialift as in Duty bound fhall ever pray."

Deborah Gannett

The foregoing petition was presented to the House of Representatives, and by them referred to a committee, consisting of Dr. William Eustis of Boston (afterwards Governor), Benjamin Hitchborn of Dorchester, and James Sproat of Middleborough. This Committee reported favorably on the petition, and consequently the following Resolve was passed: —

"Commonwealth of Maffachufetts:

Houfe of Reprefentatives, Jan. 19th 1792.

" On the petition of Deborah Gannet, praying compenfation for fervices performed in the late Army of the United States.

" Whereas it appears to this Court that the faid Deborah Gannet inlifted, under the name of Robert Shirtliff, in Captⁿ Webb's company, in the 4ᵗʰ Maffachufetts Regiment on May 20, 1782, and did actually perform the duty of a foldier in the late Army of the United States to the 23ᵈ day of October 1783, for which fhe has received no compenfation :

"And whereas it further appears that the faid Deborah exhibited an extraordinary inftance of female heroifm by difcharging the duties of a faithful, gallant foldier, and at the fame time preferving the virtue & chaftity of her fex unfufpected and unblemifhed, & was difcharged from the fervice with a fair & honorable character.   Therefore —

"Resolved, That the Treafurer of this Commonwealth be and he hereby is directed to iffue his note to the faid Deborah for the fum of thirty-four pounds, bearing intereft from October 23, 1783.

"Sent up for Concurrence.   "D. COBB, Speaker.
"In Senate, Janʸ 20, 1792.   Read and concurred.
                                   "SAMᴸ PHILLIPS, President.

Approv'd

John Hancock

Connected with the foregoing papers is the following : —

                                   "Boston, Augᵗ 1, 1786.
"To whom it may concern.

"Thefe may Certify that Robert Shurtliff was a foldier in my Regiment in the Continental army for the town of Uxbridge in the Commonwealth of Maffachufetts & was inlifted for the term of three years : — that he had the confidence of his officers and did his duty as a faithful and good foldier, and was honorably difcharged the army of the United States.   "HENRY JACKSON, late Col.
                                          in the American Army.

"A true copy of the original delivered faid Shurtliff.
      "Attest.   "JOHN AVERY Junᴿ Sec'y."
      4

The subjoined certificate accompanies the preceding papers : —

"DEDHAM, *Decem.* 10, 1791.

"This Certifies that Mrs. Deborah Gannet inlifted as a foldier on May yᵉ 20ᵗʰ 1782 for three years and was Mufter'd yᵉ 23ᵈ of yᵉ Same Month at Worcefter and fent on to Camp foon after and as I have been inform'd did the Duty of a Good Soldier

"Pᵗ ELIPHᵀ THORP, *Capᵗ 7ᵗʰ M. Regᵗ M. Mafter*

" N. B.   Robert Shirtlief was yᵉ Name by which Mʳˢ Gannet inlifted and Mufterᵈ"

The four documents immediately preceding are on file in the office of the Secretary of the Commonwealth of Massachusetts, and were copied exactly by the editor from the originals.   They are all in one fold, and are endorsed —

"Refolve on the petition of Deborah Gannet, granting her £34 for fervices in the late Continental Army.   Janʸ 20, 1792."

The sum granted, £34, was equivalent to one hundred dollars, and a small fraction over.

In reference to these documents, a strict regard to truth compels us to offer the following observations : —

1. Deborah Gannett, formerly Sampson, the heroine of our story, in presenting to the Legislature a petition for compensation as a soldier, must have made the utmost of her case.   If she had been a soldier in 1778, or in 1781, and especially if she had been a sharer in the glorious campaign which ended in the surrender of Cornwallis, she would doubtless have said so ; and, if such were the fact, she could easily have proved it.   But the petition of 1792 says nothing of this sort.

2. As we know from her own statement in this petition that

she enlisted in May, 1782, it is scarcely possible that she could have enlisted in 1781, because, in that case, she must have enlisted for one year only. But the practice of short enlistments, which had nearly proved fatal to the American cause in the autumn and winter of 1776, had, in 1781, long been abandoned. Moreover, it appears, from the "Continental Army Books,"* in the office of the Secretary of the Commonwealth, that all the men in Colonel Shepard's regiment, as well as in the other regiments of the Massachusetts line, were enlisted "for three years, or during the war."

3. She could not have enlisted in 1778, as Mrs. Ellet affirms, because, in that case, the "Continental Army Books," just mentioned, would contain the name of Robert Shirtliff. But they do not contain it. The name of Robert Shirtliff appears in the " List of Final Settlement," a volume in the office of the said Secretary, containing the names of the soldiers who were discharged in 1783. Opposite to his name is number 40066, referring to documents sent to the War Office at Washington, and destroyed when the War Office was burned in 1814.

4. Though the petition of Mrs. Gannett affirms that she enlisted for three years, and though the same statement is made in the certificates of Colonel Jackson and Captain Thorp, yet it does not follow that she *served* three years. She says that she was discharged in October, 1783. Her actual service, therefore, if we may believe her statement in the petition of 1792, was limited to one year and five months.

5. Some of the statements, both of "The Female Review" and of the MS. memoir, seem incredible. In both of these docu-

* They contain the names of all who served in the Massachusetts reg-   iments from 1777 to 1780, and the amounts due them respectively.

ments, especially in the latter, we are conducted, with great fullness of detail, through the campaign of 1781; the siege of Yorktown; the hard work in the trenches; the taking of two formidable British redoubts by storming parties; and the final surrender of the hostile forces: and Deborah Sampson, we are assured, was a sharer in these stirring scenes. Had she forgotten her part in those memorable transactions when she presented her petition to the Legislature of Massachusetts, only ten years afterwards?   .

Further to confirm what we have now said, we offer an extract from the Records of the First Baptist Church in Middleborough; of which Church, as appears by those Records, Deborah was received a member in November, 1780:—

"Sept. 3, 1782.   The Church took action as follows:

"The Church confider'd the cafe of Deborah Sampfon, a member of this Church, who laft Spring was accufed of dreffing in men's clothes, and enlifting as a Soldier in the Army, and altho fhe was not convicted, yet was ftrongly fufpected of being guilty, and for fome time before behaved verry loofe and unchriftian like, and at laft left our parts in a suden maner, and it is not known among us where fhe is gone, and after confiderable difcourfe, it appeard that as feveral bretheren had labour'd with her before fhe went away, without obtaining fatiffaction, concluded it is the Church's duty to withdraw fellowfhip untill fhe returns and makes Chriftian fatisfaction."

A vote to "withdraw fellowship" is equivalent to a vote of excommunication.   It does not appear that Deborah was ever restored to the communion of that church, or of any other.

From this extract it seems evident that she did not "dress in men's clothes, and enlist as a soldier in the army," till the spring of 1782. If so, she did not enlist till the war was substantially over. The surrender of Cornwallis, in October, 1781, virtually closed the contest. No military operations, of any importance, were, after that event, undertaken on either side.

It must be confessed, however, that the case is not wholly free from difficulty. The heroine of the story, who best knew the facts of the case, has given her testimony on both sides of the question. In January, 1792, she makes a positive statement that she enlisted in May, 1782, and is altogether silent about her being present at the siege of Yorktown. In September, 1818, twenty-six years later, she affirms, under oath, that she enlisted in April, 1781, and was at the capture of Cornwallis (see p. xvi.). The statements subsequently made in the document obtained from the Pension Office (p. xix.), and in the Report of the Committee on Revolutionary Pensions (p. xxi), that her enlistment was in April, 1781, are evidently derived only from her declaration, in 1818, just mentioned, which was clearly an *after-thought*. The reader is left to judge as to the probabilities of the case.

After making all needful allowance for these conflicting statements, and for the exaggerations of the book before us, enough remains to invest the story of Deborah Sampson with a strange and a peculiar interest. She was certainly a woman of very marked and decided character. She is entitled, as no other female is, to be denominated " the heroine of the American Revolution." Other women, during that eventful struggle, were patriotic, and brave, and courageous. Margaret Corbin, with manly fortitude, filled the place of her husband, who was killed by her side while serving a piece of artillery, at the attack on Fort Washington, and for this act of female heroism received a pension from Congress. The story of the gunner's wife is not forgotten, who took her husband's post when he was killed at the battle of Monmouth, and did such execution, that, after the engagement, she was rewarded with a commission. Mrs. Ellet has supplied a long list of other "women of the Revolution," who rendered important services to their country's cause. Deborah Sampson alone, so far as we know, entered the ranks as a common soldier, and, during two entire campaigns, performed the arduous duties of such a position. The most remarkable feature of the case is, that during those entire campaigns, while mingling constantly with men, night and day, in all their exercises, through so many months, she maintained her virtue unsullied, so that her sex was not even suspected. That such was the fact, we are assured by the Resolve of the Legislature of Massachusetts, and by many other concurrent testimonies. Her example in enlisting as a soldier is certainly not to be commended to the imitation of our fair countrywomen ; but her inflexible resolution and firm self-control, after she enlisted, are deserving of high praise. Indeed, we know not whether, in all respects, the world's history affords a parallel to the case. Women are always found in camps, sometimes in great numbers ; not always, however, for worthy ends. Women in men's clothes were found dead at Waterloo, and on other battlefields in Europe. Many remarkable instances of female courage and heroism occurred in our late civil war. Several ladies of culture and refinement exposed themselves to far greater risks, in the "secret service," both of the Federal Government and of the rebel army, than were assumed by our heroine.* Woman, we

* Mrs. Smith, wife of Captain Smith of the Army of the Cumberland, left a life of luxury for the utmost hardships of the camp and the field, to accompany her husband, and serve the cause of the Union. She distinguished

well know, may have a manly heart. Many women have excelled in manly qualities and in manly exercises, often bearing off the palm from the stronger sex.

> Ducit Amazonidum lunatis agmina peltis
> Penthesilea furens, mediisque in millibus ardet,
> Aurea subnectens exsertæ cingula mammæ
> Bellatrix, audetque viris concurrere virgo.

But Penthesilea and the Amazons never existed, save in epic poetry ; and the story of Semiramis, long believed, is now fully exploded.   Boadicea, the British warrior-queen, "rushed to bat-tle, fought, and died." Jane of Montfort, clad in complete armor, performed prodigies of valor, and, in her little castle of Henne-bon, successfully withstood the arms of France.   Joan of Arc,

> "The maid with helméd head,
> Like a war-goddess, fair and terrible,"

retrieved the desperate affairs of the French realm.   Elizabeth

herself as a scout, and performed sev-eral extremely bold exploits. She once captured, single-handed, three rebel soldiers, with their horses, which they were leading to water. At anoth-er time she defeated a plan of the rebels for the capture of her hus-band's company and the regiment, by a ride of more than thirty miles on a stormy night, encountering many dangers on the way. Pauline Cush-man, an actress well known in the West, a woman of great energy and fine personal appearance, rendered very effective and valuable aid to the operations of the Western armies. Both as a scout and as a spy, she was engaged in many daring adventures in the cause of the Union, unravell-ing, by her uncommon talents, more than one deeply-laid plot of the rebels, and bringing to the leaders of our armies much useful information from the camps of the enemy. Mrs. Brown-ell, wife of Orderly-sergeant R. S. Brownell, of the Fifth Rhode-Island Regiment, accompanied her husband to the war. She was at the battles of Bull Run, of Roanoke Island, and of Newbern, exhibiting great pres-ence of mind, attending to the wound-ed, and encouraging the soldiers by her fortitude. When a standard-bear-er fell, she seized the banner, and, carrying it across the field, received a wound.—[*U. S. Ser. Mag., Sept.,*1865.]

of England, and Catharine of Russia, nearer our own times, extended their influence and their renown into distant regions.

The following extract of a letter from Hon. William Ellis, formerly a Senator in Congress, may form a fitting conclusion to
these introductory remarks. It was furnished to the editor by
Hon. Peter Force of Washington, D. C., and is dated Dedham,
Feb. 4, 1837 : —

"From my own acquaintance with Deborah Gannett, I can truly say
that she was a woman of uncommon native intellect and force of character. It happens that I have several connections who reside in the
immediate neighborhood where Mrs. Gannett lived and died ; and I
have never heard from them, or any other source, any suggestions against
the character of this heroine. Her stature was erect, and a little taller
than the average height of females. Her countenance and voice were
feminine ; but she conversed with such ease on the subject of theology,
on political subjects, and military tactics, that her manner would seem
to be masculine. I recollect that it once occurred to my mind that her
manner of conversation on any subject embraced that kind of demonstra-
tive, illustrative style which we admire in the able diplomatist."

THE

FEMALE REVIEW:

OR,

MEMOIRS

OF AN

AMERICAN YOUNG LADY;

WHOSE LIFE AND CHARACTER ARE PECULIARLY DISTIN-
GUISHED—BEING A CONTINENTAL SOLDIER, FOR NEARLY
THREE YEARS, IN THE LATE AMERICAN WAR.

DURING WHICH TIME,
SHE PERFORMED THE DUTIES OF EVERY DEPARTMENT,
INTO WHICH SHE WAS CALLED, WITH PUNCTUAL EXACTNESS,
FIDELITY AND HONOR, AND PRESERVED HER CHASTITY IN-
VIOLATE, BY THE MOST ARTFUL CONCEALMENT OF HER SEX.

WITH AN
APPENDIX,
CONTAINING
CHARACTERISTIC TRAITS, BY DIFFERENT HANDS; HER
TASTE FOR ECONOMY, PRINCIPLES OF DOMESTIC EDUCA-
TION, &c.

———

By a CITIZEN of MASSACHUSETTS.

D E D H A M :
PRINTED BY
NATHANIEL AND BENJAMIN HEATON.
FOR THE *AUTHOR.*

M,DCC,XCVII.

TO THE

P A T R O N S AND *F R I E N D S*

OF

COLUMBIA's CAUSE;

THE F E M A L E R E V I E W

Is DEDICATED:

THOUGH *not with intentions to encourage the* like paradigm *of* FEMALE ENTERPRISE—*but becauſe ſuch a thing, in the courſe of nature, has occurred; and becauſe every circumſtance, whether natural, artificial, or acciden- tal, that has been made conducive to the promotion of our* INDEPENDENCE, PEACE, *and* PROSPERITY—*all through* DI- VINE AID, *muſt be ſacredly remembered and extolled by every one, who ſolicits the* PERPETUITY *of theſe invaluable* BLESSINGS.

THE AUTHOR.

PUBLISHED
ACCORDING to ACT of CONGRESS.

PREFACE.

THERE are but two degrees in the characters of mankind, that feem to arreft the attention of the public. The firft is that of him, who is the moft diftin-guifhed in laudable and virtuous achievements, or in the promotion of general good. The fecond, that of him, who has arrived to the greateft pitch in vice and wick-ednefs.

NOTWITHSTANDING thefe characters exhibit the greateft contraft among mankind, it is not doubted but each, ju-dicioufly and properly managed, may render effential fervice. Whilft the former ever demands our love and imitation, the other fhould ferve to fortify our minds againft its own attacks—exciting only our pity and detef-tation. This is the only method, perhaps, by which good may be faid to come out of evil.

MY firft bufinefs, then, with the public, is to inform them, that the FEMALE, who is the fubject of the follow-ing MEMOIRS, does not only exift in theory and imagina-tion, but in reality. And were fhe not already known to the public, I might take pride in being the firft to divulge —a *distinguifhed Character*. Columbia has given her birth; and I eftimate her natural *fource* too highly, to prefume fhe is difhonoured in the acknowledgement of fuch an offspring.

HOWEVER erroneous this idea may be deemed, I fhall

here state only two general traits in her life to corroborate its truth. The criterion will still remain to be formed by a candid and impartial public.

SHE was born and educated in humble obfcurity—dif-tinguilhed, during her minority, only by *unufual* propen-fities for learning, and *few* opportunities to obtain the ineftimable prize. At the age of eighteen, fhe ftepped forward upon a more exalted ftage of action.* She found Columbia, her common parent, enveloped and diftracted with confufion, anguifh and war. She commiferated, as well as participated, her fufferings. And as a proof of her fidelity and filial attachment, fhe voluntarily offered her fervices in the character of a *Continental Soldier*, in defence of her *caufe;* by which, fhe feemed refolved to refcue the reft of her brothers and fifters from that flagrant deftruction, which, every inftant, feemed ready to bury them in one general ruin; or, to perifh, a noble facrifice, in the attempt.

HAVING noted the leading traits of this illuftrious *Fair*, I haften to give a concife account of the defign and exe-cution of the work.

JUSTICE, in the firft place, demands that I fhould men-tion the reluctance, with which fhe has confented to the publication of this *Review* of her life. Though it has become more fafhionable, in thefe days of liberty and lib-

* The heroine was in her twenty-fecond year when "fhe ftepped for-ward upon a more exalted ftage of action." — EDITOR.

erality, to publifh the lives of illuftrious perfons; yet fhe refufed the folicitations of a number of literary characters to publifh her own, till after her exit. She is not a ftickler for tradition; yet this is againft her.

ABOUT fixteen months ago, by defire of a friend, I made her a vifit for this purpofe. She did not, pofitively, difcard my requeft. Being indifpofed, fhe faid, fhould fhe recover, if I would again be at the trouble to call on her, fhe would in the interim take advice, confult matters with herfelf, and come to a final decifion. This was the firft of my acquaintance with her.

IN a few weeks, I again waited on her. Having critically weighed her own feelings, and wifhing to gratify the curiofity of many, of whom fhe had taken advice—with extreme *modefty* and trembling *diffidence*, fhe confented to take a public *Review* of the moft material circumftances and events of her life. She relies on that candor and impartiality from the public, that now attend the detail of her MEMOIRS.

I INTENDED to have executed this work at leifure; as indeed, I have. I had no other way; as the materials were moftly to be collected. This, with other preffing avocations in life, brings me under the neceffity to apologize to my worthy *Patrons*, for the delay of its publication a few weeks longer than the intended time.

SENSIBLY impreffed with the idea, that every fubject intended for public contemplation, fhould be managed with intentions to promote general good; I have, in every inftance, in the FEMALE REVIEW, indefatigably, labored for this important end. But perhaps I differ from moft biographers in this refpect. I have taken liberty to interfperfe, through the whole, a feries of moral reflections, and have attempted fome literary and hiftorical information. However fingular this is, I have the vanity to think it will not be deemed ufelefs.

As an impartial writer, I am bound to handle thefe MEMOIRS in a difinterefted manner. But where a total facrifice of truth does not forbid, I take pride in publicly avowing, in this place, my defire, (as every one ought) to extol *virtue*, rather than give the leaft countenance to *vice* under any name, pretext or fanction. Both may be reprefented and difcuffed—*Vice* expofed—Virtue cherifhed, revered and extolled.

THE authorities, upon which I have ventured, for the fupport of *facts* related in the following MEMOIRS, are not merely the words of the lady's own mouth. They have been detailed to me by perfons of veracity and notoriety, who are perfonally, acquainted with the circumftances. But I particularly refer my readers to the documents accompanying the appendix.

IT would be almoft incredibly ftrange, fhould no idle, capricious and even calumnious tale take rife with refpect to the *reputation* of the female, diftinguifhed as fhe is, who is the fubject of thefe fheets. Being aware of this,

fhe has already anticipated, and perhaps, in fome meafure, experienced it. Her precaution now is, to prepare
for the worft. She dreads no cenfure—no lafh of afperfion more than that of the judicious and virtuous. My
own wifhes are in this refpeét, as in all others, that truth,
candor and charity may be our ruling principles. When
we ferioufly confider the horrors, dangers and general
fare of *war*—that it is unavoidably attended with many
irregularities, to which fhe was expofed in common with
the reft; and yet, if it be found that decorum and propriety of conduét predominated in her general purfuits, we
may bear to palliate a few foibles, from which we, even in
our moft fequeftered, happy and ferene retirements, are
not, always, exempt.

THERE are but two fides to a perfon's charaéter any
more than there are to his garments—the *dark* and
bright. In my refearches in the FEMALE REVIEW, though
I have, decidedly, declared my choice for virtuous and
laudable aétions; yet, I have endeavoured to pay proper
attention to their opponents, when they happened to
make me vifits. But if I muft hereafter fuffer the lafh of
afperfion from either fex for having fhown partiality, I
fhall rejoice in the confcientious fatisfaétion of having
given the preference to the *Bright Side.*

PERHAPS, there is not one *new* idea, in the courfe of
thefe MEMOIRS, advanced or hinted on the important
bufinefs of education. But fhould I be fo fuccefsful, as

6

to roufe the minds and excite the attention of the *inat-tentive* to thofe principles, which have before been deemed ufeful; I fhall efteem it the moft agreeable and ample compenfation for my endeavours.

Suspicious, from my firft engagement, that the Female Review would be a fubject as *delicate*, efpecially for the Ladies, as it is *different* from their purfuits; I have ftu-dioufly endeavored to meliorate every circumftance, that might feem too much tinctured with the rougher, mafcu-line virtues. This, however, has not been attempted with the duplicity of a facetious courtier; but with a diction foftened and comported to the tafte of the *virtuous* fe-male. And although I am a well-wifher to their whole circle, it is the *caufe* of this clafs, only, I wifh to promote.

I cannot difapprove their vehement attachment to many novels—even to the productions of our own foil. Whilft they touch the paffions with all that is captivating and agreeable, they infpire manly thoughts, and irrefifti-bly gain our affent to virtue. As the peculiar events, that have given rife to the Female Review, ftand with-out a rival in American annals; I, alfo, hope my endea-vours to render it agreeably entertaining and ufeful to them may not prove fallacious nor in vain. I readily yield the palm of ftyle to the rapturous and melting ex-preffions of the novelift: But I muft vie with him in one refpect:—What he has painted in *embryo*, I have repre-fented in *expanfion*.

THIS gallant HEROINE has been reared under our own fofterage: and to reject her now, would be difowning a providential circumftance in our revolutionary epoch; which the annals of time muft perpetuate.

EUROPE has exhibited its chivalry and wonders. It now remains for America to do the fame: And perhaps the moft fingular is already paft—her *beginning* in *infancy!* It is a wonder, but a truth full of fatisfaction, that North America has become *free* and *independent.* But a few years have elapfed fince this memorable era; yet, even the face of nature has affumed a new and beautiful afpect. Under the foftering—powerful hands of induftry and economy, art and fcience have taken a rapid growth. The wreath of *Virtue* has fprung up; and *Liberty* delights in twining it round her votary's brow.

HAPPY in the poffeffion of fuch a *Source* for improvement, we fhould be barbarians to ourfelves to be inattentive to its promotion. Whilft other nations may envy us the enjoyment of fuch diftinguifhed rights and felicity——Heaven grant, we may vie with them only for *that*, which dignifies and promotes the CHARACTER of MAN.

MASSACHUSETTS, *July*, 1796.

THE

FEMALE REVIEW:

OR,

MEMOIRS

OF AN

AMERICAN YOUNG LADY.

C H A P. I.

A laconic History of Mifs SAMPSON's *extraction.—Local, and other fituations of her parents.—Her endowments —natural temper and difpofition.—Her propenfities for learning.*

DEBORAH SAMPSON was born in Plympton, a fmall village in the county of Plymouth in New-England, December 17, 1760.[1] She is a regular defcen-

---

[1] Her pedigree on the father's fide is as follows : —

I. ABRAHAM SAMPSON[1] came to Plymouth either in Auguft, 1629, or in May of the following year. He was then a young man, and appears to have belonged to the Englifh congregation at Leyden, in Holland, and to have come over with fuch mem-

bers of that congregation as chofe to remove to America after the death of their paftor, Rev. John Robinfon. There can be no doubt that he was a brother of Henry Sampfon, who came in the Mayflower, when a boy, in 1620. Abraham Sampfon fettled in Duxbury, where Henry alfo refided, and died there, at an advanced age,

dant of the honorable family of WILLIAM BRADFORD,[2] a
native of England, a man of excellent, natural endow-

about the year 1690. He had four
fons, who became heads of families, —
Samuel[2], George[2], Abraham[2], Ifaac[2].*

II. Ifaac Sampfon[2], the youngeft
fon, was born in Duxbury, in 1660.
He was one of the firft fettlers of
Plympton, a town originally a part
of Plymouth, but incorporated as a
feparate municipality in 1707. He
died in Plympton, Sept. 3, 1726. His
wife was Lydia Standifh[3], daughter of
Alexander Standifh[2], and grand-daugh-
ter of MILES STANDISH[1], the military
leader of the Pilgrims. The mother
of Lydia Standifh was Sarah Alden[2],
daughter of JOHN ALDEN[1], that
"hopeful young man," as Bradford
calls him, who joined the Pilgrim
company at Southampton, in Auguft,
1620, and fpent a long life in important fervices to the Plymouth Colony,
dying, in 1687, at the age of eighty-
eight.

III. Jonathan Sampfon[2], the fecond fon of Ifaac Sampfon[2] and of
Lydia Standifh[3], was born in 1690,
and lived in Plympton all his days.
Like his father and grandfather, he
was a tiller of the foil. His wife was
Joanna Lucas. He died in Plympton, Feb. 3, 1758, aged 68. He had
but one fon, who arrived at mature
years, named for himfelf, to wit : —

IV. Jonathan Sampfon[4], junior, who

was born in Plympton, April 3, 1729.
He was, by his wife Deborah Bradford[4], the father of Deborah Sampfon,
the heroine of this ftory.—[See Sampfon Genealogy, in the "Giles Memorial," iffued, in 1864, by the editor.

[2] WILLIAM BRADFORD[1] was born
at Aufterfield, in Yorkfhire, England,
in 1588. His father and grandfather
lived in the fame place, and bore the
fame name. About 1608, he went
with Mr. Robinfon's congregation to
Amfterdam, and in 1609 to Leyden.
He came to Plymouth in the Mayflower, accompanied by his wife,
whofe maiden name- was Dorothy
May. This lady, however, never
reached Plymouth, but was acciden-
tally drowned, Dec. 7, 1620, while the
Mayflower remained in the harbor of
Provincetown. His fecond wife, married Aug. 14, 1623, was the widow
Alice Southworth, who had juft arrived in the Ann. After the death
of Carver, in April, 1621, Mr. Bradford was chofen Governor of the infant colony. He was re-elected to
that office every year till 1657, except
five years, — 1633, '34, '36, '38, '44.
In thofe years he was chofen Affiftant.
For thirty-feven years, he was the
foremoft man in Plymouth Colony.
He was acquainted not only with the
Dutch and French languages, but
with the Latin, Greek, and Hebrew.
For an unfelfifh public fpirit, and a
general noblenefs of character, he has

---

* This expreffion, Ifaac[2], denotes that Ifaac[2]
was of the fecond generation, counting from and
including the firft American anceftor.

ments; upon which, he made great improvement by
learning. He emigrated to America whilſt young; where
he was, for many years alternately, elected Governor of
the Colony of Plymouth. In this department, he pre-
ſided with wiſdom and punctuality, and to the unanimous
ſatisfaction of the people under his charge. He married
an American lady of diſtinction; by whom he had conſiderable iſſue.—As he lived beloved and reverenced, he
died lamented by all, 1756.

HER grand-father, ELISHA BRADFORD,[3] was a native of
Plymouth in New England. He poſſeſſed good abilities,

had among men no ſuperior. At his
death, which took place May 9, 1657,
(not 1756, as ſtated in the text), he
was "lamented by all the colonies
of New England, as a common bleſſ-
ing and father to them all." By his
ſecond wife, he was the father of William[2], who diſtinguiſhed himſelf as a
commander of the Plymouth forces
in "Philip's War," and was ſeveral
years Deputy Governor of the colony;
and of Joſeph[2], who was born in 1630,
and married Jael, daughter of Rev. Peter Hobart, firſt miniſter of Hingham,
in 1664. Joſeph Bradford[2] lived in
Kingſton, then a part of Plymouth, on
Jones River, half a mile from its mouth.

3 Eliſha Bradford[3] was the ſon of
Joſeph Bradford[2], laſt mentioned, and
grandſon of the Governor. His firſt
wife was Hannah Cole; his ſecond,
Bathſheba Le Broche, as in the text.
The Bradford Genealogy gives, as
the date of the ſecond marriage, Sept.

7, 1718, which muſt be correct, as the
firſt child by this marriage was born
in April, 1719. His children were—
By firſt wife:— Hannah[4], who married Joſhua Bradford[4], b. June 23,
1710, ſon of Iſrael Bradford[3] of Kingſton, who was a ſon of Major William
Bradford[2], and grandſon of the Governor. Joſhua Bradford[4] removed from
Kingſton to Meduncook, now Friend-
ſhip, Maine, where, on May 27, 1756,
both himſelf and wife were killed by
a party of Indians, who carried their
children to Canada, where they remained in captivity till the conqueſt
of that province by the Engliſh, in
1759. They then returned to Meduncook. By ſecond wife:— Han-
nah[4], b. April 10, 1719.* Joſeph[4], b.
Dec. 17, 1721. Nehemiah[4], b. July
27, 1724. Laurana[4], b. March 26,

* Inſtances are not wanting in our early records
of the giving of the ſame name to another child
in the ſame family during the lifetime of the firſt.

and explored many fources, that led him to literary diftinction. As he was eminent in property; fo piety,
humanity and uprightnefs were the diftinguifhing char-
acteriftics of his life. He was married, September 7,
1719, to BATHSHEBA LE BROCHE, a French lady of elegant extraction and accomplifhments. Her father was
a native of Paris. He left a large iffue; of which, Mifs
SAMPSON'S mother is one.—But Mr. BRADFORD, for one of
his benevolent offices, being bound for a fhip and rich
cargo belonging to a merchant of the fame town, had the
misfortune to lofe the greater part of his intereft. Thus
deprived, at once, of what he had learned to prize by the
induftry and economy it coft him; it is natural to fuppofe,
it was no fmall difcouragement to him, and that the face
of things wore a different afpect around him: efpecially,
when we reflect, that the fulfilment of thofe principles,
which exert themfelves in acts of benevolence and affection towards all perfons, depend, greatly, on wealth. Being at this time confiderably advanced in years, this circumftance, together with the lofs of his eldeft fon, preyed
faft upon his conftitution: And he did not long furvive
to mourn the lofs of what feemed not in his power to
remedy.

1726; married Elijah McFarland of
Plympton. Mary⁴, b. Aug. 1, 1727.
Elifha⁴, b. Oct. 6, 1729. Lois⁴, b. Jan.
30, 1731. Deborah⁴, b. Nov. 18, 1732;
married Jonathan Sampfon, jr.: fhe
was the mother of Deborah Sampfon.
Alice⁴, b. Nov. 3, 1734; married ——
Waters of Sharon, Mafs. Afenath⁴,
b. Sept. 15, 1736. Carpenter⁴, b. Feb.
7, 1739. Abigail⁴, b. June 20, 1741.
Chloe⁴, b. April 6, 1743. — [Bradford
Genealogy, in *Gen. Reg.*, vol. iv., p. 48.

Miss Sampson's parents, though endowed with good abilities, cannot, in an eminent degree, be diftinguifhed, either by fortune or fcientific acquifition. Her father was an only fon, and heir to no inconfiderable eftate. And if it be afked, why her parents had not a more liberal education? the anfwer may be a general objection: —Different perfons are actuated by different objects of purfuit. Some, it is evident, have leading propenfities for the accumulation of lucrative gain: whilft others, who poffefs it, gladly embrace the opportunity for their advancement in literature.

It was, doubtlefs, the intention of Mr. Bradford to have given his children good education. ˙ But whether the wreck in his fortune, or whether his numerous progeny reftrained the liberality of his beftowments in this refpect, I pretend not to affirm. It is, however, more than probable, that her mother's, and perhaps her father's, education, in fome refpects, was fuperior to that of the commonalty.

It is no difhonorable trait in the character of any in America to be born *farmers;* even if they purfue the occupation through life. Their aim, however, muft be to furnifh themfelves with the requifites, which will render them ufeful and happy, and thofe who are round about them. Had the latter of thefe bleffings been confered on Mifs Sampson's father, he might, peradventure, have furmounted difficulties, which, it is thought, tended to

7

make him fickle, and perhaps, too loofe in his morals. He met with a fad difappointment in his father's eftate, occafioned by the ill defigns, connivings and infinuations of a brother-in-law.[4] Thus, he was difinherited of a portion that belonged to him by hereditary right. This circumftance, alone, made fuch impreffions on his mind, that, inftead of being fired with a juft fpirit of refentment and emulation, to fupply, by good application and economy, that of which he had been unjuftly deprived, he was led into oppofite purfuits, which fhe laments, as being his *greateft misfortune.*

SUCH was her father's local fituation after his marriage with her mother. She informs, that fhe had but very little knowledge of her father during her juvenile years. Defpairing of accumulating an intereft by his domeftic employments, his bent of mind led him to follow the feafaring bufinefs, which, as her mother informed her, he commenced before her birth. However great his profpects were, that fortune would prove more propitious to his profperity and happinefs upon the ocean, than it had

[4] His father, Jonathan Sampfon, fenior, died in 1758. In the divifion of the eftate, which took place in 1759, a brother-in-law managed to deprive him (Deborah's father) of what he expected as his fhare of the property. Whether the expectation were well founded or not, does not appear. For aught that appears on the Probate Records, the diftribution was fair, though it may have been otherwife. The difappointment occurred only the year before Deborah's birth, and feems to have made him defperate. Mortified pride feems to have driven him from home. He appears to have fallen into habits of intemperance. His wife was an eftimable woman.

done on the land, he was effectually difappointed :—For
after he had continued this fruitlefs employment fome
years, he took a voyage to fome part of Europe, from
whence he was not heard of for fome years. At length,
her mother was informed, he had perifhed in a fhipwreck.

By this time, his unfuccefsful fortune, both by land
and fea, had the tendency to break up his family. Her
mother, however, by her induftry and economical management, kept her family together as long as poffible
after her husband's fuppofed cataftrophe. But fhe, meeting with ficknefs, and other providential misfortunes, was
obliged, at length, to disband her family and to fcatter
her children abroad.[5]

It may, perhaps, be remarked, that nothing uncommonly fingular has attended Mifs SAMPSON in the primeval ftages of her life : Yet, the inquifitive and curious
mind, which is never tired in tracing the events and per-
formances of the moft diftinguifhed charaĉters, is wont to
extend its refearches ftill further, and to enquire *where*
and *how* they have *lived*, and by what *methods* and *grada-
tions* they arrived at the fummit of their undertakings.
I believe it is a truth, to which we may generally affent,

5 There were five children, two fons
and three daughters, viz. : Robert
Shurtleff. Ephraim. Sylvia, who
married, April 6, 1799, Jacob Cufhman, b. Feb. 29, 1747–8, fon of Benjamin Cufhman of Plympton. — See
Cufhman Genealogy. Deborah, b.
Dec. 17, 1760, the heroine of our ftory.
The fifth child was a daughter, whofe
name is to us unknown.

that moſt illuſtrious characters originate, either from very *low* or very *high* birth and circumſtances.—I, therefore, beg the reader's indulgence, whilſt I trace the moſt ſingular circumſtances and events that occured to Miſs SAMPSON during her juvenility; which may not be deemed wholly uſeleſs and unentertaining.

SHE was ſcarcely five years old, when the ſeparation from her mother was occaſioned by indigent circumſtances.[6] The affectionate and prudent parent can beſt deſcribe the emotions experienced by the mother and her daughter upon this occaſion. The young Miſs SAMPSON had, already, contracted an attachment to letters; and in many other reſpects, promiſed fair to crown the inſtructions and aſſiduity of a parent, or patroneſs, with the moſt deſirable ſucceſs. And it was with pain, her mother ſaw theſe flattering ſymptons without being able to promote, or ſcarcely to encourage them by the foſterage of parental care and affection. Nor was the darkneſs of the ſcene diſſipated, until a diſtant relation of her mother's, an elderly maiden, by the name of FULLER, proffered to adopt her into her family, and take the charge of her education.[7]

6 Notwithſtanding the "indigent circumſtances" out of which our heroine emerged, it ſhould be borne in mind that ſome of the beſt blood of the Old Colony flowed in her veins. A deſcendant of JOHN ALDEN, of MILES STANDISH, of PETER HOBART, and of WILLIAM BRADFORD, and a couſin-german of Captain Simeon Samſon, one of the diſtinguiſhed naval commanders of the Revolution,—there was much in her family connections to gratify an honeſt pride.

7 Thus was Deborah, in the tender period of childhood, when the heart is moſt open to impreſſions, and when

THIS was a very honeft and difcreet lady. She fhewed her young pupil many tokens of care and affection. But as Mifs SAMPSON remarked—"*As I was born to be unfortunate, my fun foon clouded.*" She had not continued in this agreeable fituation fcarcely three years, before her benefactrefs was feized with a violent malady, which, in a few days, proved fatal.

ALTHOUGH fhe was, at that time, not more than eight years old, fhe was much affected with the lofs of her patronefs.—She deemed it almoft irreparable;—confidered herfelf without a home, or fcarcely a friend to procure her one. But this fcene was too diftreffing to laft long. Her mother, hearing of her circumftances, endeavored to obtain a fuitable place for her, till fhe fhould come of age. She was put into one Mrs. THACHER'S family in Middleborough, where fhe continued about two years.[8] This lady took particular care to gratify her favor-

it moft needs the counfels and the reftraints of parental love, virtually bereft of both her parents. The lofs fhe now fuftained could never be repaired. She had already exhibited indications of talent, and a thirft for knowledge. She had, under the tuition of her mother, begun to read. Her perceptions were quick, her imagination lively, her affections warm. Could her talents have been developed by proper culture, fhe might have adorned an elevated pofition in fociety.

[8] It has been fuppofed, and not without reafon, that this lady was the widow of Rev. Peter Thacher, the third minifter of Middleborough. Mr. Thacher was born in Milton, Oct. 6, 1688, and was fon of Rev. Peter Thacher of that place, and grandfon of Rev. Thomas Thacher, firft minifter of the Old South Church in Bofton. He was paftor of the Church in Middleborough from 1709 till his death, in 1744, in the 56th year of his age. If the fuppofition juft mentioned be correct, Mrs. Thacher muft have

ite propenſity for reading, &c. but as ſhe was of a ſlender
conſtitution, her mother removed her to Mr. JEREMIAH
THOMAS'S, of the ſame town.[9]

Is it, indeed, ſadly true, that nature, our common ſource
of being, is unequal in her intellectual beſtowments on
the human ſpecies ? If not, the apparent difference muſt
be in the manner, in which they are exhibited. This I

been, at the time when Deborah was
in her family, more than eighty years
of age, as ſhe died in 1771, aged 84.
In this caſe, ſervices may have been
required which a child ten years old
was not able to perform. Plympton
has Middleborough on the ſouth-weſt,
joining it.

9 The *Hiſtory of the Firſt Church in
Middleborough*, printed about twelve
years ſince, contains a liſt of all who
have been members of that church
from its organization, in 1695, to 1853.
This liſt appears to have been compiled with uncommon care. It contains the name of only one Jeremiah
Thomas; and he died in 1736, æ. 77.
The individual intended in the text
muſt have been *Benjamin* Thomas,
who was choſen deacon in 1776, and
died Jan. 18, 1800, æ. 78. In the MS.
memoir of Deborah Sampſon, he is
called "Deacon Thomas," without
any mention of his baptiſmal name,
which Deborah had evidently forgotten. The following facts are related
of him in the *Hiſtory of the Firſt
Church*, already mentioned: "Deacon Thomas, though not of a cultivated mind in other reſpects, was well

verſed in the Scriptures, of inflexible
virtue, of ſound and clear orthodoxy,
and conſcientious in the performance
of known duty ; holding on upon the
old landmarks, and refuſing to let
them go. In 1782, he was a repre-
ſentative in the Legiſlature, and, in
1788, a member of the Convention
which adopted the Federal Conſtitution. A bill was under diſcuſſion for
repealing the law of primogeniture.
The deacon expreſſed his doubts on
the matter, becauſe the Scriptures
ſhowed ſpecial favors to the *firſt-born*.
A Boſton gentleman ſaid that 'the
deacon miſtook the Scriptures ; for
they ſaid that Jacob, though the
younger brother, inherited the birthright.' The deacon replied, ' The
gentleman had forgotten to tell us
how he obtained it, — how Eſau ſold
his birthright for a mess of pottage,
and how Jacob deceived his father,
pretending to be Eſau, and how his
mother helped on the deception, —
he had forgotten all that !' The
laugh, which was at firſt againſt the
deacon, was now turned againſt the
gentleman from Boſton." The deacon was more than a match for him.

am inclined to believe: and the greateſt remedy is education.—Hence the ſhrewd ſaying—"*Learning keeps him
out of fire and water.*"—An excellent ſtimulation for every
one.—Logicians, I truſt, will allow me to form an eſtima-
tion of Miſs SAMPSON's endowments, even before ſhe had
reached her teens. This I do, without a deſign to flatter
her into vain conceits of herſelf, or to wheedle any one
of the human ſpecies into her favor, or eſteem of the
writer. It is a juſt tribute of reſpect due to the *illuſtrious
poor.*

CERTAIN it is, that ſhe early diſcovered, at leaſt to every
judicious obſerver, tokens of a fertile genius and an aſpir-
ing mind: a mind quick of perception and of ſtrong pen-
etration. And if it be allowable to judge of things past,
by their preſent aſpect, I heſitate not to announce, that
her primeval temper was uniform and tranquil. Though
deſtitute of many advantages of education, ſhe happened
to fix on many genuine principles. She may be noted
for a natural ſweetneſs and pliability of temper—a ready
wit, which only needed refinement—a ready conformity
to a parent's, or patroneſs' injunctions—a native modeſty
and ſoftneſs in expreſſion and deportment, and paſſions
naturally formed for philanthropy and commiſeration.

A FURTHER enumeration might give occaſion for a new
apology. Nor have I a right to deſcribe her abilities in
proportion to the improvements ſhe has ſince made. I
might fall into groſs errors. Nature might complain of

injuſtice for making a wrong eſtimate of her bounties. And it is a truth, too often to be lamented, that ſhe oftener complains of *uncultivated* talents, than for not *giving any* for cultivation. Our endowments, of courſe, muſt be equal, if not ſuperior, to our improvements.— Should the contrary be urged, thoſe principles, which have dictated her exertions, might loſe a part of their energetic influence; in which ſhe ſtill delights. Had ſhe ſhared greater advantages in education, ſhe might have much exceeded the proficiency in erudition, but ſcarcely the ſingularity of character, which ſhe has ſince attained.

IT was a circumſtance peculiarly unhappy with Miſs SAMPSON, during her minority, that ſhe found leſs *oppor_ tunities*, than *inclinations*, for learning. The inſtances I ſhall adduce to corroborate this aſſertion, will be com- priſed in the next chapter;—where the reader will find a general ſketch of her education during this period.

I SHALL only add, that many of our humble peaſantry in America, would have thanked fortune, if this evil had been confined to her. It is not ſo great a wonder, as it is a lamentable truth, which, obſervation in many families may evince, that they have amaſſed together a greater bulk of riches than of uſeful ſcience; whilſt, perhaps, the man, who never could obtain a mediocrity of wealth, only needed it to vie with them in every thing uſeful and orna- mental.—Thus, the moſt fertile genius, like that of ſoil, which for want of proper cultivation, is overrun with noxious weeds, becomes corrupted by neglect and vicious habit: and the *inherent* beauties, that might have eclipfed a more than ordinary fhow, lie dormant.

WHERE then, could the GUARDIANS of fcience have been fecreted! or, had they not taken an univerfal charge of this growing empire!—Inftances of this kind, however, are more rarely met with than formerly. And this error will always find the beft apology in the population of new countries, where the means for fubfiftence unavoidably demand the moft attention. But affluence, without being regulated by refined education, cloys the fight of the beholder; and the poffeffors are unqualified for duty. The minds of people are now roufed by the introduction of new fcenes and objects. And it is here to be repeated, to the honor of the citizens of New England, and the United States in general, that they are, with fuccefs, endeavoring to counterbalance this once prevailing evil; at leaft, they would make an equilibrium between their wealth and literature.

LET not, therefore, any who have talents for improvement, defpair of fuccefs in any fituation. Though a FRANKLIN has become extinct, a WASHINGTON furvives. Our native land fmiles under the foftering *hand* of induftry and economy. It will ftill produce our men of government, our guardians of fcience, and our encouragers and promoters of virtue.

8

C H A P. II.

Miss Sampson's *propenfities for learning, and the obfta-cles fhe met with in it, contrafted.—View of her educa-tion during her juvenility—in which time, fhe contracts a* taste *for the ftudy of* nature *or* natural philoso-phy; *which teaches her regular ideas of* Deity—*the neceffity of* morality *and* decorum *in her purfuits.*

WE are now to view Mifs Sampson advancing into the bloom and vigor of youth. In this feafon, comes on the trial of virtue and of the permanency of that foundation, upon which improvements have begun. The paffions having affumed greater degrees of vigor, and ftill fufceptible of quick and delicate impreffions from their natural attachment to the fexes, and other alluring objects of purfuit; it becomes accountable, that fo many of both fexes, efpecially thofe deprived of genuine educa-tion, fail of that uniform courfe of improvement in knowl-edge and virtue, which is the only barrier againft vice and folly, and our fureft guidance through life. If fhe be found, at this age, perfevering in thefe duties and fur-mounting the principal allurements to indecorum and vice, I need not hefitate to announce her a fingular para-digm for many in better circumftances and in higher life.

From the time fhe went to live in Mr. Thomas's fam-

ily,[10] till fhe was eighteen, it may be faid fhe lived in common with other youth of her own fex; except in two
very important refpeĉts:—She had *ftronger* propenfities
for improvement, and *lefs* opportunities to acquire it.
Induftry and economy—excellent virtues! being hereditary in this family, fhe was, of courfe, inured to them.
And as their children were numerous, and chiefly of the
mafculine fex, it is not improbable, that her athletic exercifes were more intenfe on that account. As they appeared more eager in the amaffing of fortune, than of
fcientific acquifition, fhe was obliged to check the bud,
which had already begun to expand, and to yield the
palm of the fulfilment of her duty to her fuperintendants
in the manner they deemed beft, to the facrifice of her
moft endearing propenfities. But painful was the thought,

[10] Deborah lived in the family of
Deacon Thomas from the age of ten
to that of eighteen. His houfe was
in a retired fpot, about two miles eaft
of the central village of Middleborough Four Corners. It was a fub-
ftantial building, the timbers and
roof-boards being made of white-oak.
Here Deborah was well clad, and her
phyfical wants were well supplied.
The deacon had a good farm, and
he and his family were good livers.
Deborah's health became confirmed,
and fhe acquired a bodily vigor which
fitted her to encounter the hardfhips
of fubfequent years. She became
acquainted with almoft all kinds of
manual labor proper to her fex. She
learned to fpin and weave, accomplifhments which were then thought
indifpenfable to a young woman. She
could alfo, when occafion required,
harnefs the family horfe, and ride him
to plough, or to the village on errands.
She was not only familiar with the
work of the dairy, but, when a fhower
was coming up, could rake hay, and
help to ftow it away in the barn. She
was, moreover, a tolerable mechanic.
If fhe wanted a bafket, a milking-ftool,
or a fled, fhe could make it. Indeed,
fhe acquired the habit of adapting
herfelf to exifting circumftances, whatever they might be.

that fhe muft fuffer the bolt to be turned upon this, her
favorite purfuit. Wounding was the fight of others going
to fchool, when fhe could not, *becaufe fhe could not be
fpared.* Her reflections were fingular, confidering her
age, when contrafting *her* privileges with thofe of *other*
children, who had parents to take the charge of their
education.   It was a circumftance effectually mortifying
to her, that fhe could not hold familiarity, even with the
children of the family, on their fchool-topics. But the
ambition that agitated her mind, made her wont to believe her lot as good as that of orphans in general.

HAPPY it was for her, at this age, that neither mortification nor prohibition impeded her inherent propenfity
for learning.   This, inftead of being weakened, was
ftrengthened by time; though fhe had not devifed any
effectual method to gratify it. She had often heard—
that *a forward and promifing youth is fhort lived:* But
fhe did not believe it.   And, in this refpect, her longevity
was refted on as good fafety, as was that of the wifeft
man: Nor have I the leaft inclination to cenfure either.
The preceptor knows it is a tafk to kindle fparks of emulation in moft children; and reafon informs him, when
they are *naturally* kindled, it is an injurious engine that
extinguifhes the flame.

IT is the pride of fome undifciplined, tyrannical tem-
pers to triumph over fuppofed ignorance, diftrefs and
poverty.   In this, our better-deferving orphan found a

fource of mortification." But magnanimity and hope—
ever foothing companions! elevated her above defpair.
The ideas of being rivalled by her mates in learning and
decorum, guarded their proper receptacle, and prompted
the eftablifhment of the following maxims:—*Never neglect the leaft circumftance, that may be made conducive to
improvement: Opportunity is a precious companion;* which
is too often fadly verified by the fool's companions, *folly*
and *procraftination*—thieves, that rob the world of its
treafure.

HER method was to liften to every one fhe heard read
and fpeak with propriety. And when fhe could, without
intrufion, catch the formation of a letter from a penman,
fhe gladly embraced it. She ufed to obtain what fchool
books and copies fhe could from the children of the
family, as models for her imitation. Her leifure interims
were appropriated to thefe tafks with as little reluctance,
as common children went to play.

AVAILING herfelf of fuch methods with unremitted
ardor, together with promifcuous opportunities at fchool;
fhe, at length, found herfelf miftrefs of pronunciation and

There is no reafon to fuppofe that any thing of this fort was true of Deacon Thomas or any of his family. He was a moft worthy man, careful and confcientious in all things; but, like moft of the New England farmers of that age, he could not comprehend the value of learning, except as it contributed to immediate practical refults. Deborah was bound to him till the age of eighteen; and he confidered himfelf entitled to her fervices whenever they were wanted. She attended fchool a part of the time; and, when out of fchool, fhe induced the children of the family to teach her. The fcanty opportunities allowed, fhe improved to the utmoft.

fentences to fuch a degree, that fhe was able to read, with propriety, in almoft any book in her language. The like application, in procefs of time, qualified her to write a legible hand. As foon as fhe could write, fhe voluntarily kept a journal of common occurrences; an employment not unworthy the humbleft peafant, or the most renowned fage.[12]

THE anxiety and afpirations of her mind after knowledge, at length, became more notorious to many, who made learning their element. As catechetical tuition, in fome refpects, was more in use thirty years ago, than now, fhe committed to memory, at an early age, the Catechifm by the Affembly of Divines, and could recite a prolix proof of it verbatim.[13] By this, fhe fecured the efteem and approbation of her village curate;[14] which he expreffed by many flattering expreffions, and a donation of a few books. And to mention the epiftolary corre-

[12] She kept this journal on the fingular plan of recording her good deeds on the firft, third, fifth, &c., pages, and her bad deeds on the oppofite pages. As might be expected, the oppofite pages were fooneft filled.

[13] The Catechifm was doubtlefs committed to memory by all the young members of the family. This was a family of the good old Puritan ftamp, exact in the obfervance of the Sabbath, regular attendants on public worfhip, punctual in their daily devotions. The parents difapproved, and indeed prohibited to thofe under their care, all gay and frivolous amufements; and taught them, both by precept and example, the ftricteft leffons of morality and virtue. But fo much ferious religion was irkfome to the buoyant fpirit of Deborah; and fhe contracted a difrelifh for it which remained in after-life.

[14] "Her village curate" — ftrange expreffion!— was Rev. Sylvanus Conant. He was paftor of the Firft Church in Middleborough from March 28, 1745, till his death, Dec. 8, 1777.

fpondence, which fhe commenced at the age of twelve, with a young lady of polite accomplifhments, who had not only offered to fupply her with paper, but with whatever inftructions fhe could, would be reminding her of a debt which fhe could only repay by her gratitude for fuch obliging condefcention. The correfpondence was of much utility to her in her future employments.

THUS, fo much genius and tafte were not always to remain fequeftered, like a pearl in the bowels of the deep, or in an inacceffable place. Nor muft I infinuate that fhe was here deprived of many other principal advantages of education. She fared well for food and raiment; and that, fhe reflected, was better than could be faid of many of her furrounding companions. It is with refpect and gratitude fhe fpeaks of her fuperintendants on many other accounts. She has often faid with emotion, that the moft mortifying punifhment fhe ever received from her mafter, was—" *You are always hammering upon fome book—I wifh you wouldn't fpend fo much time in fcrabbling over paper.*" Had he been poffeffed of Mifs Hannah More's beautiful fatire, he might, more politely, have recited the same ideas:

" I wifh fhe'd leave her books, and mend her clothes :
I thank my ftars, I know no verfe from profe."

They not only carefully habituated her to induftry and domeftic economy in general; but from them, her miftrefs in particular, fhe experienced leffons of morality and virtue; which, fhe thinks, could not have failed to have been beneficial to any one, whofe heart had not been too much tipped with adamantine hardnefs, or whofe faculties had not been totally wrapped in inattention. Indeed, the laborious exercifes, to which fhe was accustomed, during her ftay in this family, may be confidered of real fervice to her. They added ftrength and permanency to her naturally good conftitution; kept the mind awake to improvements (for the mind will doze, when indolence feizes the body); and thus prepared her to endure the greater hardfhips, which were to characterize her future life.

It is with peculiar pleafure, I here find occafion to fpeak of Mifs Sampson's *tafte* for the ftudy of *Nature*, or *Natural Philofophy*. More agreeable ftill would be my tafk, had fhe enjoyed opportunities, that her proficiency in it might have been equal to her relifh for it.

That *Philofophy* fhould ever have been treated with indifference, much lefs, with intentional neglect, is an idea, that affords fingular aftonifhment to every rational mind. The *philofopher* has been confidered as—*not a man of this world; as an unfocial and unfit companion*, and *wanting* in the general *duties* of *life*.* Such ideas muft

---

* I here particularly allude to a fmall performance, which contains, among thefe, many excellent moral maxims. It was written by a female, and entitled—"The whole Duty of Woman."

have been the refult of a very erroneous acceptation of the word; or, of a mind not a little tinctured with prejudice.—I have always conceived, that *philofophy* is a *fcientific fphere*, in which we are enjoined to act by nature, reafon and religion; which ferve as a directory, or auxiliaries to accelerate us in it. The *philofopher*, then, inftead of being rendered a *ufelefs object* in fociety, and *wanting* in the general *duties* of life, is the perfon moft eminently qualified for a *ufeful member* of fociety, the moft agreeably calculated for an *intercourfe* and *union* with the fexes, beft acquainted with the focial and enjoined *duties* of life; and is thus preparing himfelf for a more refined BEING in futurity.

IT muft then have been, merely, from the *abftrufenefs*, which many people have falfely imagined attends this moft plain and ufeful of all fciences, that they have been deterred from the purfuit of it, But however reprobated and ufelefs the ftudy of philofophy may have been deemed for the man of fenfe, and much more dangerous for the other fex; it is certain, that it is now emerging from an obfolete ftate, to that of a fafhionable and reputable employment. Ignorance in it being now the thing moftly to be dreaded. And many of both fexes are not afhamed of having the appellation conferred on them in any fituation in life.

I LEARN from Mifs SAMPSON's diurnals, and from the credibility of others, that fhe early difcovered a *tafte* for

9

the contemplation of the objects and appearances exhibited in creation. She was notorious for her frequent in-
terrogatories relative to their nature, ufe and end. Nor
is this, in a degree, unnatural for children in general.
Natural Creation is a fource that firft excites the notice
and attention of all. I have myfelf obferved, even in-
fants, after long confinement, appear reanimated and
filled with admiration on being again brought into the
refulgence of the Sun or Moon, the fpangled appearance
of the ftars, the enamelled mead, the afpiring grove, or a
fingle floweret. Thus, they make it a voluntary act to
enquire into their origin, ufe and end: Whereas, it
often happens, that the fame child, by reafon of fome
nurfed, ill habit of temper, will brook no controul by the
beft moral precept or example, except it be from the
dread of corporeal punifhment.—This, therefore, fhould
rouze the attention of parents. As the firft dawning of
reafon in their children difplays itfelf in this way, they
fhould make it their peculiar care to affift and encourage
it in every refpect. Nature, indeed, may be confidered
as a general monitor and inftructor: But it is from experience and practical experiments, that we are facilitated
in the acquifition of knowledge.

HER tafte for the cultivation of plants and vegetable
productions in general, appears to have been fomewhat
confpicuous in her early years. And fhe has intimated
an idea of this kind, which, from its juftnefs, and the

delicate effects it has on many of the softer passions, in-
duces me to notice it.—It has been a source of astonish-
ment and mortification to her, that so many of her own,
as well as of the other sex, can dwell, with rapture, on a
romantic scene of love, a piece of painting or sculpture,
and, perhaps, upon things of more trivial importance;—
and yet can walk in the stately and venerable grove, can
gaze upon the beautifully variegated landscape, can look
with indifference upon the rose and tulip, or can tread on
a bank of violets and primroses, without appearing to be
affected with any peculiar sensations and emotions. This
certainly proceeds from a wrong bias of the mind in its
fixing on its first objects of pursuit. And parents cannot be too careful in the prevention of such errors, when
they are forming the minds of their offspring for the
courses which are to affect the passions, and give sway
to the behavior during life.

I KNOW not whether it was from her mental application to books, instructions from public or private precep-
tors, or from her own observations on *nature*, that she acquired the most knowledge of philosophy and astronomy.
Perhaps, it was from some advantage of the whole. I
am, however, authorized to say, both from her infant
memorandums and verbal communications, that she did
obtain, during her juvenility, many just ideas respecting them. She has assured me, the questions she used
to ask, relative to the *rising* and *setting* of the Sun,

Moon, &c. never ceafed agitating her mind, till fhe had formed proper ideas of the fpherical figure of the Earth, and of its diurnal and annual revolutions. In this manner, fhe acquired a fmattering of the *Solar Syftem*. But fhe has no wifh even now, for having the appellation, *philofopher*, or *aftronomer*, conferred on her. But my readers may conclude, it is, merely on account of her fancied *ignorance* of thofe fublime fciences.

SHE frequently made it her cuftom to rife in the morning before twilight. During the Spring, Summer and Autumn, it feems, fhe was peculiarly attached to rural fpeculation. And, as though fhe had been a Shepherdefs, fhe was frequently feen in fome adjacent field, when the radiant orb of day firft gleamed on the hill tops to cheer and animate vegetable nature with his prolific and penetrating rays.

THE ftudious and contemplative mind can beft interpret her motive in this, and the utility of it. To thofe, who have feldom or never enjoyed the delicious repafts of this tranquil hour, it may be faid—the mind, like the body, having refted from the toils and buftle of the day, awakes in a ftate of ferenenefs the beft calculated for contemplation, for the reception and impreffion of ideas, which this feafon, above all others, feems capable of affording.—The phyfician may alfo inform, that *early rifing* is a cordial and prefervative of health. It creates a lively carnation on the cheek, adds vigor and activity to the

69

limbs and fenfes; which no one wishes to exchange for the languifhing conftitution, the pallid countenance, and mind ftaggering with the weight of an inactive body of him, who takes too much repofe on his downy pillow.

THE dawning of day—when the fun is diffipating the darknefs, all nature affuming reanimation, each tribe of inftinct haftening to its refpective occupation, and man, who had been confined in morbid inactivity, reaffuming ftrength and cheerfulnefs—is emblematic of CREATION rifing out of its original chaos, or non-exiftence. Surely, then, this fcene cannot fail of filling the *philofophic mind* with juft and fublime ideas, and with the pureft love and gratitude to that BEING, who caufed them to exift and who ftill regulates and fuperintends the whole.

MISS SAMPSON has repeatedly faid, that her mind was never more effectually impreffed with the power, wifdom and beneficence of DEITY than in the contemplation of his CREATION. It affords *ideas* the moft familiar and dignified, and *leffons* the moft ftriking, captivating and beautifully fublime.

THE Earth, which is computed to be 25,038 Englifh miles in circumference, and to contain about 199,512,595 fquare miles of furface, is indeed a large body.* The thoughts of its conftruction, of its convenient fituations for its innumerable fpecies of inhabitants, and of the

* SEE Efq. GUTHRIE's and Dr. MORSE's Geographies.

abundance of good it affords them, are fufficient to warm the human breaft with all that is tender and benevolent.

BUT our creative faculties in their refearches are not limited to this globe. The fight is attracted into bound-lefs ether, to roam amongft the other revolutionary orbs and fpangled fituations of the fixed ftars.* In this, *nature* is our prompter, and *reafon* our guide. Here we are led to believe, without doubt, that fuch orbs, as are vifible to the eye, occupy immenfity. And the prob-ability is, that millions, yea, an infinite number, of fuch bodies are peopled by inhabitants not diffimilar to our own. And when we further confider the immenfe dif-tance there is between each of thefe planets, ftars or funs, and the certainty of the regularity and mutual harmony, that for ever fubfifts between them, although they are per-petually whirling with the moft inconceivable velocity;— what auguft and amazing conceptions do we have of that BEING, who has fabricated their exiftence! Surely then the mind, that is not loft to all fenfe of rectitude and de-corum, muft be filled with ideas the moft dignified, with fentiments and paffions the moft refined, and with grati-tude the moft abundant and fincere.

As MISS SAMPSON had a natural attachment to the ftudy of *creation*, it would have been unnatural, and even crimi-nal, to have been negligent in forming an acquaintance

---

* CONSIDERED by modern philofophers and aftronomers, as SUNS.

with her own nature—with its important ufe and end. Every thing in nature, as well as in reafon, enjoins this as a duty. The uniformity every where obfervable in creation, doubtlefs, was influential and fubfervient to the regulation of her moral and civil life. This may excite an idea of novelty with thofe, who do not ftudioufly attend the *lectures* of Nature. But had we no other directory, by which we could regulate our lives and conduct, and were it not poffible to deviate from this, there would be lefs danger of the confufion fo often vifible among mankind, of immorality, and of the fword, which is, even now, deluging fuch a part of the world in blood.

From an habitual courfe of fpeculations like thefe, fhe may be faid to have been feafonably impreffed with the following theoretical conclufions drawn from them : That human nature is born in imperfection; the great *bufinefs* of which is *refinement*, and conftant endeavors of approximation to perfection and happinefs ;—That ignorance and the general train of evils are the natural offspring of inattention, and that all tend to the degradation of our nature ;—And that diligent application is the great requifite for improvement; which, only, can dignify and exalt our nature and our character.

These traits, I venture to affirm, are fome of the primeval exertions of thofe endowments, which are fo peculiarly characteriftic of our rectitude and worth. They are *leading principles* of life. I take the liberty to call them *fpontaneous;* becaufe they are, more or lefs, *nat-ural* to every one.

IMPELLED by defires to promote virtue and decorum, as well as by juftice, I here mention one more trait of her juvenility: and I could wifh it might not diftinguifh her from others at this day.—During this feafon, it may be faid, fhe was generally a ftranger and fhowed an aver-fion to all irregular and untimely diverfions. Nor is fhe more deferving a panegyric on this account than her fuperintendents. She defpifed revelry, goffipping, detrac-tion and orgies, not becaufe fhe was, originally, any bet-ter than others, but becaufe genuine nature exhibits no fuch examples—becaufe they were unfafhionable in her neighborhood;—and, efpecially, becaufe her mafter and miftrefs not only difapproved, but prohibited them. This theory is certainly good, however bad her practice here-after may appear. Their *practice*, rather than their *name* fhould be ftruck out of time.

PERHAPS I make a greater diftinction, than many do, between what is called the univerfal ruin of nature, and that occafioned by wrong education. We call *nature* corrupt: inftead of which, we may fay *corporeal fub-ftance.* The immortal part of man is pure; and it is the pride of genuine nature to keep it fo. It is em-barraffed many times by a vicious body: but it will re-main uncontaminated, though the body tumbles into dif-folution.

Custom bears great fway; even the palate may be made to relifh any diet by cuftom. But this argues not, that any thing can be received by the ftomach without danger. We are the pilots of our children; and on us they depend for fafety. They learn by imitation, as well as by precept. And I have either read, heard or thought, (no matter which) that children will always be gazing on the *figns* their parents have *lettered.*—We wifh for reformation in youth; but let age be careful to lay the foundation ftone.

It is not prefumed, that Mifs Sampson was, at this age, without her particular blemifhes and foibles. Like others deftitute of principal advantages of education, fhe was doubtlefs culpable for the mifimprovement of much time and many talents. Whilft her fuperintendents may corroborate this, they are ready to do her the juftice of faying, that fhe was a lover of order in their family—punctual in the fulfilment of her duty to them, and affiduous to heighten their regard for her. And that her obligations of this nature did not terminate here, many of her cotemporaries, I dare fay, can teftify. Studious to increafe a reciprocity of affection with her relations and furrounding companions, fhe was fuccefsful. To behave with temperance to ftrangers, is what fhe deemed a ftep of prudence: But to fhow an indifference, or actually to difoblige a friend or companion, could only be repaid by

10

redoubled attention to reftore them to her favor, and by acknowledged gratitude for their lenity.

On the whole, we muſt look upon her endowments, in general, during her juvenility, as the ſtatuary may look upon his marble in the quarry; or as any one may look upon a rich piece of painting or ſculpture, which combines uniformity with profuſion; yet where the hand of the artiſt has not diſcovered every latent beauty, nor added a finiſhing poliſh to thoſe that are apparent.

CHAP. III.

Analyſis of Miſs Sampson's *thoughts on the riſe and progreſs of the* American war, *with a conciſe account of the Lexington and Breed's Hill engagements—including a remarkable dream.*

THE motives, that led to hoſtilities between North America and Great Britain, and the period that terminated our *relation* to, and *dependence* on, that nation, are events the moſt ſingular and important we have ever known :—*ſingular*, becauſe, in their very *nature*, they were *unnatural;—important*, becauſe, on them depended the future welfare and luſtre of America.

The operations of theſe affairs, both before and after the firſt engagement at Lexington, are well known to have affected the minds, even of both ſexes, throughout the Colonies, with fenfations and emotions different from whatever they had before experienced. Our progenitors had fuffered almoſt every hardſhip in their firſt fettlement of this country, and much bloodſhed by the Aborigines. But thefe are events that naturally attend the population of new countries; and confequently, naturally anticipated. But when our property, which our anceſtors had honeſtly acquired, was invaded; when our inherent rights were either prohibited or infringed, an alarm was univerfally given; and our minds were effeƈtually awakened to the keeneſt fenfe of the injuries, and naturally remained in diſtrefs, till we became exempt from their jurifdiƈtion.

PERHAPS the public may not be furprifed, that events, fo intereſting and important, ſhould arreſt the attention of any one.—But when either of the fexes reverfes its common fphere of aƈtion, our curiofity is excited to know the caufe and event. The field of war is a department peculiarly affigned to the hero. It may, therefore, appear fomewhat curious, if not intereſting to many, when they are informed, that *this* uncommonly arreſted the attention of a YOUNG FEMALE of low birth and ſtation. Mifs SAMPSON is the one, who not only liſtened to the leaſt information relative to the rife and progrefs of the late American War; but her thoughts were, at times, engroffed with it.—I will analyze them, as I find them fketched in her credentials, or as I learn them from credible authorities.

BEFORE the blockade of Bofton, March 5th, 1775, by the Britifh, the Colonies had been thrown into great confufion and diftrefs by repeated acts of oppreffion by the Britifh, that produced riots, which, in Bofton, were carried to the greateft extremities. It was not till this time, that Mifs SAMPSON obtained information of the arrival of the King's troops, and of the fpirited oppofition maintained by the Americans. She juftly learned, that it was the Acts of the Britifh Parliament to raife a revenue, without her confent, that gave rife to thefe cruel and unjuft meafures.[15]   Had fhe poffeffed information and experience on the fubject, like many others, fhe would doubtlefs, like them, have feen the impropriety, that England fhould have an unlimited controul over us, who are feparated from her by the vaft Atlantic, at leaft, three thoufand miles.

BUT fo it was.—From the firft eftablifhed fettlement in North America, to the *Declaration* of our *Independence*, we acknowledged the fovereignty of the Britifh Government; and thus continued tributary to her laws.   And as though it had not been enough, that fhe had driven

[15] There was no "blockade of Bofton, March 5, 1775," afide from the clofing of the port, under the " Bofton Port Bill," which went into effect June 1, 1774. Several Britifh regiments were ftationed in Bofton from the middle of June, 1774. "Without her confent!"   Without *whofe* confent?

many of our anceftors from their native clime, by the
intolerant and unrelenting fpirit of her religious perfe-
cution, to feek a new world, and to fuffer the diftrefs
naturally confequent—they infifted ftill, that our *property*, our *conduct* and even our *lives* muft be under their
abfolute controul. Thus, we remained fubject to the
caprice of one, the influential chicanery of a fecond, and
the arbitrary decifion of the majority. And it is not my
prerogative to fay, we fhould not have remained loyal
fubjects of the Crown, to this day, had not our affections
been alienated by the adminiftration of *laws*, in their
nature, unjuft, and calculated to injure none, but thofe
the leaft deferving of injury.

PERHAPS, there is no period in our lives, in which the
principles of humanity and benevolence can better take
root, than in that of the juvenile age. And it has been
a rare inftance, that the fituation of any nation has been
fo effectually calculated to bring thefe to the act of experiment, as ours was at the juncture of our revolution.
The diftreffed fituation of the inhabitants of Maffachufetts, and particularly of thofe in the metropolis, after the
paffing of the *Port-Bill*, can never be remembered without ftarting the tear of humanity, and exciting the indignation of the world.

MISS SAMPSON, though not an eye-witnefs of this diftrefs, was not infenfible of it. She learned that the inhabitants of Bofton were confined by an unprovoked

enemy; that they were not only upon the point of perifhing for want of fuftenance, but that many had been
actually maffacred, their public and private buildings of
elegance fhamefully defaced, or quite demolifhed ; and
that many of her own fex were either ravifhed, or de-
luded to the facrifice of their chaftity, which fhe had
been taught to revere, even as dear as life itfelf.

THESE thoughts filled her mind with fenfations, to
which fhe had hitherto been unaccuftomed—with a kind
of enthufiafm, which ftrengthened and increafed with the
progreffion of the war; and which, peradventure, fixed
her mind in a fituation, from which, fhe afterwards found
it impoffible to be extricated, until the accomplifhment of
the object, after which it afpired.

DURING her refidence in Mr. THOMAS's family, they
granted her many domeftic privileges ;—fuch as the ufe
of a number of fowls, fheep, &c. upon condition, that fhe
would appropriate the profit arifing from them to the
attainment of objects ufeful and ornamental. This was
an effectual method to inure her to *method* and a proper
ufe of money. She applied herfelf to the bufinefs with
diligence and fuccefs. And, at this time, fhe had accu-
mulated a fmall ftock, which was appropriated, agreeably to her notion, perfectly coincident to the injunction.
The poor people of Bofton were reduced to the piteous
neceffity of afking *charity,* or *contribution* from the country inhabitants. This was no fooner known to her than

fhe experienced an anxiety, that could brook no controul, until fhe had an opportunity of *cafting in her mite:* Upon which, fhe fincerely congratulated herfelf, not upon the principle, that any one owed her any more gratitude; but upon the confcioufnefs of having endeavoured to relieve the innocent and diftreffed.

THOUGH I am as much difinclined to have faith in com- mon dreams as in any invented fable, or to fpend time in reciting their ominous interpretations; yet as they proceed from that immortal part of man, which no one ought to flight, they may fometimes be of ufe. I can- not help noticing, in this place, a phenomenon prefented to the mind of Mifs SAMPSON during her nocturnal re- pofe, April 15, 1775, in the fifteenth year of her age, and but four days before the battle at Lexington. I infert the principal part of it in her own language, and fome of the latter part, verbatim.[16]

"As I flept, I thought, as the Sun was declining be- neath our hemifphere, an unufual foftnefs and ferene- nefs of weather invited me abroad to perambulate the *Works* of *Nature.* I gladly embraced the opportunity;

[16] In the MS. memoir of Deborah Sampfon, fhe is reprefented as having had this dream on three fucceffive nights, the laft of which immediately preceded the "Lexington Alarm." *Credat Judaeus Apella, non ego.* In that memoir, the dream is told with much enlargement, and in extremely high-flown language. It is there rep- refented as a prophecy of the Amer- ican Revolution. Pretty well for a girl of fourteen! It is difficult to believe that this dream ever had any exiftence, fave in the brain of Herman Mann. It is a pity to fpoil with it fo much white paper.

and with eager fteps and penfive mind, quickly found
myfelf environed in the adjacent fields, which were decorated with the greateft profufion of delights. The gentle
afcending ground on one fide, upon which were grazing
numerous kinds of herds; the pleafant and fertile valley
and meadow, through which meandered fmall rivulets on
the other; the afpiring and venerable grove, either before
or behind me; the zephyrs, which were gently fanning
the boughs, and the fweet caroling of the birds in the
branches; the husbandmen, intent upon their honorable
and moft useful employment, *agriculture;* the earth, then
cloathed with vegetation, which already filled the air
with ravifhing odours;—all confpired to fill my mind
with fenfations hitherto unknown, and to direct it to a
realization of the AUTHOR of their being whofe power,
wifdom and goodnefs are, as they manifeft, as infinite as
they are perpetual.

STUDIOUS in contemplating the objects that furrounded
me, I fhould have been barbarous, and perhaps, have deprived myfelf of advantages, which I never might again
poffefs, had I abruptly quitted my ramble. I prolonged
it, till I found myfelf advanced upon a lofty eminence
that overlooked a far more extenfive and beautiful profpect, both of the ocean and continent.

HAVING reached the fummit, I fat down to indulge
fuch thoughts as the fcene feemed altogether capable of
infpiring.—How much, thought I, is it to be regretted,

that I am not always filled with the fame fenfations, with fuch fublime ideas of CREATION, and of that BEING, who has caufed it to exift! Indeed, I fancied, I could joyfully have fpent my life in refearches for knowledge in this delightfome way.

BUT how great was my aftonifhment and horror at the reverfion of the fcene! An unufual appearance, different from whatever my eyes beheld, or imagination fuggefted, was, at once, caft on every thing that furrounded me. The fky, which before was fo pleafant and ferene, fuddenly lowered, and became, inftantaneoufly, veiled with blacknefs. Though not altogether like a common tempeft, inceffant *lightning* and tremendous peals of *thunder* feemed to lacerate the very vaults of nature. The ambrofial fweets of vegetation were exchanged for the naufeous ftenches of fulphur and other once condenfed bodies, that feemed to float in ether.

HAPPENING, at this inftant, to caft my eyes upon the liquid element, *new amazement* was added to the fcene. Its furface, which before was unruffled, was now properly convulfed, and feemed piled in mountains to the fky. The fhips, that before were either anchored, or riding with tranquillity to their harbors, at once difmafted, dafhing againft rocks and one another, or foundering amidft the furges. The induftrious farmers, many of whom were vifited by their conforts in their rural occupations, feemed difperfed, and flying for refuge to the neareft

11

place of fafety.   And the birds and beftial tribes feemed at a lofs where to go, being in as great confufion as the elements.

FILLED with aftonifhment at this diftraction of the elements, without any fixed precaution what method to take for fafety; on the one fide, the earth, a volcano, which fhook with the perpetual roar of thunder; and on the other fide, the liquid element foaming to the clouds —my reafon feemed entirely to forfake me, on beholding the moft hideous *ferpent* roll itfelf from the ocean.   He advanced, and feemed to threaten *carnage* and *deftruction* wherever he went.   At length, he approached me, with a velocity, which I expected would inftantly have coft me my life.   I happened to be directed homeward; but looking back, and perceiving the *ftreets*, through which he paffed, *drenched in blood*, I fell into a fwoon.   In this condition, I know not how long I remained.   At length, I found myfelf, (as I really was) in my own apartment; where I hoped not to be again fhocked with the terrific and impending deftruction of the *elements* or *monfter*.

BUT to my repeated grief and amazement, I beheld the door of the apartment open of itfelf; and the *ferpent*, in a more frightful form and *venomous* in looks, reappeared. He was of immenfe bignefs; his mouth opened wide, and teeth of great length.   His tongue appeared to have a *fharp fting* in the end.   He entered the room; but it was not of fufficient dimenfions for his length.   As he advanced towards my bed-fide, his head raifed, as nearly as I conjectured, about five or fix feet, his eyes refembled *balls* of *fire*. I was frightened beyond defcription. I thought I covered my head and tried to call for affiftance, but could make no noife.

AT length, I heard a voice faying, "*Arife, fand on your feet, gird yourfelf, and prepare to encounter your enemy.*"—This feemed impoffible; as I had no weapon of defence. I rofe up, ftood upon the bed; but before I had time to drefs, the *ferpent* approached, and feemed refolved to fwallow me whole. I thought I called on God for affiftance in thefe diftreffing moments: And at that inftant, I beheld, at my feet, a bludgeon, which I readily took into my hand, and immediately had a fevere combat with the enemy. He retreated towards the door, from whence he firft entered. I purfued him clofely, and perceived, as he lowered his head, he attempted to ftrike me with his tail. His tail refembled that of a *fifh*, more than that of a *ferpent*. It was divided into feveral parts, and on each branch there were *capital letters* of yellow gilt. I purfued him, after he left the apartment, feveral rods, ftriking him every opportunity; till at length, I diflocated every joint, which fell in pieces to the ground: But the pieces reunited, though not in the form of a *ferpent*, but in that of an *Ox*. He came at me a fecond time, roaring and trying to gore me with his horns. But I renewed the attack with fuch refolution, and beat him in fuch a manner, that he fell again in pieces to the ground. I ran to gather them; but on furvey, found them nothing but a *gelly*.—And I immediately awoke."

THIS very fingular *Dream* had an uncommon effect on her mind, and feemed to prefage fome great event. The novelty and momentous ideas it infpired, induced her to record it; but fhe kept it fecreted from others. At that time fhe attempted no particular interpretation of it.

ALTHOUGH the nature and limits of thefe MEMOIRS will not admit of a connected fketch of the American War; yet, as the motives that led to open hoftilities, and the actions, in which the firft blood was fhed, fo peculiarly occupied the mind of a young FEMALE, I cannot help following the example: efpecially, as thefe were the opening of the great DRAMA, fo fingular in its *nature* and *important* in its *confequences;* and in which fhe afterwards became fo diftinguifhed an ACTRESS.[17] Thefe, added to a prompt regard and honor to the memory of thofe HEROES, who fell the firft facrifices in the CAUSE of their COUNTRY, induce me to dwell, for a few minutes on thofe fcenes; the remembrance of which, while they fire the mind and paffions with genuine love of LIBERTY and PATRIOTISM, muft bring up recollections, fhocking and melancholy to every tender mind.

[17] The long account which follows of the opening events of the American Revolution is omitted in the MS. memoir, as wholly irrelevant. It was evidently inferted here merely to fill up the fpace.

REVIEW.   85

THE repeated and unjuſt *Acts of Parliament*, which
they more ſtrenuouſly endeavoured to enforce on the Colonies, ſeemed to threaten general deſtruction; unleſs they
would, in *One mutual Union*, take every effectual method
of reſiſtance. For this purpoſe, a CONGRESS had been
formed; whoſe firſt buſineſs was to remonſtrate and petition for redreſs. At the ſame time, they had the precaution to take methods for defence, in caſe their voice
ſhould not be heard in Parliament. Great encourage-
ment was given for the manufacture of all kinds of military ſtores and apparatus. The militia were trained to
the uſe of arms.

WHILST things were going on in this manner, a detachment of troops commanded by Colonel SMITH and
Major PITCAIRN were ſent from Boſton to poſſeſs or de-
ſtroy ſome ſtores at Concord, twenty miles from Boſton.
At Lexington, a few companies were collected for the
purpoſe of manœuvring, or to oppoſe the incurſions of
the Britiſh. Theſe, as ſome accounts ſay, were ordered
by the Britiſh commander, with the epithet of *damn'd
rebels*, to diſperſe. Whether they ſo readily complied
with the injunction as he wiſhed, or not, he ordered his
troops to fire upon them; and *eight men* were inſtantly
the victims of death.

AFTER the diſperſion of the militia, the troops proceeded to Concord and deſtroyed a few ſtores. But by
this time the militia had collected from the adjacent

towns, and feemed unanimoufly refolved to avenge, by fevere retaliation, the death of their innocent brethren. This the troops effectually experienced during their pre-cipitate march to Bofton.

WHO but the actors and fpectators, being themfelves unaccuftomed to fcenes of this kind, can beft defcribe the anguifh of mind and emotions of paffion excited by it! The lofs of the Americans was fmall compared to the Britifh. But view them once tranquil and happy in the midft of focial and domeftic compact. No mufic more harfh than the note of the fhepherd, of friendfhip and in-nocent glee. With the lark, each morn was welcomed, as a prelude to new joy and fatisfaction.—Now behold the reverfe of the fcene! As if nature had been con-vulfed, and with juft indignation had frowned on fome unpardonable offence, their peace, and every focial and private endearment was, at once, broken up. But *fhe* ftands acquitted; whilft the *pride* of *man* could be fatiated only with the dear price of the *fcourge*—the *havoc* of *war*. On that fatal day, when their fields and ftreets, which had fo often re-echoed with rural felicity, fuddenly affumed the afpect of the regular *battalia*, refounding with nothing but the din of war, and the agonies of expiring relatives and friends, the Earth feemed to precipitate her diurnal revolution, and to leave the Sun in frightful afpect. The fhepherd's flocks ftood aghaft. Birds forgot to carol, and haftened away with aftonifhed mutenefs. And think—

while the tender *female* breaſt turned from the ſcene in diſtraction, how it muſt have humanized the moſt ſavage temper, and have melted it into ſympathy, even towards a relentleſs enemy.

THE news of this battle ſpread with the rapidity of a meteor. All America was rouſed. And many companies of militia, from remote parts, marched day and night, almoſt without intermiſſion, to the relief of their friends in Maſſachuſetts. Thus, in a ſhort time, the environs of Boſton exhibited, to the view of the enemy, the formidable appearance of 20,000 men.

THIS event had the ſame effect on the mind of Miſs SAMPSON, as it had on thoſe of every one, that was *awake* to the introduction of objects ſo intereſting and important; and whoſe feelings were ready to commiſerate the ſufferings of any of the human race.

ON June the 5th, the ſame year, Congreſs unanimouſly appointed GEORGE WASHINGTON, Eſq. to the chief command of the American Army. He is a native of Virginia: And though he is a *human being*, his abilities and improvements can never be called in queſtion. He had acquired great reputation in the execution of a Colonel's commiſſion in the French war. He accepted this appointment with a *diffidence*, which, while it beſt interpreted his wiſdom, evinced the fidelity of his heart, and his patriotic zeal for the fulfilment of the impor tant *truſt* repoſed in him.*—Of this illuſtrious *perſonage*, I may have further occaſion to ſpeak in the progreſs of theſe MEMOIRS.

LEXINGTON battle was ſoon ſucceeded by that of Breed's Hill in Charleſtown, Maſſachuſetts, a mile and an half from Boſton.

THE 16th of this month, a detachment of Provincials under the command of Col. PRESCOTT, was ordered to intrench on Bunker's Hill the enſuing night. By ſome miſtake, *Breed's Hill* was marked out for the intrench-ment, inſtead of *Bunker's:* It being high and large like it, and on the furthermoſt part of the peninſula next to Boſton. They were prevented going to work till mid-night. They then purſued their buſineſs with alacrity: And ſo profound was their ſilence, that they were not heard by the Britiſh on board their veſſels lying in the harbour. At day-break, they had thrown up a ſmall re-doubt; which was no ſooner noticed by the Lively, a man of war, than her cannon gave them a very heavy ſalute.

THE firing immediately rouzed the Britiſh camp in Boſton, and their fleet to behold a novelty they had little expected. This diverted their attention from a ſcheme they meant to have proſecuted the next day; which was now called to drive the Americans from the hill.

NOTWITHSTANDING an inceſſant cannonade from the

* He arrived at Head Quarters in Cambridge on the 2d of July fol-lowing.

enemy's fhips, floating batteries and a fort upon Cop's
hill in Bofton, oppofite the American redoubt, they continued laborious till noon, with the lofs of only one man.
By fome furprifing overfight, one detachment had labored, inceffantly, four hours, without being relieved, or
fupplied with any refrefhment.

By this time the Americans had thrown up a fmall
breaft-work, extending from the eaft fide of their redoubt
towards the bottom of the hill; but were prevented completing it by the intolerable fire of the enemy.

Just after twelve o'clock, the day fair and exceffively
hot, a great number of boats and barges were filled with
regular troops and apparatus, who fail to Charleftown.
The Generals, Howe and Pigot, take the command.
After they were landed, they form, and remain in that
pofition, till they are joined by another detachment, confifting of infantry, grenadiers and marines; which make
in all, about 3000.

During thefe operations, the Generals, Warren and
Pemeroy, join the American force. General Putnam
continues ambitious in giving aid as occafion requires.[18]

---

[18] General Jofeph Warren was on
the field that day, but with no afferted
authority. On entering the redoubt
thrown up by the troops, Colonel
Prefcott offered him the command;
but Warren replied that he had not
received his commiffion, and fhould
ferve as a volunteer. He had been
chofen major-general by the Provincial Congrefs of Maffachufetts only
three days before. He gave no order
during the action, though his prefence
and example were of great fervice.
He took a mufket, and mingled in

They are ordered to take up a poft and rail fence, and to fet it not quite contiguous to another, and to fill the vacancy with fome newly mown grafs, as a flight defence to the mufketry of the enemy. They are impatiently waiting the attack.

In Bofton, the Generals, CLINTON and BURGOYNE, had taken their ftand on Cop's Hill to contemplate the bloody operations now commencing. General GAGE had previoufly determined, when any works fhould be raifed in Charleftown by the Americans, to burn the town: And whilft his troops were advancing nearer to the American lines, orders came to Cop's Hill for the execution of the refolution. Accordingly, a carcafs was difcharged, which fat fire to the hither part of the town; which, being fired, in other parts by men for that purpofe, was, in a few minutes, in a general flame.

WHAT fcenes are now before us! There, a handfome town, containing 300 houfes, and about 200 other buildings, wrapt in one general conflagration; whofe curling flames and fable fmoke, towering to the clouds, feem to befpeak heavy vengeance and deftruction! In Bofton,

the thickeft of the fight. — [Frothingham's *Siege of Bofton;* Loring's *Hundred Bofton Orators.*]

General Seth Pomeroy, a veteran who had behaved with great gallantry at Louisburg, alfo ferved as a volunteer on Bunker Hill, and fought in the ranks with a mufket in hand. He was at the rail-fence. General Ifrael Putnam was alfo at the rail-fence, in command of the Connecticut troops, and rendered important fervice. — [Frothingham's *Siege of Bofton.*]

fee the houfes, piazzas and other heights crowded with the anxious inhabitants, and thofe of the Britifh foldiery, who are not called upon duty! Yonder, the adjacent hills and fields are lined with Americans of both fexes, and of all ages and orders.—Now turn to the American lines and intrenchments. Behold them facing the moft formidable enemy, who are advancing towards them with folemn and majeftic dignity! In a few moments, muft be exhibited the moft horrid and affecting fcene, that mankind are capable of producing!

ALTHOUGH the Americans are ill fupplied with ftores; and many of their mufkets without bayonets; yet they are generally good markfmen, being accuftomed to hunting. The Britifh move on flowly, inftead of a quick ftep. The provincials are ordered to referve their fire, till the troops advance within ten or twelve rods; when they begin a tremendous difcharge of mufketry, which is returned by the enemy, for a few minutes, without advancing a yard. But the ftream of American fire is fo inceffant, and does fuch aftonifhing execution, that the regulars break and fall back in confufion. They are again with difficulty rallied; but march with apparent reluctance to the intrenchments. The Americans at the redoubt, and thofe who are attacked by the Britifh infantry in their lines leading from it to the water, are ordered, as ufual, to referve their fire.—The fence proves a poor fhelter: and many are much more expofed than neceffity obliges. So that the Britifh cannot, in future, ftigmatize them with the name of *cowards*, who will fly at the fight of a *grenadier's cap*, nor for fighting in an unfair manner. They wait till the enemy is within fix rods; when the earth again trembles with their fire. The enemy are mown down in ranks, and again are repulfed. General CLINTON obferves this, and paffes over from Bofton without waiting for orders. The Britifh officers are heard to fay, "*It is downright butchery to lead the troops on afrefh to the lines.*" But their *honor* is at ftake; and the attack is again attempted. The officers are feen to ufe the moft violent geftures with their fwords to rally their troops: and though there is an almoft infuperable averfion in them to renew the attack, the officers are once more fuccefsful.—The Americans are in want of ammunition, but cannot procure any. Whilft they are ordered to retreat within the fort, the enemy make a decifive pufh: the officers goad on the foldiers with their fwords—redouble their fire on all fides; and the redoubt is attacked on three fides at once. The Americans are, unavoidably, ordered to retreat: But they delay, and fight with the butt end of their guns, till the redoubt is two thirds filled with regular troops.—In their retreat, which led over a neck leading from Cambridge to Charleftown, they were again in the greateft jeopardy of being cut off by the Glafgow man of war, floating batteries, &c. But they effected it without much lofs, and with greater regularity, than could be expected from men, who had never before feen an engagement. General WARREN, being in the rear, was fhot in the back part of his head; and having clapped his hand to the wound, dropped down dead.

THE number of Americans engaged, including thofe who dared to crofs the neck and join them, was only 1500. Their lofs was fmall compared with the Britifh. The killed, wounded and miffing were 453; of which, 139 were flain. Of the Britifh, the killed and wounded were 1054; of which, 226 were killed.[19]

IT has been faid by a veteran officer, who was at the battles of Dettingen, Minden, and feveral others, in Germany—that for the time it lafted, he never knew any thing equal it. The Britifh difplayed great heroic bravery: And there was a perpetual fheet of fire from the Americans for half an hour; and the action was intenfely hot for double that time.

AMONG the flain of the Britifh, they particularly lament the deaths of Lieut. Col. ABERCROMBY, and Major PITCAIRN, who occafioned the firft fhedding of blood at Lexington. Among the Americans, we lament, in particular, the fall

---

[19] The Britifh force in the battle was ftated by General Gage, in his official account, as fomething over 2,000. It would feem, therefore, that half their number were killed or wounded. Stedman, Biffett, and Lord Mahon, Britifh hiftorians, fay the Britifh force was 2,000; Marfhall, Ramfay, and Barry, Americans, and Thacher, in his "Military Journal," fay 3,000. Contemporary MSS., and the Journal of the Provincial Congrefs, fay, between 3,000 and 4,000. The American force was about 1,500.

of General WARREN, the Colonels, GARDNER, PARKER, CHELMSFORD, &c.²⁰ But the fall of General WARREN is the moſt effectually felt. By his fall, the public ſuſtain the loſs of the warm patriot and politician, the eminent orator and phyſician; with which were blended the other endearing and ornamental accompliſhments. And though an amiable conſort and a number of ſmall children had rendered his exiſtence more deſirable; he diſtinguiſhed himſelf *this day*, by fighting as a *volunteer;* and fell an illuſtrious EXAMPLE in the CAUSE of LIBERTY and the RIGHTS of MAN.

ABOUT this time, the country inhabitants, near Boſton, were frequently alarmed by idle and ignorant reports, that the Britiſh troops had broken through the American lines, were penetrating, with the greateſt rapidity, into the country, ravaging, plundering and butchering all before them. And more than once, was Miſs SAMPSON perſuaded to join her female circle, who were as ignorant of what paſſed in the armies as herſelf, to ſeek ſecurity in the dreary deſert, or deſerted cottage. But ſhe peculiarly noted the day of Breed's Hill engagement, as did many

²⁰ General Warren was killed juſt as the Americans were leaving the well-conteſted field. It was with the greateſt reluctance that he left the redoubt. He was retreating ſlowly, which brought him next to the Britiſh. Colonel Thomas Gardner of Cambridge, and Lieutenant-colonel Moſes Parker, were mortally wounded. Gardner died, July 3; Parker died, a priſoner, July 4. Major Willard Moore, who that day led Doolittle's regiment, was alſo mortally wounded. There was no officer of the name of Chelmsford in the battle, (See Frothingham's *Siege of Boſton.*)

others, by the inceffant roar of the cannon. A fertile eminence, near which fhe lived, is a ftanding monument of the penfive thoughts and reflections fhe experienced during the melancholy day.²¹ She has faid, that, for fome days after the battle, having had an account of it, fleep was a ftranger to her. It feems, her attention was of a different nature from that of many of her fex and youth. Whilft they were only dreading the *confequences*, fhe was exploring the *caufe* of the eruption. This, as fhe had heard, or naturally apprehended would terminate, at leaft, in New-England's wretchednefs or glory.

It is, indeed, too much to fport with the *lives* of any animals. But when a large number of *men*, many of whom, perhaps, are involuntarily led into the field, and many more, without knowing or caring for what reafon,— march within a few paces of each other, that their *lives* may be made a fairer *mark* for the *fport* of the avarice, pride and ambition of a few licenced incendiaries—*nature* muft recoil, or the whole fyftem of intellects forget there is a higher dignity of man.

She had frequent opportunity of viewing the American foldiers, as they marched from one part to another.—One

²¹ The meaning is, fhe heard the cannon, on the day of the battle, from a hill near her refidence. The diftance is at leaft thirty miles. Befides the firing from the Britifh fhips and floating batteries, and from Copp's Hill, a furious cannonade was kept up on the American lines in Roxbury, to divert the attention of the right wing of the American army, and to prevent reinforcements being fent to the troops on Bunker Hill.

day, having gone fome diftance to fee a number of regiments, her curiofity was arrefted by an officer, who boafted
much of his courage and heroic achievements. A young
female domeftic being near him, he thus addreffed her :—
"You *Slut*, why are you not better *dreffed* when you come
to fee fo many *officers* and *foldiers !*"—Mifs SAMPSON feeing her confufed, thus replied to the arrogant coxcomb :
—" Elegance in drefs, indeed, Sir, becomes the *fair*, as
well as your fex. But how muft that foldier feel, who
values himfelf fo highly for his courage, his great ex-
ploits, *&c.* (perhaps where there is no danger,) fhould
they *for fake* him in the *field* of *battle !* "

HOSTILITIES having commenced throughout the Colonies, a new and effectual *fchool* was opened for the hero,
politician and ftatefman ; and which was a ftimulation,
even to the philofophic moralift. The confequence of
which, was the declaration of our *Independence*, July 4,
1776. This momentous event took place two hundred
and eighty four years after the difcovery of America by
COLUMBUS—one hundred and feventy, fince the firft eftablifhed fettlement in Virginia—and a hundred and fifty
fix, fince the fettlement of Plymouth in Maffachufetts ;
which were the firft permanent fettlements in North America. And whilft this *Era* will forever be held a *Jubilee*
by every votary of *American Freedom*, it muft bring to
our minds *two* very affecting periods :—Firft, the time
when we, with the moft *heart-felt* fatisfaction, acknowl-

edged the *fovereignty* of our *parent country :* And fecond-
ly, when we were *diftreffed*, and like her *dutiful offspring*
afked her *lenity* and *compaffion*—but could not *fhare*, even
in her *parental affection !*

BUT out of great *tribulation*, it is believed, *anguifh* has
not been the greateft refult. Thofe neceffitous events
were, doubtlefs, conducive to the raifing our Empire to
that rare height of perfection in the *moral*, as well as in
the *political* world ; in which it now fo confpicuoufly
fhines.

C H A P. IV.

MISS SAMPSON *continues in Mr.* THOMAS's *family after
fhe is of age, without meeting any incidents more uncommon, than her increafing propenfities for learning and
the mode of interefting herfelf in the* CAUSE *of her*
COUNTRY.—*Engages in a public fchool part of two years
fucceffively.—An outcry of religion in her neighborhood.
—Her thoughts upon it.—Summary of what fhe deemed
the trueft religion.*

WE are now to view the ftate of Mifs SAMPSON's
mind comparable to him, who has planned fome
great achievement, which, he believes, will be of the
greateft utility and importance to him ; but, who finds

13

his opportunities, rather than abilities, inadequate to its completion.

I KNOW not that fhe ever was deferving the name of *ficklenefs* in her purfuits; yet, I have the ftrongeft reafon to conclude, that her mind, during her juvenility, was fo crowded with inventive ideas for improvements, as to throw it into uncommon anxiety. And notwithftanding her invention propofed many fchemes; yet, as they tended to the fame comparative objeft, they ought rather to be applauded than afperfed. Neither would I think it gratifying to any, to account for this upon any other fcore. To affign no other motive for thefe intelleftual exertions, than the attainment of gewgaws, fuperfluity in drefs and the night confumption, would not only be doing injuftice to her, but mentioning a train of evils, which, it muft be confeffed, charafterize too great a part of our youth at this day; and which, every legiflator fhould difcourage, and every parent prohibit.

BEFORE this time, Congrefs had taken effeftual methods to encourage the manufafture of our own apparel, and every other confumption in America. And the refleftion is pleafing, that Mr. THOMAS's family was not the only one, who had not the reformation to begin. As though they had always been apprehenfive of the utility and honor they fhould gain by it, they had always practifed it; and the voice of Congrefs was only a ftimulation: So that Mifs SAMPSON's employments were not much altered. And fhe has, fomewhere, fuggefted—that had we continued this moft laudable and ever recommendable employment, in the fame degree, to this day, we fhould not only have increafed commerce with many foreign nations; but, have retained immenfe fums of money, which are now piled fhining *monuments* of the opulence of other nations, and of our own *vanity* and *inattention*. In this opinion, I am confident, every well-wifher to his country is ftill ready to concur.*

NECESSITY, our *dreadful*, but *ufeful*, friend, having taught us the advantages of our own manufactures for the fupport and conveniences of life, continued ftill favorable to our intellectual powers, and prompted them to the ftudy of arts and fciences. The propriety of this is ratified by our Independence. Nor was Mifs SAMPSON the only one, who realized it: But fhe has often faid, fhe hoped every one, who had, or may have, the fame propenfities for it, may have freer accefs to it. Her fituation of mind was very applicable to the maxim—"*Learning has no enemy but ignorance*." She was not now of age; but

---

* MISS SAMPSON has juft fhown me pieces of *lawn* and *muflin*, which were manufactured with her own hands, foon after the commencement of the war. I confider them as nothing more than fpecimens of COLUMBIAN *abilities, genius* and *tafte*. It is wounding to me to hear—"We can *buy cheaper* than we can *make*." No doubt—And fo long as we encourage *foreign manufacture* by fending them our *fpecie*, there is no doubt, but *they* can *fell cheaper* than *we* can *make*. And even when they have entirely drained us of our *money*, there will be one cheerful certainty left— they will *laugh* at our *credulity*.

fhe refolved, when that period fhould arrive, to devife fome more effectual method to attain it.

IT is natural for *fear* to fubfide, when *danger* flees out at the door. This, doubtlefs, was the cafe with many good people in Maffachufetts, after the feat of war was removed to diftant parts; when they were not fo fuddenly alarmed by its havoc. To whatever degree this may have been the cafe with Mifs SAMPSON, it appears, that its firft impreffions, inftead of being obliterated by time, were more ftrongly impreffed on her mind. In fact, it feems, fhe only needed a different formation to have demonftrated in *actions* what fhe was obliged to conceal through re-ftraint of nature and cuftom.

JUST before fhe was eighteen, 1779, fhe was employed, much to her liking, fix months in the warm feafon, in teaching a public fchool in Middleborough.[22] In this

[22] This fchool was taught in the warm feafon of 1779, when Deborah had *completed* her eighteenth year. Until the age of eighteen, fhe was bound to the fervice of Mr. Thomas. Her term of fervice was now expired, and fhe was at liberty. The fchool taught by her was at the village of Middleborough Four Corners, two miles from the houfe of Deacon Thomas. The houfe in which fhe taught ftood on the fpot where Major Tucker now refides ; the building having fubfequently been removed to Water Street, and occupied as a dwelling-houfe. At this time, fhe boarded in the houfe of Abner Bourne, which now ftands oppofite to Peirce Academy. — [*Rev. Stillman Pratt.*]

The range of ftudy in her fchool was not extenfive ; and it may be taken as a fpecimen of the fummer fchools generally in New England at this time. The books ufed were "The New-England Primer," here and there a Spelling-Book, "The Pfal-ter," and a few Teftaments. A fheet of paper was fometimes allowed to the boys for the exercife of penman-fhip, while the chief occupation of the girls was to learn to knit and few ! One forward lad brought to fchool a

bufinefs, experience more effectually convinced her, that her *education*, rather than her *endowments*, was inadequate to the tafk. But her fuccefs more than equalled her expectations, both with regard to the proficiency of her pupils, and the approbation of her employers.

THE next feafon her engagement was renewed for the fame term in the fame fchool. She now found her tafk eafier, and her fuccefs greater, having had the advantage of a good man fchool the preceding winter. The employment was very agreeable to her; efpecially, as it was a fource of much improvement to herfelf.

NOT far from this time, there began to be an uncommon *agitation* among many people in her neighborhood; as had been, or foon followed, in many towns in New-England. This penetrating diforder was not confined to old age. It violently feized on the middle-aged, and as fhe remarked, even *children* caught the contagion. There are but few mifchiefs, that *war* is not capable of effecting.[23]

dilapidated copy of Fifher's "Young Man's Beft Companion." A few books which Deborah brought to the fchool for her own improvement completed the catalogue. Such is the account fhe gives in the MS. memoir, where it is implied, though not exprefsly ftated, that "The Affembly's Catechifm" was taught in this, as in other fchools, every Saturday. When the editor taught fchool, forty years ago, this was the practice in Maffachufetts.

[23] It is to be hoped that very few readers of this volume will fympathize with the irreligious fpirit exhibited in thefe remarks, and in thofe which follow. They are very properly omitted in the MS. memoir. The facts of the cafe, derived from authentic fources, were the following: —

During the enfuing autumn and winter, there was in Middleborough, and in feveral other towns, an unufual

BUT fome well-minded people were ready to term this *the working of the Spirit, of the Holy Ghoft—a reforma-*

intereft felt in the great concerns of religion. Notwithftanding the heavy preffure of the war, many of the people were led to feel that there are higher interefts than thofe which pertain merely to the prefent life. Nothing, furely, could be more rational, nothing more capable of a fatisfactory vindication. A revival of religion is the greateft blefling which can be beftowed upon any people. It is a mark of ftupendous madnefs when immortal beings, ruined by fin, and haftening to the judgment, can remain, year after year, wholly indifferent and thoughtlefs. *They* are the fanatics who neglect the great falvation !

Many, both old and young, in Middleborough, at this time, were making the earneft inquiry, " What fhall I do to be faved ? " Among the number thus tenderly and folemnly affected was Deborah Sampfon, the fubject of our ftory, then nineteen years of age. At length fhe entertained the hope that fhe had experienced renewing grace, and that her fins were forgiven. Ever fince coming to live in Middleborough, at the age of eight years, fhe had attended public worfhip with the Firft Congregational Church in that town, whofe meeting-houfe was at the " Upper Green," fo called. This church, at the time indicated in the text, had no fettled paftor.* The

Rev. Abraham Camp, who was then preaching there, is faid to have entertained a high opinion of Deborah's talents and character, and to have regretted her departure from the congregation ; for, as the revival extended into other fections of the town, it was greatly promoted by the labors of Rev. Afa Hunt,† a Baptift minifter in the south part of Middleborough, at a locality known as " The Rock," on the borders of Rochefter. Deborah was induced to attend on his preaching, and not long after joined herfelf in covenant with his church. The Records of the Firft Baptift Church in Middleborough fhow that fhe was received by them as a member, Nov. 12, 1780. She continued in that relation lefs than two years. It appears that fhe renounced her covenant with the Church, and learned to fpeak lightly of experimental religion.

church had long exifted. Rev. Sam'l Fuller, their firft minifter (fon of the excellent Dr. Samuel Fuller of the Mayflower), had preached in the town from 1679, and probably from the incorporation of the town in 1669. After the death of the Rev. Sylvanus Conant, in 1777, there was no fettled minifter there till 1781. Mr. Abraham Camp, a graduate of Yale College in 1773, was preaching to this church at the time mentioned in the text. The people were greatly interefted in his preaching, and gave him a unanimous call to be their paftor, in February, 1779, and again called him, by a vote of twenty-two to five, in November, 1780. He concluded not to fettle in Middleborough.

* The Firft Church in Middleborough was organized Dec. 26, 1694, although materials for a

† Mr. Hunt was from Braintree, and was ordained at Middleborough, Oct. 30, 1771; d. Sept. 2, 1791.

tion in religion. Whether it originated from the unufual and influential exertions of the clergy, who took advantage of this unparalleled crifis to add to their number of converts in the Chriftian religion; or, whether it was a voluntary act of the mind, or a natural cachexy;—or whether it is a characteriftic trait of the *Divine Character* —I have not time here to conjecture.

She was in the midft of it, and was excited to obferve its operations. But fhe had the wife precaution to ftudy well its purport, rather than to fuffer the *fugitive* to take her by furprife. But let its tendency have been what it might, it anfwered a good purpofe for her. It ferved to rouze her attention; and to bring about thefe important enquiries:—From whence came man? What is his bufinefs? And for what is he defigned? She confidered herfelf as having been too inattentive to religion; which, as fhe had been taught, and naturally conceived, is the moft indifpenfable duty enjoined on man, both with regard to his *well-being here*, and to the *eternal welfare* of his immortal part.

But from her beft conclufive arguments drawn from a conteft of this nature, fhe faw no propriety in it. Reafon being perverted or obftructed in its courfe, the whole fyftem of intellects is thrown into a delirium. This being the cafe, as fhe conceived, in this *outcry* of *religion;* its fubjects were of courfe, not only difqualified for ufeful bufinefs, which was, certainly, wanted at that time, if ever, but rendered totally incapacitated for the adoration and worſhip of DEITY, in a manner becoming his dignity, or the dictates of ſound reaſon.

AT this age, ſhe had not, profeſſionally, united herſelf to any religious denomination;[24] as was the practice of many of her cotemporaries. She conſidered herſelf in a ſtate of probation, and a free agent; and conſequently at liberty, to ſelect her own religion. In this, ſhe was, in a meaſure, miſtaken. Had her mind been free from the manacles of *cuſtom*, and unſwayed by *education*, ſhe might have boaſted of an advantage ſuperior to all others, and might, peradventure, have entertained the world with a ſet of opinions, different from all other ſects and nations. But theſe were her combatants. As ſhe advanced on the ſtage of life to eſtabliſh a religion, her proſpect was that of the *Chriſtian world:* And her aſſent to it was at once urged by her mode of education. Indeed, this was the only religion of which ſhe had any knowledge, except that which ſimple *nature* always teaches.

BUT her reſearches in Chriſtianity did not occaſion ſo much ſurpriſe to its votaries as they did to herſelf. On ex-amination, inſtead of finding only *one* denomination, ſhe muſt have been entertained—more probably, alarmed, on finding almoſt an infinite number of ſects which had ſprung out of it, and in each ſectary, a different opinion—

---

[24] So far is this from being true, that ſhe profeſſed to be a ſubject of the revival, and united herſelf to the Baptiſt Church, as already ſtated.

all right, infallibly right, in their own eftimation. A great diverfity of fcenery in the fame drama, or tragedy, upon the ftage, perhaps, has nothing in it wonderful or criminal. But a religion, which is believed to be of divine origin, even communicated directly from GOD, to *Man*, confequently, intended for the equal good of all, but ftill fubject to controverfy—differently conftrued and differently practifed—fhe conceived, has every thing of the marvellous, if not of an inconfiftent nature. Thus, when fhe would attach herfelf to *one*, the fentiments of a *fecond* would prevail, and thofe of a *third* would ftagnate her choice: and for a while fhe was tempted to reject the whole, till thorough examination and the aid of HIM, who cannot err, fhould determine the beft. And I am not certain, there are not many, who have made their profeffion, who ought to difapprove her refolution.

To have called in queftion the validity and authenticity of the Scriptures would only have been challenging, at leaft, one half America, and a quarter of the reft of the globe to immediate combat: For which fhe had neither abilities, nor inclination. She began to reflect, however, that, the being bound to any fet religion, by the force of man, would not only be an infraction of the laws of *Nature*, but a ftriking and effectual blow at the prime root of that *liberty*, for which our nation was then contending.

I WOULD not leave the public to furmife, that fhe derived no advantage from Chriftianity. Though divines

14

utterly difallow, that the plan of the Gofpel can be attained by the dim light of nature, or by the boafted
fchools of philofophy; yet, we have already found in thefe
MEMOIRS, that, as feeble as they are, they lead, without
equivocation, to the knowledge and belief of DEITY, who,
every one acknowledges, is the firft and great objeƈt of
our reverence and devotion. Chriftian morality, fhe acknowledges with more warmth, than I have known in
many, who have had greater advantages of education.
Setting afide the doƈtrines of *total depravity*, *eleƈtion*, and
a few others, which were always inadmiffible by her reafon, fhe is an adherent to its creed. By her diffidence,
fhe is willing, however, that her ignorance fhould be fo
far expofed to the public, as to declare, that fhe knows
not whether it is more from the *light* of *Gofpel revelation*,
or the *force* of *education*, that fhe is led to the affent of
the fundamental doƈtrines of Chriftianity.[25]

THIS view of her religious fentiments will be concluded
by the following fummary of what fhe now believes to be
genuine religion: And under whatever denomination it
may fall, it muft always continue without a precedent.

THAT religion, which has a tendency to give us the
greateft and moft direƈt knowledge of DEITY, of his attri-
butes and works, and of our duty to HIM, to ourfelves and
to all the human race, is the trueft and beft; and by which,
only, we can have *confciences void of offence*.

[25] The author here delivers his own
fentiments rather than thofe of Deborah Sampfon. He reminds us of the
fable of the viper biting the file.

REVIEW. 107

I TAKE the liberty to clofe this chapter with a few digreffional remarks.

SENSIBLE I am, that when we can be made fenfible that religion, in its trueft fenfe, ought to be made the ultimate end and object of our purfuit—that it is the greateft requifite for our general felicity, both here and in futurity;—or, fhould it be found, that, as we difregard, or attend to it, our temporal intereft will be effected, as it is by our legiflative government—I am inclined to believe, not a myftery, or hidden part in it will long remain unexplored, but eftablifhed or rejected, as it may be deemed genuine. Civil government and religion have, briefly, this difference:—Civil government ferves as a directory neceffary for the accumulation and prefervation of temporal intereft and conveniencies for life: religion teaches us how to fet a proper eftimate on them, and on all other enjoyments in life. It expands and elevates the mind to a fenfe and knowledge of DEITY, and to the dignity of human nature. It pervades the whole foul, and fills it with light and love. It is a fource, from which, only, can be derived permanent fatisfaction, and teaches us the true end of our exiftence. For want of a knowledge or realization of this, into how many grofs errors and abfurdities have mankind inadvertently fallen, or inattentively been led: When impofitions of this kind have been multiplied upon them, when they have been ftigmatized by this name, or by that, in matters of fentiment; it feems, they have refted comfortably eafy, without enquiring into their truth or juftice, or paffed them off with flighty indifference. But touch our *intereft*—that bright, momentary gem! the cheek is immediately flufhed, and the whole heart and head are upon the rack—fet to invention for redrefs. So contracted and interwoven with lucrative, fantaftical gain are the views and purfuits of men.

C H A P. V.

Remarkable anxiety of Mifs SAMPSON'S *mind relative to the War, and to gain a knowledge of her country.—For once, fhe is tempted to fwerve from the fphere of her fex, upon the mere principle of gratifying curiofity and of becoming more effectually inftrumental in the promotion of good.—There are but two methods for the accomplifh-ment of this, in which her inclinations lead her to con-cur.—The firft is that of travelling in the character of a gentleman.—The fecond, that of taking an effective part in the* CAUSE *of her* COUNTRY, *by joining the Army in the character of a voluntary foldier.—The latter, after many fevere ftruggles between prudence, delicacy and vir-tue, fhe refolves to execute.*

IT is impoffible to conjecture what would have been Mifs SAMPSON'S turn of mind, had fhe obtained the moft refined education. But it requires no great force of logic to difcover her leading propenfities in her prefent fituation. She was formed for *enterprife:* and had for- tune been propitious, fhe might have wanted limitations.

AMONG all her avocations and intervening occurrences in her juvenility, her thirft for knowledge and the prevail- ing American conteft, appear, by her diurnals, to have held the moft diftinguifhed and important fway in her mind:—*Diftinguifhed,* becaufe they were *different* from the generality of her fex;—*important,* becaufe on *that* depended the future welfare and felicity of our country. Her refolutions on thefe accounts, and the execution of them will now employ our attention.

FROM the maturity of her years, obfervation and expe- rience, fhe could determine, with more precifion, on the nature of the war and on the confequence of its termina- tion. This may be faid to be her logic:—If it fhould terminate in our fubjeótion again to England, the aboli- tion of our *Independence* muft follow; by which, we not only mean to be *free,* but to gain us the poffeffion of *Lib- erty* in its trueft fenfe and greateft magnitude: and thus fecure to ourfelves that illuftrious *name* and *rank,* that adorn the nations of the earth.

THIS, and her propenfities for an acquaintance with the geography of her country, were, alternately, fevere in her mind. Her tafte for geography muft have been chiefly fpontaneous; as the ftudy of it in books was unfafhiona- ble among the female yeomanry.—I am happy to remark

here, that this ufeful and delightfome fcience is now become a polite accomplifhment for ladies.

It was now a crifis with her not often to be experienced: and though it was painful to bear, it was, doubtlefs, conducive to improvement. Invention being upon
the rack, every wheel in the machine is put in motion,
and fome event muft follow. It produced many perti-
nent thoughts on the education of her fex. Very juftly
did fhe confider the female fphere of action, in many refpects, too contracted; in others, wanting limits. In
general, fhe deemed their *opportunities*, rather than *abilities*, inadequate for thofe departments in fcience and the
bellef-lettres, in which they are fo peculiarly calculated to
fhine.—From this, let me infer—that, although *cuftom*
conftitutes the general *ftandard* of female education; yet,
the beft method that occurs to my mind to be ufed in
this important bufinefs, is that dictated by reafon and
convenience.

But the public muft here be furprifed in the contemplation of the machinations and achievements of *female*
heroifm and virtue: which if not the moft unparalleled,
are the moft fingular, that have ever fprung out of Columbia's foil. And it is but reafonable, that we exercife
all that candor and charity, that the nature of the circumftances will admit. By ideally putting ourfelves in fimilar
circumftances, the reafonablenefs will be fully evinced.
Though independent and free, *cuftom* in many refpects,

rules us with defpotic fway: And the perfon who greatly deviates from it, expofes himfelf to numberlefs dangers. An indelible ftigma may doom him to infamy; though perhaps, his original defign was to effect fome ufeful and important event. But on the other hand, *liberty* gives us fuch afcendancy over old *habit*, that unlefs it bind us to fome apparent and permanent good, its iron bands are fubject to diffolution. We have, in fome meafure feen Mifs SAMPSON's motives for achievement; the reft will be illuftrated in the fequel.

HAVING come of age, her former refolution[*] remained to be executed.[26] For this purpofe, fhe planned many fchemes and fabricated many caftles; but, on examination, found them chimerical, or of precarious foundation. Every recent information of the geography of the continent, ferved only to ftimulate propenfities, which fhe had no defire to ftifle. But the news of the war ferved but to engrofs her mind with anxieties and emotions fhe had long labored to fupprefs. And it muft here be mentioned to her honor, that fhe ufed arguments *for*, and *againft*, herfelf in every important propofition drawn for enterprife. Her chief problems for folution may have been thefe:—Muft I forever counteract inclination and ftay within the compafs of the fmoke of my own chimney?

[*] SEE CHAP. IV.

[26] Her refolution to travel, and to obtain a knowledge of her country, induced her to enlift in the Continental army.

Never tread on different foils; nor form an acquaintance with a greater circle of the human race? Stifle that fpirit of *heroic patriotifm*, which no one knows but HIM who foreknows all events, but may terminate in the greateſt good to myſelf, and, in fome degree, promote the CAUSE of my COUNTRY? Yield the palm of *cuſtom* to the *force* of that *philanthropy*, which ſhould warm the boſoms of both ſexes and all ages?—In faĉt, ſhall I ſwerve from my ſex's ſphere for the ſake of acquiring a little uſeful acquifition; or, ſhall I ſubmit (without reluĉtance, I cannot) to a priſon, where I muſt drag out the remainder of my exiſtence in ignorance: where the thoughts of my too cloiſtered fituation muſt forever harraſs my boſom with liſtleſs purſuits, taſteleſs enjoyments, and reſponfive difcontent?

CONTRASTING this argumentation with the fuperior advantages of many of the human race for acquiring knowledge, ſhe was ready, for a moment, to find fault with her *formation:* but happily, it was but momentary. As if ſhe had been inſtantly cured of a frenzy, ſhe could fcarcely be reconciled with herſelf for ſuch preſumption. It being not only an indignity to her own ſex, but the baſeſt ingratitude to her MAKER, and derogatory to his laws. Her humble folicitations were, that ſhe never might be fo loſt to all fenſe of virtue and decorum, as to aĉt a part unworthy her *being*, thereby not only bring infamy on herſelf, but leave a blemiſh and ſtigma on the female world. .

For this purpofe, fhe refolved to think no more of projecting adventures, of leaving the tranquillity of her domeftic retirement—her endearing circle of relations and
friends, to vifit diftant parts; as the good fhe anticipated
in the refult was uncertain, and might, in a fatal manner,
prove fallacious. Her flights of imagination had furnifhed a clue the moft requifite for the maxim, which
every one more or lefs needs—"*When fancy rides, let
reafon hold the reins.*" She likewife refolved to fufpend
all further enquiries and anxiety about the war. Vain
attempts! The prohibitions proved a fource of mortification and difcontent. And it feems, a prevention of thefe
enquiries would have been as much impoffible as it would
to have brought the war to a clofe without negotiation,
or by inaction itfelf. It feems, fhe could not *hear* of its
fuccefs without *feeling* the *victory*. She had heard of
many beautiful cities, rich foils, healthy climates and different cuftoms with the inhabitants: And the thought of
being prohibited from augmenting her acquaintance with
them, was but anticipating her diffolution too foon.[27]

[27] While Deborah, as in the text, is pondering her future courfe, let us confider what fhe was at this time.

She was now a few months over twenty years of age; had been de-prived of the advantages refulting from a proper training under the pa-rental roof, and, in great meafure, of opportunities for intellectual improve-ment. She had good natural capaci-ty; was of a ftudious, contemplative turn of mind; an ardent lover of na-ture; a careful obferver of paffing events. She was fond of adventure, and had a great deal of energy. Her temper was bold, enterprifing, inde-pendent, fearlefs; and fhe was dif-pofed to have her own way. regard-

15

In this dilemma she continued several months without any fixed resolution. At length, her propensities for viewing distant places, &c. gained such a perfect ascendancy over cooler reason, that her propensities could brook no controul. She determined to burst the bands, which, it must be confessed, have too often held her sex in awe, and in some mode and measure, stretch beyond the boundaries of her own neighborhood; by which means she might be convinced whether what she had read or heard be true—" *That one half of the world does not know how the other half lives.*" But here fresh scenes of difficulties awaited her; though many had been before

less of consequences. The sphere in which she had hitherto moved she found too quiet and too narrow for her aspiring temperament: she longed for something higher and better, she knew not what. Under proper culture and discipline, she might have become an ornament to her sex and a blessing to the world. But she had none to guide, to train, to admonish her, scarcely any to sympathize with her. Consequently, her efforts were misdirected, her energies misemployed. To a considerable extent, she was a day-dreamer, and a builder of castles in the air. She had a strong desire to see the world, to visit distant regions, to behold society in new lights and under unusual aspects. She determined that she would, at all events, quit the ignoble employments to which she had been accustomed in

a farmer's family in Middleborough, —of feeding pigs and poultry, of plying the spinning-wheel and the loom.

She resolved, therefore, to put on male attire, and travel; and to this end spun and wove, with her own hands, cloth, which (she says) she employed a tailor to make up as a suit for a gentleman, pretending that it was for a young man, a relative of hers, who was about leaving home for the army. She found these garments became her so well, that even her mother, whom she visited at Plympton in this costume, did not know her. This is the statement which is made in the MS. memoir, where it is also stated that she procured and put on these garments several times, to try them, in the autumn of 1780. It was certainly a year later when this was done.

anticipated. Prudence, as ufual, appeared in her plain, but neat, attire, and called her refolution in queftion. Delicacy trimmed her diflocated hair; and virtue brought her amaranthine wreathe. The thought of travelling without a companion or protector, was deemed by *prudence*, a ftep of prefumption. Not to have travelled at all, might have deprived her of much good, with increafing anxiety: And there was an avenue to it both ways. But her greateft obftacle was the want of that current fpecie, which is always fure to gain the efteem of all people. Without it, fhe muft have been liable to have incurred the appellation of an idler, a bonaroba, or a vagabond: And fo have failed in her defign; which was the acquifition of knowledge without the lofs of reputation.

WHILST fhe was deliberating on thefe matters, fhe privately dreffed herfelf in a handfome fuit of man's apparel and repaired to a prognofticator.[28] This, fhe declares, was not to ftimulate, but to divert her inclinations from objects, which not only feemed prefumptuous, but impracticable. She informed him, fhe had not come with an intention to put entire confidence in his delufory fuggeftions; but it was partly out of principle, but moftly out of curiofity. He confidered her as a blithe and honeft young gentleman. She heard his preamble. And it was either by art or accident, that he told her, pretty juftly,

---

[28] Or fortune-teller. Her interview with him undoubtedly contributed much to ftengthen and confirm her refolution.

her feelings—that fhe had propenfities for uncommon enterprizes, and preffed to know why fhe had held them in fufpenfion fo long.—Having predicated, that the fuccefs of her adventures, if undertaken, would more than compenfate a few difficulties, fhe left him with a mind more difcompofed, than when fhe found him. But before fhe reached home, fhe found her refolution ftrengthened. She refolved foon to commence her ramble, and in the fame clandeftine plight, in which fhe had been to the necromancer. She thought of bending her firft courfe to Philadelphia, the metropolis of America.

IN March, 1781, the feafon being too rough to commence her excurfion, fhe propofed to equip herfelf at leifure: and then appoint the time for her departure. A handfome piece of cloth was to be put to a use, of which fhe little thought, during the time fhe was employed in manufacturing it.—Ye fprightly Fair, what is there in your domeftic department, that neceffity, ingenuity and refolution cannot accomplifh?—She made her a genteel coat, waiftcoat and breeches without any other affiftance, than the uncouth patterns belonging to her former mafter's family. The other articles, hat, fhoes, &c. were purchafed under invented pretexts.[29]

[29] During her abode in the family of Mr. Thomas, he had allowed her the income arifing from a number of fowls and fheep, with the underftanding that it fhould be applied to ufeful purpofes. The burning of Charlestown and the fiege of Bofton had occafioned fevere fuffering to the inhabitants of thofe places; and Deborah had contributed out of her fcanty

BEFORE fhe had accomplifhed her apparatus, her mind
being intent, as the reader muft imagine, on the *uſe* to
which they were foon to be appropriated; an idea, no
lefs fingular and furprifing, than true and important, determined her to relinquifh her plan of travelling for that
of joining the American Army in the character of a voluntary foldier.[30]   This propofal concurred with her inclinations on many accounts.   Whilft fhe fhould have equal
opportunities for furveying and contemplating the world,
fhe fhould be accumulating fome lucrative profit; and in
the end, perhaps, be inftrumental in the CAUSE of LIBERTY,
which had for nearly fix years, enveloped the minds of
her countrymen.

ftock for their relief. This fmall fund
alfo enabled her to purchafe the materials for a fuit of mafculine apparel.
During feveral weeks of the winter,
fhe was employed in fpinning and
weaving a piece of handfome woollen
cloth. As fpring advanced, and the
weather became more comfortable,
fhe retired, as we are informed, to a
beautiful recefs in the grove above
the Borden Hills, and there, with the
aid of patterns, cut and made for herfelf a coat, veft, and breeches. Pan-
taloons reaching to the ankles were
not then worn. — [*Rev. S. Pratt.*]

30 Her original plan of travelling as
a gentleman was foon laid afide, from
the lack of that very neceffary article,
which, as the royal preacher well fays,
"anfwereth all things." There re-

mained no other method for gratifying the roving propenfities which had
now acquired full poffeffion of her
mind, but this, — to enlift as a foldier
in the Continental army. There is
no need of denying that fhe felt alfo
the impulfe of earneft and genuine
patriotifm ; but this feems not to have
been the principal motive. From the
beginning of the Revolutionary ftruggle, fhe had, though a young girl, fym-
pathized intenfely with the caufe of
liberty, and had, with deep emotion,
liftened, from a hill near her refidence, to the boom of cannon on the
day of Bunker Hill.

It feems very clear that an enliftment as a foldier was not the original
plan, nor patriotifm the original impulfe.

Here I might bring forward her former monitors, and reprefent the affecting dialogues, which no virtuous mind wifhes to difpute, fhe held with them on this trying occa-fion. But I leave this for the poet, novelift, or fome more able pen. Suffice it to fay, the following motto is the chief refult of her debates:—" *There may be an heroic* INNOCENCE *as well as an heroic* COURAGE." *Cuftom*, not *virtue*, muft lofe its name by tranfition; unlefs *cuftom* be made the *criterion* of virtue. She debated, with all the force of eloquence, that a fenfe of duty to a parent or miftrefs could produce, whether to communicate her in-tentions to them, or to make a confident of any one in fo important an undertaking. She refolved in the negative, for this reafon:—If her purfuits fhould terminate in an event, that fhould caufe her to lament her engagement, fhe fhould not reflect upon herfelf for having gone coun-ter to their advice and injunctions; though fhe might, for not afking and adhering to them. In either cafe, fhe meant to make an expiation.

Females! *you* have refolutions, and you execute them. And you have, in a degree, the *trial* of the virtues and graces, that adorn your fex. Then, by ideal fimilitude, put yourfelves in the fituation of our *Heroine*, (for thus fhe muft be diftinguifhed in future) and then grant her fuch favors as you might wifh from her. I am your friend, and would do honor to that, which dignifies your character, and renders you the amiable companions of man. Heaven, who has aided *Columbia's Caufe*, recognize my fincerity! And although it has been purchafed, moftly, at the dear expenfe of her *fons; you* have not remained uninterefted nor without the pang of the diftreffed lover.—I cannot defire you to adopt the example of our Heroine, fhould the like occafion again offer; yet, we muft do her juftice. Whether that *liberty*, which has now cemented us in fo happy an union, was purchafed through direct, or indirect means; we certainly owe the event to HEAVEN. And enterprife in it can better be difpenfed, than in many other eminent cafes.—Let your imagination, therefore, travel with me through the toils and dangers fhe has paffed. And if you exercife that propriety and fweetnefs of temper, which I have known in many of you, in the contemplation of other lefs interefting fcenes and objects, I am fure, I fhall never be tired with your company.

C H A P. VI.

The time prefixed for her perfonating the SOLDIER.—*Reflections on her bidding adieu to her relations, friends,
&c.—Takes a Weftern, circuitous rout for Bofton.—Is
hired for a clafs of Uxbridge, as a foldier, for three
years, or during the War.—Her mode of joining the
Army at Weft-Point.—Is put into the Fourth Maffachufetts' Regiment.*

IN April, 1781, having obtained what requifites fhe
could for her new, but hazardous, expedition, warm
weather being generally fettled—fhe allowed herfelf but
a few days to compromife matters with herfelf, and to
take a private leave of her agreeable circle, before her
departure.³¹ The thoughts of being put into a kind of
transformation were not fo alarming, as the dread fatality,
which fhe knew not but it might produce. Whilft moft
females muft recoil at the commencement of an undertaking of this nature, few can have refolution to attempt
a fecond trial. And had I a tragi-comic pen, it might
find ample fcope in the fcenes now before me.

SEVERAL circumftances concurred, in this interim,
which could not have failed to excite peculiar emotions.

³¹ It has been fatisfactorily and   tion, by official documents, that "her
conclufively fhown in the Introduc-   departure" was in May, 1782.

She knew her mother had long doated on her future
felicity, with a young gentleman of fortune, and agréeable
deportment; and with whom fhe had contracted an intimate and endearing acquaintance. He had given her
many cordial proofs of the fincerity of his attachment
and lafting affections. And had' her mind been difen-
cumbered with a higher object in view, fhe might, doubtlefs, have united her affections in the happieft alliance
for life.[32] Already did fhe confider a parent not only difappointed in her warmeft wifhes, but diftracted with anguifh by the elopement, and for aught fhe knew, the fatal
and untimely cataftrophe of a daughter. She felt for
thofe who had taken the charge of her youth;[33] whofe
affections had not been alienated by her difobedience.

[32] That this talk about the "young
gentleman of fortune" is mere "moon-
fhine," will be apparent from a quota-
tion from the MS. memoir, to which I
have repeatedly referred. She fays,—
"I did not, however, in this vernal
feafon of raptures and defpairs, efcape
the addreffes of a young man, of
whom my mother, I believe, was paf-
fionately fond, and feemed ftruck with
wonder that I was not. She confidered him regenerated. I had not her
eyes to fee fuch perfection in this
lump of a man, or that he poffeffed
qualities that would regenerate *me*.
I had no averfion to him at firft, and
certainly no love, if I have ever underftood that noble paffion. At any
rate, this marry, or not to marry, was

decided thus: On a certain parade-
day he came to me, with all the *fang
froid* of a Frenchman, and the filli-
nefs of a baboon, intoxicated, not
with *love*, but with *rum*. From that
moment I fet him down a fool, or in
a fair way to be one."
This will ferve to fhow that "The
Female Review" cannot, in matters
of detail, be fafely trufted.
It is quite probable that a wifh to
efcape the addreffes of this young
man — though he is doubtlefs groffly
mifreprefented in the extract juft
made — was one of the motives which
operated in inducing her to leave home
fecretly, and join the army.
[33] The family of Deacon Thomas,
next to her mother, her beft friends.

16

For him, who loved her, fhe felt with emotions, that had not before alarmed her. Indeed, fuch groups of ideas, that hurried upon her mind, muft have been too much for a breaft naturally tender. She retired to indulge the effects of nature: And in this feclufion, refolved, fhould her purfuit fucceed, to write to her mother in a manner, that might pacify her mind without difclofing the delicate ftratagem.

But neither the rigor of a parent to induce her marriage with one, whom fhe did not diflike, nor her own abhorrence of the idea of being confidered a *female candidate* for conjugal union, is the caufe of her turning volunteer in the American War; as may hereafter, partly, be conjectured by an anonymous writer. This muft be the greateft obftacle to the magic charm of the novelift. She did not flight love; nor was fhe a diftracted inamorato. She confidered it a divine gift: nor was fhe deceived. For, ftrike *love* out of the *foul*, life becomes infipid and the whole body falls into lethargy. Love being, always, attended by hope, wafts us agreeably through life.—She was a *lover;* but different from thofe, whofe love is only a fhort epilepfy, or for the gratification of fantaftical and criminal pleafure. This, I truft, will be demonftrated by a fact, to which, but few can appeal. Her love extended to all. And I know not, but fhe continues to have this confoling reflection, that no one can tax her for having coveted the prohibited enjoyment of any individual. This is that love, whofe original fource and motive induced Columbia's fons to venture their property, endearments—their lives! to gain themfelves the poffeffion of that heaven-born companion, called *liberty:* and which, when applied to conjugal union, is the fame thing, only differently combined with the other paffions. And whatever effect it may then have had on her, fhe has fince been heard to fay, without referve—That fhe deemed it more honorable for one to be *fuffocated* with the *fmoke* of *cannon* in the *Caufe*, in which fhe was then embarked, than to wafte a ufeful intended exiftence in defpair, becaufe Heaven had juftly denied the favorite of a whimfical and capricious fancy. The perfeverence for the object, dictated by love, in both cafes, corroborates, beyond doubt, its efficacy and utility.

JUST before her departure, fhe received a polite invitation to join a circle of her acquaintance for rural feftivity. She was cheerful; and the reft of the company more fo. Among many lively topics, it was remarked that Mr. ———, brother to a lady not prefent, had been killed in the battle at Long-Ifland, in New-York. It was brufhed into oblivion, by concluding—his fweetheart was again courted. It drew involuntary tears from our intended heroine, which were noticed. In the evening, fhe returned home with emotions, that might affect a lover.

NEXT day, the weather was exceedingly pleafant; and nature fmiled with the feafon. Mifs SAMPSON performed

her bufinefs with much affected gaiety and fprightly converfation : But the night was to be big with the important event.[34]

[34] I am forry to fpoil a good ftory ;
but there is another account given of
her affumption of male attire, far lefs
romantic than that given in the text,
and far more truftworthy. It was
given to my friend, Rev. Stillman
Pratt, by a perfon in Middleborough
who remembered Deborah Sampfon.
It is alfo for fubftance confirmed by
that diftinguifhed antiquary, Mr. Samuel G. Drake of Bofton, whose firft
wife was a near relative of Capt.
Leonard. The account is as follows :—

During the war of the Revolution,
Capt. Benjamin Leonard, a diftant
connection of Hon. Daniel Leonard of
Taunton, the author of the famous letters figned " Maffachufettenfis," refided in Middleborough, eaftwardly from
what are now known as the Upper
Namafket Works. A negro woman
of the name of Jennie, daughter of
a flave of Judge Oliver, was an in-
mate of his family. Here Deborah
Sampfon was ftaying for a time. By
the aid of this negro woman, Deborah dreffed herfelf in a fuit of clothes
belonging to a young man named
Samuel Leonard, a fon of Capt. Benjamin Leonard. Thus clad, fhe repaired to a recruiting - office, kept
at the houfe of Mr. Ifrael Wood.
There fhe enlifted as a foldier under
the affumed name of Timothy Thayer,
and received the bounty. Having

now plenty of money, fhe went, thus
attired, to a tavern near the meeting-
houfe, two miles eaft of Middleborough
Four Corners ; called for fpirituous
liquors ; got excited ; and behaved
herfelf in a noify and indecent manner. During the night, fhe returned
home ; crept to bed with the negro ;
and, when morning came, refumed
her female attire, and returned to her
female employments, as if nothing
had happened.

She enlifted at this time, it is fuppofed, partly to have a little frolic,
and to *fee how it would feem* to put on
a man's clothing, but chiefly for the
purpose of procuring a more ample
fupply of fpending money. Some of
the money fhe now received was
fpent for female wearing apparel. A
few nights after this adventure, fhe
appeared at a finging-fchool, held at a
houfe near the prefent refidence of
Mr. Earle Sproat, dreffed out in a
fomewhat gaudy ftyle. On this occafion, fhe made a prefent of a pair of
long gloves to a young lady of her
acquaintance, to whom fhe felt indebted for fpecial kindnefs in a time of
ficknefs.

She had doubtlefs long meditated
the defign of becoming a foldier, but
was not yet quite prepared to join the
army. It was now either in the winter feafon, or the early fpring of 1782 ;
and it feemed beft to wait a while.

HAVING put in readinefs the materials fhe had judged
requifite, fhe retired, at her ufual hour, to bed, intending
to rife at twelve. She was, doubtlefs, punctual. But

When the time came for the foldiers newly enlifted in Middleborough to join their regiment, Timothy
Thayer, to the furprife of the recruiting-officer, could not be found. His
identity with Deborah Sampfon was
difcovered in this manner: When the
fuppofed Timothy was putting his
name to the articles of enliftment, an
old lady, who fat near the fire card-
ing wool, remarked that he held the
pen juft as Deb. Sampfon did. Deborah, having by means of a felon, or
whitlow, loft the proper ufe of her
fore-finger, was obliged to hold a pen
awkwardly when fhe wrote. This
was well known in the neighborhood
where fhe had kept fchool, and where,
of courfe, fhe had often been feen to
ufe a pen. This circumftance led to
a ftrong fufpicion that fhe and Timothy Thayer were the fame perfon.
Inquiry being made, black Jennie difclofed the part fhe had acted in dreffing Deborah in men's clothes. Deborah, thus expofed, was obliged to
refund that portion of the bounty-
money fhe had not fpent, and to keep
herfelf out of fight for a time, left
punifhment fhould overtake her.
Tradition affirms that Samuel Leonard was fo fhocked at the idea of his
clothes having been ufed by a woman,
that he never wore them afterwards.

There is no reafon, however, to
doubt that fhe provided herfelf with

a fuit of mafculine apparel, by the labor of her own hands, in the manner
already ftated. If her fcheme was to
be put in execution, fhe muft, of courfe,
have a fuit of her own. The clothes
of Samuel Leonard were put on merely for the occafion, and fhe had no intention of keeping them. The frolic
in which they were ufed occurred fome
months before her fecond enliftment.

The affurance given by the fortune-
teller whom fhe vifited, as ftated on
page 115, that fhe would fucceed in
the plan fhe was meditating, feems to
have contributed to confirm her refolution to join the American army.
Her repeated experiments in male attire had been fuccefsfull: fhe had
paffed for a man without fufpicion;
and, as fhe fays in the MS. memoir,
fhe found men's clothes more convenient than thofe worn by her own fex.
It was not without confiderable hefitation and mifgiving that the final
refolution was taken. The family of
Deacon Thomas had been kind to
her; fhe had not alienated their affections even by her wayward conduct; and to leave them utterly coft
her a fevere ftruggle. What troubled her moft of all was the thought
that her mother, who ftill lived in
Plympton, would be diftreffed at her
difappearance. At laft, however, fhe
came to the fixed determination to join
the army, and abide the confequences.

there was none, but the INVISIBLE, who could take cogni-
fance of the effufions of paffion on affuming her new
garb; but efpecially, on reflecting upon the *ufe*, for which
it was affigned—on leaving her connections, and even
the vicinity, where the flower of her life had expanded,
and was then in its bloom. She took her courfe towards
Taunton, in hopes of meeting with fome ftranger, who
was going directly to Head-Quarters, then at the Southward.[35]—Having walked all night, fhe was juft entering
the Green in Taunton, when the bright luminary of day,
which had fo often gleamed upon her in the rufticity of
a fhepherdefs, then found her, not, indeed, impreffed only
with the fimple care of a brood of chickens, or a bleating
lamb—but with a no lefs important CAUSE, than that, in
which the future felicity of America was then fufpended.
The reflection ftartled her: but female temerities were
not to be palliated.

AT this inftant, fhe unwelcomely met Mr. WILLIAM
BENNETT, her near neighbor. Surely, an apoplexy could
not have given her a more fudden fhock.[36] Though fhe
was not pofitive he had difcovered her mafquerade; yet,
fhe knew if he had, fhe fhould be purfued when he
reached home.—After fome refrefhment, and fupplying

---

35 Taunton Green, which is the
principal village in Taunton, is eight
or ten miles from Middleborough,
on the weft.

36 Her eye met his; her heart pal-
pitated: fhe feared that fhe was
known; but fhe paffed by him without difcovery.

her pockets with a few bifcuit, fhe haftened through the town; but determined not to bend her courfe directly for the Army, till fhe fhould know what had been done about her clandeftine elopement. Fatigued with walking, fhe took an obfcure path, that led half a mile into a thicket of wood; where the boughs of a large pine ferved for her canopy during her repofe till evening. Surprifed when fhe awoke on finding it dark, with difficulty, fhe regained the road; and by the next peep of dawn, found herfelf in the environs of her former neighborhood.[37]

DEJECTED at the fight of the place where fhe had enjoyed fo much rural felicity, fhe half refolved to relinquifh all thoughts of further enterprize, and to palliate what had paffed, as a foible, from which females are not always exempt. The debate was not long. As ufual, fhe muft perfevere, and make the beft of what might prove a bad choice. The groves were her fanctuary for meditation that day and the fucceeding night. After the birds had fung their evening carols, fhe lay down with intentions to fleep: but neceffity, our old alarming friend, roufed her attention. Impelled by hunger, during the tranquillity of the village, fhe repaired to a houfe fhe had much frequented, with intentions to appeafe the cravings

[37] Her heart now began to fail her. Fearing that Mr. Bennett had penetrated her difguife, and that her friends would ftart in hot purfuit, fhe retraced her fteps to Middleborough to learn if any thing of the kind were in progrefs. Finding no evidence of purfuit, fhe refolved to perfevere in her romantic undertaking, but ftarted in another direction.

of nature. Going to a pantry, where victuals was wont to be depofited, and meeting with no better fuccefs than a cruft of bread, fhe again retired to her folitary afylum. —The caroling of the feathered tribe having again notified her of day, fhe refumed her ramble, and foon loft fight of thofe

> Adjacent villas, long to her endear'd,
> By the rough piles our anceftors have rear'd.

SHE reached Rochefter that day, and the next, Bedford, a feaport town in Maffachufetts; which had been much diftreffed by the Britifh in 1778—79. She here met with an American, Commander of a Cruifer; who, after much importunity and proffered emolument, gained her confent to go his waiter to fea. But fhe was informed, that, although he ufed much plaufibility on the fhore, it was changed to aufterity at fea.[38] She, therefore, requefted him to keep her month's advance, and leave to go into town on bufinefs; and, that night, lodged in Rochefter, and was careful not to fee him afterwards.*

* It has been reported, that fhe enlifted, as a Continental Soldier, for a clafs in Middleborough—that fhe received a part of the ftipulated bounty—that fhe was immediately difcovered, and refunded the bounty. I have no account of this from her; nor is the report in the leaft authenticated. It probably has fince taken its rife from this circumftance.[39]

[38] Rochefter joins Middleborough on the fouth. At a tavern in that place, where fhe fpent the next night, fhe faw fome of her town's-people, without being known by them. The next day fhe reached New Bedford, where fhe enlifted on board of a privateer, but abandoned the defign on being informed of the captain's bad treatment of his men.

[39] For proof of the correctnefs of this "report," fee note 34.

HEARING nothing concerning her elopement, fhe con
cluded to take a circuitous ramble through fome of the
Weftern towns, and vifit Bofton, the capital of Maffachufetts, before fhe joined the army. This was partly to
gratify curiofity, and partly to familiarife herfelf to the
different manners of mankind—a neceffary qualification
for a foldier, and perhaps, not detrimental to any, whofe
minds are properly fortified, and whofe eftablifhed maxim
is—*To do good.*

SHE left Rochefter on Friday. The next night and
the fucceeding, fhe tarried at Mr. MANN's tavern in
Wrentham. From thence, fhe vifited fome of the Weftern towns in the State.[40] Finding herfelf among ftrangers, her fear of being difcovered fubfided; and fhe found
herfelf in an element, from which, fhe had long, involuntarily, been fequeftered. She, doubtlefs, had awkward
geftures on her firft affuming the garb of the man; and
without doubt, more awkward feelings. Thofe, who are
unacquainted with mafquerade, muft make a difference between that, which is only to heighten beauty for fantaftical amufement and pleafure—and that of fex, which is to
continue, perhaps, for life, to accomplifh fome important

[40] This is not true. From Wrentham, where fhe fpent two days, fhe
went to Bofton, travelling, as before,
all the way on foot. She then paffed
through Roxbury, Dedham, and Medfield, to Bellingham; wifhing to proceed a confiderable diftance from
home before fhe enlifted. In Bellingham fhe met with a recruiting-officer;
and, being at this time almoft deftitute
of money, fhe enlifted as a foldier,
under the affumed name of ROBERT
SHURTLIFFE. This was the name of
her elder brother. — [*MS. Memoir.*]

event. She acted her part: and having a natural tafte for refinement, fhe was every where received as a blithe, handfome and agreeable young gentleman.

It may be conjectured, whether or not, fhe meant to fee the army before fhe enlifted. By what follows, it appears fhe did not. She doubtlefs chofe to engage for Maffachufetts; not becaufe fhc could render any more fervice, but becaufe it is her native State, and which had been the opening of the firft fcene of the horrid *drama*, and had fuffered moft by its actors.

In Bellingham fhe met with a fpeculator; with whom, for a certain ftipulated bounty,* fhe engaged for a clafs of Uxbridge as a *Continental Soldier.*†⁴¹ Inftead, then, of going to Bofton, fhe went back, and was immediately conducted to Worcefter; where fhe was muftered. She was enrolled by the name of ROBERT SHURTLIEFF. The general mufter-mafter was, doubtlefs, glad to enrol the

* General Wafhington refufed any pecuniary pay for his fervices during the war. Our Heroine needed, at leaft, his wealth, to have followed the example.

† Thofe are called *Continental Soldiers*, who engaged for three years, or during the war.

41 The male population of every town, capable of bearing arms, was at that time divided into *claffes*, as they were called ; and each clafs was obliged to furnifh a foldier for the army. The clafs fometimes paid a very confiderable bounty. Deborah enlifted, and was accepted, for a clafs in Uxbridge. The enliftment was for three years, or during the war. Bellingham is feparated from Uxbridge by the town of Mendon. The man who enlifted Deborah is called a fpeculator, becaufe he withheld from her a part of the bounty-money to which fhe was entitled.

name of a youth, whofe looks and mien promifed to do
honor to the caufe, in which fhe was then engaged.[42]
Ah, females—we have too long eftimated your abilities
and worth at too mean a price! Pardon an inadvertent
mifapplication of our intellects; as our profeffion is improvement, and our propenfities to redrefs all wrongs.

On May 13th, fhe arrived at Weft-Point in company
with about fifty other foldiers, who were conducted there
by a ferjeant fent for that purpofe.[43] Weft-Point was
then an important poft, where was ftationed a large divifion of the American army. It guarded a paffage in
the river Hudfon, fixty miles from the city of New-York.
Weft-Point will forever remain diftinguifhed by the infa-
mous treafon of General ARNOLD in 1780. His conduct,
the preceding winter in the city of Philadelphia, had

---

[42] The mufter-mafter was Capt. Eliphalet Thorp of Dedham, whofe certificate has already been given in the
Introduction. From his certificate it
appears that fhe enlifted May 20, 1782;
more than a year later than is ftated
in the context, page 120.

The ftory told by Mrs. Ellet about
Deborah's paffing feven weeks after
her enliftment in the family of Capt.
Nathan Thayer in Medway, and
the "love paffage" between the fuppofed Robert Shurtliffe and a girl vif-
iting the family, appears to be deftitute of any foundation.

[43] In the MS. memoir, fhe fays that
this march of ten or twelve days was

very fatiguing to her. At the clofe
of a chill and drizzly day, on approaching a fire in a tavern, fhe fainted, and fell upon the floor. Recovering, fhe found herfelf furrounded by
kind fpirits miniftering to her relief. Particularly fhe noticed a beautiful young woman, the innkeeper's
wife, who offered her cordials and re-
frefhments, with many expreffions of
pity and fympathy that one fo young
and tender fhould fuffer the hardfhips
of fuch a march. This amiable lady
infifted that the delicate young recruit
fhould take her place in the bed with
her husband. In the memoir, the account of the march is highly colored.

been cenfured; which gave him offence. The confequence was—he fought for revenge. He confpired with
Sir HENRY CLINTON to deliver Weft-Point and all the
American army into the hands of the Britifh; which he
meant to accomplifh during General WASHINGTON's abfence in Connecticut. But the plot was, providentially,
difconcerted. Major ANDRE, Adjutant General in the
Britifh army, an illuftrious young Officer, had been fent
as a fpy to concert the plan of operations with ARNOLD.
On his return he was overtaken, condemned by a court
martial, and executed.*   ARNOLD made his efcape by get-
ting on board the Vulture, a Britifh veffel : But his character wears a ftigma, which time can never efface.

IN the morning, fhe croffed the Hudfon, near Fort
Clinton. This is one of the moft beautiful and ufeful
rivers in the United States. It takes its name, as do
many others in America, from its difcoverer. Its fource
is between the lakes Ontario, and Champlain, running in
a Southern direction two hundred and fifty miles, till it
falls into the ocean; where it forms a part of New-York
harbor. It is navigable for fhips of almoft any burthen to
the city of the fame name, a hundred and thirty fix miles
from its mouth.

THEY marched on level land, and quickly had orders

* A particular account of his behaviour, from the time he was captured to his execution, would heave the moft ftubborn bofom, and affect
the magnanimous mind.

to parade for infpeĉtion.—The foldiers were detached into their proper companies and regiments. It fell to her lot to be in Capt. WEBB's company of light infantry, in Col. SHEPARD's regiment, and in General PATTERSON's Brigade.[44]

THE fecond day, fhe drew a French fufee, a knapfack, cartridge-box, and thirty cartridges. Her next bufinefs was to clean her piece, and to exercife once every morning in the drill, and at four o'clock, *P. M.* on the grand parade. Her garb was exchanged for a uniform peculiar to the infantry. It confifted of a blue coat lined with white, with white wings on the fhoulders and cords on the arms and pockets; a white waiftcoat, breeches or overhauls and ftockings, with black ftraps about the knees; half boots, a black velvet ftock, and a cap, with a variegated cockade, on one fide, a plume tipped with red

[44] Our heroine enlifted in the Fourth Maffachufetts Regiment, commanded at that time by Col. William Shepard of Weftfield, but foon afterwards by Col. Henry Jackfon of Bofton. This regiment was the old Ninth. Col. Shepard had command of it from 1777 to 1782. George Webb was one of the captains.

Col. William Shepard was born Dec. 1, 1737, fon of Deacon John Shepard. He entered the army at the age of feventeen; was, in 1759, a captain under Gen. Amherft in the old French war; and was in various battles, as at Fort William Henry, Crown Point, &c. He married Sarah Dewey, who was his wife fifty-feven years. Entering the army of the Revolution as lieutenant-colonel, he was colonel in 1777, and in 1782 a brigadier-general. He fought in twenty-two battles. He was afterwards major-general of the militia. From 1797, he was a member of Congrefs fix years. For thirty-four years he was a profeffor of religion, and a conftant attendant upon public worfhip. His houfe was a houfe of prayer. He died at Weftfield, Mass., Nov. 11, 1817, aged nearly eighty. — [Allen's *Biog. Diĉt.*, 3d edit.]

on the other, and a white fafh about the crown. Her martial apparatus, exclufive of thofe in marches, were a gun and bayonet, a cartridge-box and hanger with white belts. She says, fhe learned the manual exercife with fa-cility and difpatch, though fhe loft her appetite; which, through favor, fhe afterwards recovered.

HER ftature is perhaps more than the middle fize; that is, five feet and feven inches. The features of her face are regular; but not what a phyfiognomift would term the moft beautiful. Her eye is lively and pene-trating. She has a fkin naturally clear, and flufhed with a blooming carnation. But her afpect is rather mafculine and ferene, than effeminate and fillily jocofe. Her waift might difpleafe a coquette: but her limbs are regularly proportioned. Ladies of tafte confidered them hand-fome, when in the mafculine garb.* Her movement is erect, quick and ftrong: geftures naturally mild, ani-mating and graceful; fpeech deliberate, with firm articu-lation. Her voice is not difagreeable for a female.

SUCH is the natural formation, and fuch the appear-ance of the FEMALE, whom I have now introduced into a fervice—dreadful I hope, to moft men, and certainly, de-ftructive to all. Perhaps, exclufive of other irregularities,

---

* She wore a bandage about her breafts, during her difguife, for a very different purpofe from that which females wear round their waifts. It is not improbable, that the fevere preffure of this bandage ferved to com-prefs the bofom, while the waift had every natural convenience for aug-mentation.

we muft announce the commencement of fuch an enterprife a great prefumption in a *female*, on account of the
inadequatenefs of her nature. Love and propenfity are
nearly allied; and we have, already, difcovered the efficacy of both. No love is without hope: but that only is
genuine, which has for its objeƈt *virtue*, and is attended
with refolution and magnanimity. By thefe, the animal
economy is enabled to furmount difficulties and to accomplifh enterprifes and attain objeƈts, which are unattain-
able by the efforts of the other paffions. When love finks
into defpondency, the whole fyftem becomes enervated,
and is rendered incapacitated for the attainment of common objeƈts.—What is *Liberty*—I mean, in a genuine
fenfe? The love of it prompts to the expofure of our
property and the jeopardy of our lives. This is the
fureft definition of it: For interwoven with and dependent on it, are all our enjoyments. Confequently, *love*,
the nobleft paffion in man, in no other inftance, can do
more, or better fhow its effeƈts.

CHAP. VII.

March by stages from West-Point to Haerlem; from thence to White Plains.—Her company of infantry engage a party of Dutch cavalry.—Retreat and are reinforced by Col. SPROAT. Capture of the British Army under Lord CORNWALLIS at York-Town, where our HEROINE does duty during the siege.

SIX years having elapsed since our revolutionary *Epoch*, four years and ten months since our ever memorable *Independence*—COLUMBIA'S DAUGHTER treads the field of *Mars!*[45] And though she might, like Flora, have

---

[45] The time when Deborah Sampson joined the army is here declared to have been May, 1781. The same statement is made in the MS. memoir; where, after relating the manner of her leaving home in April, 1781, as she affirms; her visiting Taunton, New Bedford, Boston, Dedham, and other towns; her enlistment at Bellingham, &c.,—she adds, " It was near the last of April when we arrived at Worcester, where a regular muster and enrolment took place. . . . A large company of us then commenced our march for the camp at West Point, commanded by a sergeant, who was sent from the lines for that purpose." She then describes at considerable length, and in an animated, picturesque style, the march to the

Hudson. "We crossed the Housatonic," she says, "at New Milford, on the 12th of May." A day or two later, they crossed the Hudson at West Point, and joined the army. These statements are made by Mr. Mann as the mouth-piece of Deborah Sampson.

Notwithstanding this fulness and particularity of statement, there is much reason to believe that she did not enlist till at least a year later. In her petition to the General Court in January, 1792, she says she enlisted May 20, 1782. Capt. Thorp, the muster-master, says she enlisted on that day; the resolve of the General Court makes the same statement; the records of the First Baptist Church in Middleborough say, that, in the

graced the damaſk roſe, and have continued, peradventure, in the contemplation and unmoleſted enjoyment of her rural and ſylvan ſcenes; yet, for a ſeaſon, ſhe choſe the ſheathleſs cutlaſs, and the martial plume. She is a nymph, ſcarcely paſt her teens!—Think—females, think —but do not reſolve till you ſhall have heard the ſequel.

WE have already found, that ſhe did not engage in this perhaps unprecedented achievement, without the precaution of reflection and pathetic debates on the cauſe. And this renders her more excuſable than many ſoldiers, who ruſh, like the horſe, to the battle, before they eſtabliſh their proper *ultimatum*, which is derived only from a thorough inveſtigation of the principles of the contention. Happy for us, that a diſſemination of this knowledge is oftener the effect of a confederated Republic, than of the juriſdiction of an unlimited monarch. But neither a delirium, nor love in diſtraction, has driven her precipitate to this direful extremity. In cool blood, yet with firm attachment, we now ſee blended in her, the peerleſſneſs of enterpriſe, the deportment, ardor and heroiſm of

ſpring of 1782, ſhe put on men's clothes, and enliſted as a ſoldier. In any ordinary caſe, ſuch evidence would be deciſive. In the aforeſaid petition, ſhe would aſſuredly make the moſt of her caſe. If ſhe had participated in the campaign which reſulted in the triumph at Yorktown, ſhe would have ſaid ſo. Her ſilence proves, in our apprehenſion, that ſhe did not. But Mr. Mann deſired to make an intereſting book; and therefore included among the experiences of Deborah Sampſon the great campaign of 1781. This matter has been fully conſidered in the Introduction.

18

the veteran, with the milder graces, vigor and bloom of her fecreted, fofter fex.

On the tenth day in the morning, at reveille-beat, the company to which fhe belonged, with fome others, had orders to parade and march. They drew four days pro-vifion; which, with her large fack of clothes and martial apparatus, would have been a burthen too much for fe-males, accuftomed only to delicate labor. She left fome of her clothes, performed the march, and ufe foon be-came a fecond nature.

As the infantry belonged to the rangers, a great part of their bufinefs was fcouting; which they followed in places moft likely for fuccefs. In this duty fhe continued till they arrived at Haerlim; where they continued a few days, and then proceeded in like manner to White Plains. Here they, in their turn, kept the lines, and had a num-ber of small fkirmifhes; but nothing uncommon occurred in thefe places.

On July 3d, fhe experienced in a greater degree, what fhe had before moftly known by anticipation.[46] Captain

[46] We know of no reafon to doubt the truth of what is related in this paragraph and that immediately fuc-ceeding. A better ftatement, abridged from the MS. memoir, with fome ad-ditions, is the following : —

About the 10th of June, a detach-ment of troops, including our heroine, received orders to go out on a fcout-ing-party. They croffed the Hudfon at Stony Point. This brought them to the eaft fide of that river. Their deftination was the neutral ground between the American and Britifh armies. They halted for one night at Tarrytown, where the detachment was divided into two parties. They foon came into the vicinity of the en-

REVIEW. 139

WEBB'S company being on a fcout in the morning, and
headed by Enfign TOWN, came up with a party of Dutch
cavalry from Gen. DELANCIE's core then in Morfena.
They were armed with carabines, or fufees, and broad
fwords. The action commenced on their fide. The
Americans withftood two fires before they had orders to
retaliate. The ground was then warmly difputed for

emy's pickets, which they were careful to elude. They proceeded as far
as Haerlem, within the Britifh lines,
and only eight miles from the city of
New York, then held by the Britifh
army. After making fuch obferva-
tions of the enemy's pofitions as they
were able, they turned back to the
White Plains. About the 25th of
June, they left the White Plains, and
directed their courfe towards the Hudfon. The next day, the fkirmifh happened which is related in the text.
It took place in the neighborhood of
Tappan Bay, between Sing Sing and
Tarrytown. The party encountered
was a detachment from Col. Delancy's
regiment of dragoons, confifting chiefly, if not wholly, of Tories, and then
ftationed at Morrifania, near the
Sound. This regiment confifted in
part of defcendants of the old Dutch
fettlers : hence the phrafe in the text,
" Dutch cavalry." Delancy was an
active officer ; and his regiment made
frequent incurfions beyond the Britifh
lines, bent on rapine and often com-
mitting acts of great cruelty.
The enemy commenced the attack

by a volley from their carbines ; then
fuddenly wheeled about and gallop-
ed away. The Americans, being on
foot, had no opportunity to return the
fire. Repeating the attack, their
fecond fire was anfwered by a moft
deadly difcharge from the Continen-
tals. The enemy being re-enforced
by a party of Tories on foot, the Americans were compelled to retreat to a
piece of woods near by, ftill keeping
up a fcattering fire. They were foon
ftrengthened by the arrival of a part
of Col. Sproat's regiment, and poured
in a deftructive fire upon the enemy,
who were fpeedily compelled to a hafty
and diforderly retreat, after fuftaining
a heavy lofs.
It muft have been in this encounter that fhe was wounded, although
"The Female Review " and the MS.
memoir reprefent the wound as having been received in a fkirmifh with
a marauding party of Tories at a later
period. Both in her petition to the
General Court, January, 1792, and in
her declaration under oath, September, 1818, fhe fays fhe was wounded at
Tarrytown.

confiderable time. At length, the infantry were obliged to give way: but they were quickly reinforced by a detachment led on by Col. SPROAT, a valiant officer of the fecond Maffachufetts regiment.[47] They were then too much for the enemy, although a large number had landed from boats for their affiftance. The ground they had gained was then meafured back with precipitance, even to a confiderable diftance within their own lines; where the action terminated.

THE Americans having retired to their encampment, our fair Soldier, with fome others, came near lofing her life by drinking cold water. She fays, fhe underwent more with the fatigue and heat of the day, than by fear of being killed; although her left-hand man was fhot dead the fecond fire, and her ears and eyes were continually tormented with the expiring agonies and horrid

---

[47] This excellent officer, Col. Ebenezer Sproat, was a native of Middleborough. He was the talleft man in the brigade of Gen. John Glover, of which his regiment formed a part; being fix feet and four inches in height. Of the perils of the war he largely partook, being engaged in the battles of Trenton, Princeton, Monmouth, and many others. His fuperior excellence as a difciplinarian attracted the notice of the Baron Steuben, infpector-general of the army, who appointed him infpector of the brigade. After the war, he was one of the leaders in the enterprife of fettling the prefent State of Ohio; and was known to the Indians as the "Big Buckeye;" whence originated the term fince applied to all the people of that State. He died fuddenly, at Marietta, his refidence, in February, 1805, aged fifty-three. — [Hildreth's *Early Settlers of Ohio.*]

Our author is not careful about his fpelling. In the text we have "Gen. Delancie" for *Col. Delancy;* "core" inftead of *corps;* and *Morrifania* is transformed into "Morfena," all in a fingle line.

fcenes of many others ftruggling in their blood. She recollects but three on her fide, who were killed, JOHN BEEBY, JAMES BATTLES and NOOBLE SPERIN.[48] She efcaped with two fhots through her coat, and one through her cap.

PERHAPS, by this time, fome may be ready to tax her with extreme obduracy, and, without mercy, to announce her void of all delicacy of fentiment and feeling. And really, had this been her cuftomary plight in her kitchen at home, fhe might not have paffed for an agreeable companion : for fhe was perfectly befmeared with gunpowder. But if we reflect, that this was not the effect of indolence or fluttifhnefs, but for ought we know, of the moft endearing attachment to her country; it ought, at leaft, to awaken the gratitude of thofe, who may remain too callous to this great philanthropic paffion. It behooves every one to confider, that war, though to the higheft degree deftructive and horrid, is effectually calculated to rouze up many tender and fympathetic paffions. If the principles of humanity and benevolence are ever to be *forced* into exertion, war, which fhould be the laft refource, muft have the defired effect. And this renders it, at beft, but a neceffary evil; and the promoters of it are the fubjects of the greateft afperfion. Let us

---

[48] Others were killed and wounded, fhe knew not how many. Thefe names fhe happened to remember, as fhe was well acquainted with the perfons. The proper fpelling is John Beebe, James Battles, Noble Sperin.

be free from all other evils, to which dire neceffity does not prompt, and we may excufe, even a *female*, for taking arms in defence of all that is dear and lovely.—She, doubtlefs, once thought fhe could never look on the *battle-array.* She now fays, no pen can defcribe her feelings experienced in the commencement of an engagement, the fole objeƈt of which is, to open the fluices of human blood. The unfeigned tear of humanity has more than once ftarted into her eye in the rehearfal of fuch a fcene as I have juft defcribed.[49]

49 At this place fhe mentions, in the MS. memoir, that, juft after this fkirmifh, fhe came to be under the command of Col. Henry Jackfon, a native of Bofton. But Col. Jackfon did not affume the command of the Fourth Maffachufetts Regiment, in which fhe was a foldier, till fome time in 1782, upon the promotion of Col. Shepard, its former commander, to the rank of brigadier-general: fo that here is additional evidence that our heroine did not join the army till May, 1782.

In the MS. memoir, in immediate conneƈtion with the mention of Col. Jackfon, fhe alfo fays, "In Col. Jackfon's regiment I readily recognized Dr. James Thacher of Plymouth, our furgeon. I had before known him at his houfe and in its vicinity," &c. It appears from Dr. Thacher's "Military Journal," a work of high authority in regard to the Revolutionary War, that he was at this time furgeon of Col. Henry Jackfon's regiment. "Col. Henry Jackfon, who commands our regiment," he fays, "is a native of Bofton. He is very refpeƈtable as a commander, is gentlemanly in his manners, ftrongly attached to military affairs, and takes a peculiar pride in the difcipline and martial appearance of his regiment." The MS. memoir, from which I have fo often quoted, fpeaks of Col. Jackfon in terms of the warmeft eulogy. "There was," it fays, "an affability and yet a dignity of manner that won the hearts of all under his command. This rendered obedience to orders. and fubmiffion to difcipline, eafy."

Col. Jackfon, after the war, refided in Bofton, was we believe a brigadier-general in the militia, and had the care of Mrs. Swan's large property while her husband was a prifoner in France. He is reprefented as having

FROM this time till Autumn, nothing unufual in war happened to her. Indeed, it may be faid, every thing fhe did in this fituation was *fingular;* much of which might afford amufement and moral inferences. But the limits prefcribed to thefe MEMOIRS will not admit the detail of minute circumftances.[50]

IN Auguft, the Marquis DE LA FAYETTE had been dif-patched from the main army to contemplate the opera-tions of Lord CORNWALLIS's army in Virginia. After a multiplicity of military manœuvres between them, his Lordfhip felected York-Town and Gloucefter Point as the moft confpicuous and advantageous pofts for the feat of military operations.—York-Town lies on the river of the fame name, which empties into the Chefapeak. It forms a capacious harbor, admitting fhips of great bur-then. Gloucefter Point being on the oppofite fide, and

been an elegant and fafcinating man. He died in 1809, and his remains were depofited in Mrs. Swan's tomb in Dorchefter. He was never mar-ried.

[50] We now enter on the details of the glorious and decifive campaign of 1781. The various operations in-cluded in this campaign are related with much more fulnefs in the MS. memoir than in this volume. The account extends through eighty pages, equalling in length the previous por-tion of the memoir. But this ac-count, it is perfectly evident, was not furnifhed by Deborah Sampfon, but was taken by Mr. Mann, the com-piler, from the printed accounts of thofe tranfactions, efpecially from Thacher's " Military Journal." This work muft have been before him all the while; for he borrows from it con-ftantly, and ufes the very words of Dr. Thacher in more than twenty in-ftances; and yet Deborah Sampfon is reprefented as the fpeaker through the whole! This portion of the MS. memoir is written in a better ftyle than the preceding and fubfequent portions, indicating its origin. Dr. Thacher was prefent at the fiege of Yorktown.

projecting fo far into the river, that the diftance being but about a mile, they entirely command the navigation of it. Thither CORNWALLIS with 7000 excellent troops repaired; ftrongly fortified the places, and made other good arrangements.

ABOUT the laft of Auguft, Count DE GRASSE arrived with a powerful French fleet in the Chefapeak, and blockaded York-Town by water. Soon after, Admiral GRAVES with a fleet appeared off the capes of Virginia. The French immediately flipped their cables, turned out of their anchorage ground, and an action fucceeded; and though both fides fuftained confiderable lofs, it was not decifive.

THE Generals, WASHINGTON and ROCHAMBEAU had previoufly moved their main armies to the Southward: and when they heard of the French Admiral's arrival in the Chefapeak, they made the moft rapid marches till they arrived at the head of the Elk. Within an hour after their arrival, they received an exprefs from DE GRASSE, with the joyful intelligence of his arrival and fituation. The combined armies embarked on board the veffels which the French Admiral had previoufly prepared to tranfport them down the Chefapeak; and by the 25th of September they landed at Williamsburgh. The American and French Chief Commanders had reached Williamsburgh by exceffive travelling eleven days fooner. They immediately proceeded to vifit the Admiral on

board the Villa de Paris. A council being called, and
their plan of co-operation fettled, they returned; and all
the Americans and allied troops foon formed a collifion
at Williamsburgh.⁵¹ FAYETTE had previoufly been joined
by 3000 under the Marquis DÈ ST. SIMON: The whole
regular force thus collected, amounted to nearly 12,000
men, exclufive of the Virginia militia, which were called
to fervice, and commanded by governor NELSON. Preparations were then made with great difpatch for putting
the army in a fituation to move on to York-Town.

IT is almoft needlefs to mention the hardfhips, that
common foldiers muft have undergone in fo long and
rapid a march. The deficiency of clothing, particularly
of fhoes, but moft of all, the fcanty and wretched quality of provifions, augmented their fufferings. Our heroine fuftained her march from fome part of New-York
with good heart, and without faltering, till the day on
which fhe landed with the troops at Williamsburgh. She
was then much indifpofed; which was not the only time
fhe had experienced the inconveniences of the concealment of her fex. She puked for feveral hours without
much intermiffion; which fhe imputed chiefly to the roll-
ing of the veffel. With the reft, fhe here drew good pro-
vifion and fpirits : and by the next day, fhe was revived;
and the luftre and auguft manœuvring of the army feemed
to perfect a cure beyond the reach of medicine.

⁵¹ " Formed a junction,"—"united   their forces," the writer means to fay.
19

On the morning of the 28th of September, after parade and review, general orders were read to the armies; wherein his Excellency, Gen. WASHINGTON, emphatically enjoined—" If the enemy fhould be tempted to meet the army on its march, the General particularly enjoins the troops to place their principal reliance on the *bayonet*, that they may prove the *vanity of the boaft, which the Britifh make of their peculiar prowefs in deciding battles by that weapon*." After this, the American and French Chief Commanders perfonally addreffed their armies. Our blooming *foldier*, always attentive to underftand every new manœuvre and eventful fcene, happened to ftand fo near his Excellency Gen. WASHINGTON, that fhe heard diftinctly what he faid. He fpoke with firm articulation and winning geftures: but his afpect and folemn mode of utterance affectingly befpoke the great weight, that refted on his mind. The common foldiers were before moftly ignorant of the expedition, upon which they were going.[52] Being now informed by general orders and the affectionate addreffes of their leaders, every countenance,. even of many who had difcovered a mutinizing fpirit, wore an agreeable afpect, and a mutual harmony and reverential acquiefcence in the injunctions of their commanders were reciprocated through the whole.

THE phalanx compofed the advanced guards, and was

[52] No foldier in the American army, after reaching Philadelphia, could have been ignorant as to the defign of the expedition.

moftly commanded by DE LA FAYETTE. Our Heroine was one of thefe; and by reafon of the abfence of a non-commiffioned officer, fhe was appointed to fupply his place. Juft before the fetting of the fun, Col. SCAMMELL, being officer of the day, brought word for the army to halt two miles from York-Town. The officers and foldiers were ftrictly enjoined to lie on their arms all night.

SUCH language (ftrange to fay) was perfectly familiar to our fair foldier. It did not even excite in her a tremor: although it was a prelude to imminent danger. She had been ufed to keep her martial apparatus bright and in the beft order; as they were often prematurely wanted. Anticipating no greater danger than fhe had often actually experienced, although fhe forboded a great event, fhe acquiefced in the mandates of her officers with a calmnefs, that might have furprifed an unexperienced foldier.

NEXT morning, after roll-call, their equipments again reviewed, they went through the quick motions of loading and firing blank cartridges by the motion of the fword. They formed in clofe column, difplayed to the right and left, and formed again. The grand divifion then difplayed, formed by platoon, when they were ordered to march in the beft order. The next day, Col. SCAMMELL, approaching the enemy's works, was mortally wounded and taken prifoner by a party of horfe in ambufcade. York-Town was this day ftrongly invefted by the allied armies. Their lines being formed, the French extending from the river above the town to a morafs, where they were met by the Americans on the right, their hard fatigues begun. They continued more than a week laborious, fuftaining a very heavy cannonade from the befieged. This bufinefs came near proving too much for a *female* in her teens. Being naturally ambitious, it was mortification too fevere for her to be outdone. Many apparently able-bodied men complained, they were unfit for duty, and were relieved. Among others, fhe affected pleafure in giving them the mortifying confolation—that, although fhe believed their *fever* was fettled upon them, fhe hoped it would prove nothing worfe than the *cannon* or *gun-powder fever*.

THE fifth night, fhe was one of a party, who was ordered to work on a battery; the completion of which had been prevented by a too intenfe rain of bombs. Before morning, fhe was almoft ready to yield to the horrors of defpair. Her hands were fo bliftered, that fhe could fcarcely open or fhut them: and it was nearly twenty-four hours fince fhe had taken much nourifhment. But fhe refolved to perfevere as long as nature would make her efforts; which fhe effected almoft beyond credibility.

ON the ninth, the American intrenchments being completed, a fevere cannonade and bombardment commenced by them on the right, and continued all night without intermiffion. Next morning, the French opened their redoubts and batteries on the left; and a tremendous roar of cannon and mortars continued that day without ceafing.—Our Heroine had never before feen either of the main armies together. Being thus brought into view of them, and led on to a general engagement, doubtlefs excited in her fenfations and emotions different from what fhe had before experienced. And I fhould need the pathos of a HOMER, and the polifhed numbers of a HUME or POPE, to do juftice to her feelings, or to exceed the reality of this fcenery.—The ground actually trembled for miles by the tremendous cannonade, which was inceffantly maintained by both fides day and night. Notwithftanding it was not fo horribly deftructive as is generally the confequence of an open field action; yet, the contemplation of two immenfe armies, headed by the moft illuftrious leaders, each ftrenuoufly contending for victory, muft have afforded ideas peculiarly fhocking and auguft. The nights exhibited fcenes, to the higheft degree, folemn and awfully fublime. Perpetual fheets of fire and fmoke belched, as from a volcano, and towered to the clouds. And whilft the eye was dazzled at this, the ear was fatiated and ftunned by the tremendous explofion of artillery and the fcreaming of their fhot.[53]

I SHALL here notice a heroic deed of this gallantrefs; which, while it deferves the applaufe of every patriot and

[53] The cannonade, on the part of the Britifh, commenced Sept. 27; on the part of the allied army, not till the completion of their trenches, Oct. 9.

veteran, muft chill the blood of the tender and fenfible
female.

Two baftion redoubts of the enemy having advanced
two hundred yards on the left, which checked the progrefs of the combined forces, it was propofed to reduce
them by ftorm.   To infpire emulation in the troops, the
reduction of one was committed to the Americans, and
the other to the French.   A felect corps was chofen.
The command of the infantry was given to FAYETTE, with
permiffion to manage as he pleafed.   He therefore ordered them to remember *Cherry-Valley* and *New-London
Quarters*, and to retaliate accordingly, by putting them
to the fword, after having carried the redoubts.[54]   Our
Heroine was one of thefe!   At dark, they marched to
the affault with unloaded arms, but with fixed bayonets;
and with unexampled bravery, attacking on all fides at
once, after fome time of violent refiftance, were complete
victors of the redoubts.   There were two women in the
one attacked by the Americans, and when our fair foldier
entered, the *third* was unknown.   After entering, the carnage was fhocking for a few minutes.   She, ftanding near

[54] There is much reafon for doubt-
ing the truth of this ftatement.   Dr.
Thacher, who gives a particular account of the assault and capture of
these two redoubts, makes no allusion
to fuch orders.   He fays diftinctly—
"not a man was killed after he ceafed
to refift."   "Such was the order difplayed by the affailants, that all refiftance was soon overcome."   A New
Hampfhire captain, wifhing to avenge
the death of Colonel Scammel, threatened to take the life of Major Camp-
bell, who commanded the redoubt on
the left of the Britifh line; but Col.
Alexander Hamilton, who led the
ftorming party, would not suffer it to
be done.

one of the women, heard her pronounce *yankee,** which
was no fooner articulated, than fhe faw a bayonet plunged
into her breaft, and the crimfon, vital liquid, that gufhed
from the incifion, prevented her further utterance! After
this, they cried and begged fo on their knees for quarters,
that the humanity of the Americans.overcame all refentment, and they fpared all, who ceafed to refift; for which
they were afterwards applauded by their humane officers.
Before they left the fort, one clapped her on the fhoulder,
and faid—" *Friend, fear not; you are only disfigured behind.*" She took no apparent notice of what he faid, till
an opportunity prefented : when, happy for her, fhe found
it no worfe! The lapelle of her coat dangled by ftring;
which muft have been the effect of a broad fword, or of a
very clofe fhot.[56]

* THE derivation of this word is from farmer JONATHAN HASTINGS of
Cambridge about 1713. He ufed it to exprefs a *good quality*. Thus, a
yankee horfe and *yankee cider*, were an *excellent horfe* and *excellent cider*.[55]—
The Britifh ufed it wrongly, as a word of contempt to the Americans.
Thus, when they marched out of Bofton in 1775, they played a march,
called *Yankee doodle;* though the prediction of an active boy was—that
their retrograde march would be to *Chevy Chafe*. During this fiege,
two bombs having fell, their fufes were extracted whilft burning ; one by
a *Female*, the other by a *Soldier*. The contents of one were *fquafh*, of
the other, *molaffes*.

55 This account of the derivation
of the word "Yankee" is borrowed
from Thacher's "Military Journal," p.
19. It is, neverthelefs, wholly unfat-
isfactory. The more probable derivation is from the word "Englifh," corrupted by the Indians into *Yenglees*,
then *Yanklees*, and finally *Yankees*.
56 Was Deborah Sampfon here at
this time? Did fhe work in the trench-

Was not this enterprife, alone, in a *female*, worth the attainment of *liberty?* Yet, where is the fair one, who could again hazard it! Methinks I fee the crimfon cheek of the female turning pallid, her vigorous limbs relaxing and tottering in the rehearfal of this eventful fcene. Yet, let no one imagine I have painted it to the life. The fact is fimply narrated; and the proper coloring is left for thofe peculiar inmates of the female benevolent and he- roic breafts.—I haften to drop the fcene.

THE French commanders, whofe fervices demand the gratitude of every American, led on their troops with a heroic bravery, fcarcely to be excelled. And whilft DE GRASSE difplayed much valor, and was doing great execu- tion with his Armada, the Americans, headed by the ever dear and unrivalled WASHINGTON, redoubled their activity and refolution. Nothing, thus, but inevitable ruin, or an entire furrender, awaited CORNWALLIS: And on the 19th of October, after three weeks fevere ftorm,[57] an armiftice having taken place for twenty-four hours, he was glad to accept the terms of capitulation.—He was not permitted to march out with colors flying—an honor that had been refufed to Gen. LINCOLN the preceding winter, when he,

es, with bliftered hands, on the night of the 7th October? Was fhe one of the ftorming-party on the night of the 15th? Did fhe witnefs the furrender of Cornwallis? We confefs we have our doubts on the fubject.

57 The allied forces, about 12,000 ftrong, arrived before Yorktown Sept. 27. They were engaged till Oct. 9 in throwing up intrenchments ; fuffering all the while a fevere cannonade from the town. On the evening of the 9th they firft opened fire on the British lines.

with all the American garrifon, was captured in Charlefton, South Carolina.[58] Lincoln was now appointed to receive his fword and the fubmiffion of the royal army precifely in the mode his own had been conducted.

THE marching out of fuch an immenfe army, as prifoners of war, muft have been a fcene the moft folemn and important. The magnanimity which was difcovered in Gen. WASHINGTON upon this occafion, was inexpreffibly peculiar. Tears trickled from his eyes during the moft of the fcene.[59] And a view of him in thefe moments muft have forced a tear of reverential gratitude from the moft obdurate. He thought of his COUNTRY!—Remember the PATRIOT—remember the PHILANTHROPIST!

THUS, was the grand pillar of war, at length, broken down, and an ample foundation laid for the eftablifhment of the fo much celebrated, and wifhed for *palladium* of peace. We certainly owe this event, at leaft, in a great meafure, to our generous auxiliaries. Had they not lent us their powerful and timely aid, America, for any thing we can tell, might have ftill clanked her chain under a monarchical and defpotic fway. Muft not a remembrance of their LEADERS, particularly of FAYETTE, ftart the tear

[58] Gen. Lincoln with his army, and the city of Charlefton, furrendered to the Britifh forces under Sir Henry Clinton, May 12, 1780.
[59] Gen. Wafhington was not inclined to weep, and it is not likely that he wept on this occafion. Dr. Thacher, who was an eye-witnefs of the fcene, and defcribes it with great particularity, makes no mention of fuch want of felf-control on the part of the American commander-in-chief.

20

of gratitude, and of filial and fympathetic attachment? He generoufly and nobly made Columbia's Cause his own. Unhappy man! Happy perhaps he might have continued, had not his philanthropic defigns been baffled in his exertions to put them in execution in his native country. Difappointed in thefe, his warmeft wifhes, behold him dragging out a more ufeful intended exiftence in a loathfome dungeon!* O wretched, inhuman return for philanthropy—the beft fervices of man!

> See vegetable nature all confpire
> To make man bleft, his ultimate defire :
> Yet, mark how erring to great NATURE's plan,
> That man, made wife, fhould be unjuft to man !

Whilft our blood can never ceafe to thrill with indignation for his fufferings, may our gratitude and reverence

* Soon after the revolution in France, an accufation was decreed againft him ; and in attempting to efcape, he was apprehended in Magdeburg and imprifoned. Heaven grant, he may have been liberated before this time ! [60]

60 On the memorable 10th of Auguft, 1792, the populace of Paris rofe in arms, attacked the Palace of the Tuileries, maffacred the Swifs guards, and dethroned the king. Lafayette, who, during the earlier part of the French Revolution, had concurred in the conftitutional reforms decreed by the National Affembly, and who was at this time in command of an army ftationed on the frontiers to oppofe the Pruffian invafion, now felt his own life to be in peril from popular violence. He was, indeed, at this juncture, accufed of treafon by the popular leaders, and a price was fet upon his head. He therefore, on the 17th of Auguft, quitted the army and the territory of France with twelve officers of rank, intending to proceed to the United States. They had travelled but a fhort diftance, when they were all taken prifoners by the Pruffians ; and Lafayette was put in clofe

never cool towards this illuftrious, but diftreffed, noble-
man. May a reciprocity of friendfhip and affection con-
ciliate and cement us more ftrongly with France, our
once helpful and now fifter republic. We folicit England
to fhake hands with COLUMBIA, her natural offspring.
Let the banners of war be forever furled, the fword of
contention fheathed in its proper place; and may fhe always forget to prove inimical to her eftablifhed CAUSE.
May philanthropy become as extenfive as the nations of
the earth: Men fhall then quit their fallacious purfuits,
retire to their refpective and proper occupations, and learn
humility and propriety of conduct. Then fhall mutual
harmony, peace and profperity pervade the world.

I SHALL leave our fair Soldier, or as fhe was frequently
called, the _blooming boy_, in winter quarters not far from
Weft-Point and the banks of the Hudfon, or North River,
in what were called the York huts. She arrived at this
place in December, much debilitated and difpirited by
hard marches and fatigues. She was deftitute of fhoes,
as were moft of the foldiers during the march; except-
ing raw hides, which they cut into ftraps and faftened
about their feet. It was not uncommon to track them

confinement in the Caftle of Magdeburg, once the abode of Baron
Trenck, and was foon after imprifoned in the ftrong Fortrefs of Olmutz.
To the honor of Napoleon it fhould
be faid that one of the articles of the

Treaty of Campo Formio, Oct. 18,
1797, negotiated under the preffure of
that conqueror's great fucceffes in
Italy, ftipulated for the releafe of Lafayette, after Wafhington had interceded for him in vain.

by the bleeding of their feet on the fnow and ice.[61]   And
it appeared, their officers fared not much better; although
they ufed their greateft efforts to foothe, animate and encourage the foldiers, principally with the profpects of
peace, and the great honor they fhould gain by perfevering to the end.

JUST before their arrival, one of her company having
been feverely chaftifed for ftealing poultry, importuned
her to defert with him and two others.   But fhe not only
difdainfully refufed, but ufed all the eloquence, of which
fhe was miftrefs, to diffuade them from fo prefumptive an
attempt.   Having hazarded one defperate prefumption
herfelf, fhe chofe to take her lot in the prefent and future
ills; though, peradventure, her fex might in fome meafure, have juftified her breach of contract.   The arguments fhe enforced were—that, it would not only be an
evidence of difloyalty to their country, a token of cowardice, a breach of civil obligation, but the greateft jeopardy
of their lives.   As female eloquence is generally irrefiftible, they here yielded to its energy : although they were
infenfible, that it was articulated through *female* organs.

HAVING repaired the huts, in which bufinefs fhe froze
her feet to that degree, that fhe loft all her toe-nails, the
foldiers were culled, in order that all who had not had
the fmall pox might be inoculated.   The foldiers, who

---

[61] There is nothing of this fort in   " Military Journal."   Of courfe, there
the MS. memoir, nor in Thacher's   is exaggeration here.

were to be inoculated, paraded; when our Heroine, for the firſt time, ſhewed an averſion to it. Determined to hazard taking this malignant diſtemper unaware, ſhe would even have falſified the truth of her having had it, ſooner than have gone to the hoſpital; where the pride and glory of her ſex, the ſource of the *blooming boy*, might have been diſcloſed.[62]

SHE did duty, ſometimes as a common ſoldier, and ſome-times as a ſerjeant; which was moſtly on the lines, patrol-ling, collecting fuel, &c. As the winter was very intenſe, the ſnow the moſt of the time deep, I ſhall leave it for the conſiderate to imagine the unuſual hardſhips of a female in this ſituation. · She went cheerful to her taſks, and was never found loitering when ſent on duty or enterprize.

[62] In the MS. memoir, ſhe ſays, "Dreading the expoſure of my per-ſon, and the conſequent diſcovery of my ſex, far more than death, I told a plump lie to the ſurgeon, in the ſtatement that I had long ſince ex-perienced that diſeaſe. I preferred to hazard taking the ſmall-pox rather than go to the hoſpital. I was there-fore excuſed, and by the favor of a kind Providence eſcaped the conta-gion, though often expoſed to it."

Dr. Thacher places the inoculation of the troops for ſmall-pox in January, 1782. Of courſe, it took place before her enliſtment. He inoculated, he ſays, about two hundred, including women and children.

C H A P. VIII.

Building of the COLONNADE *on* Weſt-Point *after the open-*
ing of the Campaign.—Writes to her MOTHER.—A ſe-
vere SKIRMISH, *where ſhe receives two* WOUNDS, *and is left*
in the French hoſpital.—Returns to the army on their
lines.—Is left with a ſick ſoldier in a Dutchman's family,
who is a tory and treats her ill.—Heroic ADVENTURE *in*
her MODE *of Retaliation.—She and a party, being at-*
tacked by a party of Dutch Cavalry, are obliged to ford
a dangerous ferry.—The main Army retire to Winter
Quarters at New-Windſor.—She is one of a detachment
ſent to reinforce Gen. SCHUYLER *in ſubduing the Indians*
on the Frontiers above Albany ; where a number of hor-
rid ſcenes are exhibited.

HAVING now furniſhed a clue, by which the ſucceed-
ing common occurrences of our diſtinguiſhed FAIR,
whilſt a ſoldier, may be gathered, I ſhall not tire the patience of the reader in their enumeration. Though, as
common as they then were to her, could they be exhibited
afreſh by an indifferent female, I am confident I have not
a reader, but would think his leiſure interims luxuriantly
employed in their recital. But I haſten to a narration of
thoſe, on which to dwell muſt be luxury and wonder; but
to paſs them unnoticed, criminal injuſtice.

THOUGH peace had not longer been anticipated than
wiſhed for ; yet, the conduct of both armies after the

opening of the campaign feemed to place it as a matter of extreme uncertainty. The opening of this campaign was diftinguiſhed by the building of a Colonnade, or rather a Bowery, on Weft-Point. It was begun on the 3d of May, and completed after about three weeks fatigue. In this bufinefs, our heroic FEMALE often worked againſt the moſt robuſt and expert ſoldier: and had not the delicate texture of her frame been concealed, it would, doubtlefs, have been judged, that ſhe was very unequally mated.

WHEN this delightful building was finiſhed, the officers held a meeting of ſocial intercourſe and conviviality. The full, ſparkling bowl was here handed cheerfully round. Many toaſts of health and long life were drank to the half-divine WASHINGTON—to the true ſons of freedom and republicanifm—to the increaſe and perpetuity of our alliance with FRANCE, and giving three cheers for the new-born Dauphin of that realm, they concluded the day.[63]

[63] Dr. Thacher notices the erection of this edifice, and the magnificent feſtival in it after it was finiſhed. The feſtival was on the 31st of May, 1782. About one thouſand men were employed about ten days in the conſtruction of this curious edifice, under the direction of Major Villefranche, an ingenious French engineer. It was on the eſplanade of Weſt Point, and was compoſed of the ſimple materials which the common trees of that vicinity afforded. It was ſix hundred feet in length, and thirty in width, ſupported by a grand colonnade of one hundred and eighteen pillars made of the trunks of trees. The roof conſiſted of branches of trees curiouſly interwoven, and the walls were of the ſame materials, leaving the ends entirely open. " This ſuperb ſtructure," he ſays, " in ſymmetry of proportion, neatnefs of workmanſhip, and elegance of arrangement, has ſeldom, perhaps, been ſurpaſſed on any temporary occaſion." The feſtival held in

THE reader has long enough been in fufpenfe to know what effect her elopement had on her mother and connections, and what method fhe took to pacify, as we may fuppofe, their half diftracted minds. Though fhe received her education in obfcurity, the news of her elopement, or among other conjectures, that fhe had come to fome untimely cataftrophe, flew to a great diftance. Her mother, raifing a thoufand doubts and fears was almoft inconfolably wretched. Sometimes fhe harbored the too often poignant reflection, that her too rigorous exertions to precipitate her union with the gentleman I have before mentioned, had driven her to fome direful and fatal alternative. The like dire, alternate thoughts filled her undiffembled Lover, with emotions he could ill conceal. And like a man of fenfe and breeding, he commiferated each of their misfortunes. Frantic at times, when reflection had pictured to his imagination all her frightful groups of ideas and images, he would curfe his too overbearing importunity and too open declaration of his paffions. Thefe, he too late furmifed, were the caufe of her leaving him abruptly, (which, by the bye, is the reverfe of common circumftances) and, for aught he knew, of her cafual exit from all earthly objects; or, that the too warm pref-

this remarkable edifice was in honor of the new-born Dauphin of France and of the French alliance. The MS. memoir, from which I have often quoted, defcribes the edifice and the feftival in exact accordance with the account given by Dr. Thacher; in no less than twelve inftances, ufing his very words. Of courfe, this could not be by mere accident.

fure of his love had rendered him odious, and that fhe
had too juftly punifhed him by throwing herfelf into the
embraces of a more agreeable rival. He determined,
however, were it practicable, once more to fee her, and to
congratulate her on her union with a better companion,
than he could make;—or, fhould fhe conceive as he
once thought fhe had, a growing affection for him, he
fhould rejoice to find himfelf, in the road for that happinefs, which alone could render his exiftence fatisfactory,
or fcarcely defirable.

For this purpofe, one of her brothers made a fruitlefs
expedition a number of hundred miles to the Eaftward
among fome of her relations.[64] Her Suitor took his rout
to the Weftward. And among his rambles, he vifited the
feat of war; where he faw his half adorable object of
love. But as fortune, adverfe or propitious, would have
it, he knew not, that fhe, who appeared in martial attire, was the tender object, who occupied the moft diftinguifhed feat in his bofom. Her eyes were not deceptory;
and when fhe heard the articulation of her name in his
enquiries, it was not becaufe fhe flighted him, nor becaufe
fhe was enraptured with his love, that fhe, a fecond time,
haftened from his prefence. The big tear trembled in

[64] This brother went to Meduncook, now Friendfhip, on the feacoaft of Maine, to fee if fhe had not taken up a refidence there with the children of Jofhua Bradford, who had married her mother's eldeft fifter, Hannah Brad-ford. See note, page 47. This place is a few miles weft of Penobfcot Bay.

21

her eye; and when she turned to conceal her emotions, she silently and reluctantly bid him adieu.[65]

AFTER many wearisome steps and unsuccessful researches, he returned home; when it was concluded, that she must have crossed the wide Atlantic, or have found an untimely sepulchre in her own country.—She was preserved; and she only could cure the cruel suspense and racking sensations, which would be brutal to suppose did not pervade their bosoms on this occasion. The mind is scarcely capable of picturing a contrast more trying to the tender passions than this. And no doubt, she allotted her sequestered retirements to indulge the sorrowing, unnoticed tear; when the anguish of a mother, of her relatives and of him, whose felicity she knew was perfectly interwoven with her own, took complete possession of her mind together.—After striving a long time in vain to ease the distress of her mother, and to exonerate the too intense burden of her own mind by writing, she found an opportunity, and enclosed to her the substance of the following:[66]

[65] The account here given is not accurate. Deborah saw *him:* it is not certain that he saw *her.* Some of her comrades told her of the inquiries he was making respecting her. By this means, also, she actually heard from home; heard that her mother and other friends were well; that a great excitement had been occasioned by her elopement. She says she felt tenderly towards him, and would gladly have thanked him for his interest in her welfare; but she did not speak to him, and would not risk a discovery of herself to him. He therefore returned without success.

[66] This letter was doubtless composed, like some of Cicero's orations, long after the time when it was said to have been written. It is given

May, 1782.

DEAR PARENT,

ON the margin of one of thofe rivers, which inter-fects and winds itfelf fo beautifully majeftic through a vaft extent of territory of the United States, is the pref-ent fituation of your unworthy, but conftant and affection-ate daughter.—I pretend not to juftify, or even to palliate, my clandeftine elopement. In hopes of pacifying your mind, which, I am fure, muft be afflicted beyond meafure, I write you this fcrawl. Confcious of not having thus abruptly abfconded by reafon of any fancied ill treatment from you, or difaffection towards any; the thoughts of my difobedience are truly poignant. Neither have I a plea, that the infults of man have driven me hence : And let this be your confoling reflection—that I have not fled to offer more daring infults to them by a proffered proftitu-tion of that *virtue*, which I have always been taught to preferve and revere. The motive is truly important; and when I divulge it, my fole ambition and delight fhall be to make an expiatory facrifice for my tranfgreffion.

I AM in a large, but well regulated family. My employ-ment is agreeable, although it is fomewhat different and more intenfe than it was at home : But I apprehend it is equally as advantageous. My fuperintendents are in-

in the MS. memoir with confiderable variation in the words, and in a more ambitious ftyle. It is the compofi-tion of Mr. Mann, not of Deborah Sampfon. The ftyle differs not at all from that of the reft of the book.

dulgent; but to a punctillio, they demand a due obfervance of decorum and propriety of conduct.   By this you
muft know, that I have become miftrefs of many ufeful
leffons, though I have many more to learn.   Be not too
much troubled, therefore, about my prefent or future engagements; as I will endeavor to make that prudence
and virtue my model, for which, I own, I am much indebted to thofe, who took the charge of my youth.

My place of refidence and the adjacent country are,
beyond defcription, delightfome.   The earth is now preg-
nant with vegetation; and the banks of the river are already decorated with all the luxuriance of May.   The
cottages, that peep over the rifing grounds, feem perched
like eagles' nefts; and the nobler buildings, well cultivated plantations and the continual paffing and re-paffing
of veffels in the river below, form one of the moft pleaf-
ingly variegated and noble profpects, I may fay, in the
world.—Indeed were it not for the ravages of *war*, of
which I have feen more here than in Maffachufetts, this
part of our great continent would become a paradifiacal
elyfium.   Heaven condefcend, that a fpeedy peace may
conftitute us a *happy* and *independent* nation: when the
husband fhall again be reftored to his amiable confort, to
wipe her forrowing tear, the fon to the embraces of his
mourning parents and the lover to the tender, difconfolate
and half diftracted object of his love.—

Your affectionate   DAUGHTER.

THIS letter, being intrufted with a ftranger, was intercepted.—Let us now refume her progrefs in war.

PASSING over many marches, forward and retrograde, and numberlefs incidental adventures and hardfhips peculiar to war. I come to other MEMOIRS, which muft forcibly touch the paffions of every bofom, that is not callous to reflection and tendernefs of feeling.

THE bufinefs of war is devaftation, rapine and murder. And in America, thefe brutal principles were never more horribly exemplified, than in this war. Hence the neceffity of fcouting; which was the common bufinefs of the infantry, to which our HEROINE belonged. And fome time in June of this year, fhe, with two fergeants, requefted leave of their Captain to retaliate on the enemy, chiefly refugees and tories in New-York, for their outragious infults to the inhabitants beyond their lines. He replied— " *You three dogs have contrived a plan this night to be killed, and I have no men to lofe.*" He however confented; and they beat for volunteers. Nearly all the company turned out; but only twenty were permitted to go.[67]— Near the clofe of the day they commenced their expedition. They paffed a number of guards and went as far as Eaft-Chefter undifcovered; where they lay in ambufh to watch the motions of thofe, who might be on the plun-

67 The MS. memoir fays about thirty were permitted to go, and that they belonged to three different companies. Eaft Chefter is four miles eaft of the Hudfon. Tories were numerous thereabouts.

dering bufinefs. They quickly difcovered that two parties
had gone out; and whilſt they were contriving how to
entrap them, they difcovered two boys, who were fent for
provifions to a private cellar in the wood. One of them
informed, that a party had juſt been at his mother's, and
were then gone to vifit the *Yankees*, who were guarding
the lines. Concealing from them, that they were Americans, they accompanied them to the cellar, or rather a
cave, which they found well ſtored with provifion; fuch
as bacon, butter, cheefe, crouts, early fcrohons and jars
of honey. They made a delicious repaſt, filled their
facks and informed the boys, they were *Yankees;* upon
which, the cave loudly rung with their cries. Dividing
into two parties, they fet out centinels and again am-
bufhed in a place called, in Dutch, *Vonhoite.*

About four in the morning, a large party, chiefly on
horfeback and well armed, were faluted by one of the
centinels; which was no fooner done, than they returned
a number of piſtol and fufee ſhots at the flafh of his
gun.[68] A fevere combat enfued. The Americans found
horfes without riders: they had then light-horfe and foot.

---

[68] About two in the morning, according to the MS. memoir. The
fentinel was ſtationed by the party to
which our heroine belonged, to give
notice of the approach of the party
of refugees, who, according to the information obtained from the boy, were
expeſted foon to repair to the depôt
of provifions. The fentinel gave notice by firing his gun ; upon which,
Deborah's party fired at the party of
refugees, killing feveral, and putting
the others to flight, after a ſhort but
fevere ſtruggle.

Our GALLANTRESS having previoufly become a good horfeman, immediately mounted an excellent horfe. They pursued the enemy till they came to a quagmire, as it appeared by their being put to a nonplus. They rufhed on them on the right and left, till as many as could, efcaped; the reft begged quarters. The dauntlefs FAIR, at this inftant, thought fhe felt fomething warmer than fweat run down her neck. Putting her hand to the place, fhe found the blood gufhed from the left fide of her head very freely. She faid nothing; as fhe thought it no time to tell of wounds, unlefs mortal. Coming to a ftand, fhe difmounted, but had not ftrength to walk, or ftand alone. She found her boot on her right leg filled with blood; [69] and in her thigh, juft below her groin, fhe found the incifion of a ball, whence it iffued. — Females! this effufion was from the veins of your tender fex, in queft of that LIBERTY, you now fo ferenely poffefs.

SHE told one of the fergeants, fhe was fo wounded, fhe chofe rather to be left in that horrid place, than be carried any further. They all, as one, concluded to carry her, in cafe fhe could not ride. Here was her trial! A thoufand thoughts and fpectres at once darted before her. She had always thought fhe fhould rather die, than difclofe her fex to the army! And at that inftant, almoft in defpair, fhe drew a piftol from a holfter, and was nearly

[69] The *left* leg, according to the MS. memoir. This fhows that our author was not accurate in matters of detail.

ready to execute the fatal deed. But divine goodnefs here ftayed her hand: and the fhocking act and idea of fuicide were foon banifhed by her cooler reafon.[70]

[70] " I confidered this as a death-wound, or as being equivalent to it; as it muft, I thought, lead to the dif-covery of my fex. Covered with blood from head to foot, I told my companions I feared I had received a mortal wound; and I begged them to leave me to die on the fpot; pre-ferring to take the fmall chance I fhould in this cafe have of furviving, rather than to be carried to the hof-pital. To this my comrades would not confent; but one of them took me before him on his horfe, and in this painful manner I was borne fix miles to the hofpital of the French army, at a place called Croon Pond. On coming in fight of the hofpital, my heart again failed me. In a paroxyfm of defpair, I actually drew a piftol from the holfter, and was about to put an end to my own life. That I did not proceed to the fatal act, I can afcribe only to the interpofition of Divine Mercy.

" The French furgeon, on my being brought in, inftantly came. He was alert, cheerful, humane. 'How you lofe fo much blood at dis early hour? Be any bone broken?' was his firft falutation; prefenting me and the other wounded men of our party with two bottles of choice wine. . . . My head having been bound up, and a change of clothing becoming a wound-ed foldier being ready, I was afked by the too inquifitive French furgeon whether I had any other wound. He had obferved my extreme palenefs, and that I limped in attempting to walk. I readily replied in the nega-tive: it was a plump falfehood! 'Sit you down, my lad: your boot fay you tell fib!' faid the furgeon, no-ticing that the blood ftill oozed from it. He took off my boots and ftock-ings with his own hands with great tendernefs, and wafhed my leg to the knee. I then told him I would re-tire, change my clothing, and if any other wound fhould appear, I would inform him.

" Meanwhile I had procured in the hofpital a filver probe a little curved at the end, a needle, fome lint, a bandage, and fome of the fame kind of falve that had been applied to the wound in my head. I found that the ball had penetrated my thigh about two inches, and the wound was ftill moderately bleeding. The wine had revived me, and God, by his kind care, watched over me. At the third attempt, I extracted the ball, which, as a facred relic, I ftill poffefs.*

" This operation over, the blood was ftanched, and my regimentals,

* In the Report of the Committee of Congrefs, Jan. 31, 1837 (fee Introduction, page xxi.), it is ftated that the ball was never extracted, and "that the effect of the wound continued through life, and probably haftened her death."

HAVING refted a little, being deftitute of any refrefhment, her wounds became exceffively painful; but noth-

ftiff enough with blood to ftand alone, had been exchanged for a loofe, thin wrapper, when I was again vifited by the furgeon. In his watchful eye I plainly read doubts. I told him that all was well; that I felt much re-vived, and wifhed to fleep. I had flept fcarcely an hour, when he again alarmed me. Approaching me on my mattrefs of ftraw, and holding my breeches in his hand, dripping from the wafh-tub, ' How came this rent ? ' faid he, putting his finger into it. I replied, ' It was occafioned, I believe, on horfeback, by a nail in the faddle or holfter. 'Tis of no confequence. Sleep refrefhes me : I had none laft night.' One-half of this, certainly, was true. But I had lefs dread of receiving half a dozen more balls than the penetrating glance of his eye. As I grew better, his fcrutiny dimin-ifhed.

"Before the wound in my thigh was half healed, I rejoined the army on the lines. But had the moft hardy foldier been in the condition I was when I left the hofpital, he would have been excufed from military duty." — [*MS. Memoir.*]

There is no doubt that fhe was wounded, as now related; for it is ftated in her petition to the Legifla-ture, and in other authentic memori-als. But her petition and her decla-ration fay that fhe was wounded at Tarrytown, which place is not men-

tioned in the foregoing account. This account locates the fkirmifh at or near Eaft Chefter, four or five miles eaft of the Hudfon ; whereas Tarry-town is fituated on that river. The encounter with a party of Delancy's dragoons, related a few pages back, was therefore the occafion when fhe was wounded ; and the " Female Re-view " is here, as in many other places, inaccurate.

Mrs. Ellet fays, " She was a volun-teer in feveral hazardous enterprifes ; the firft time by a fword-cut on the left fide of the head." This muft have been in the cavalry encounter at Tarrytown. " About four months after her firft wound, fhe received another fevere one, being fhot through the fhoulder. Her firft emotion when the ball entered fhe defcribed to be a fickening terror at the probability that her fex would be difcovered. She felt that death on the battle-field were preferable to the fhame that would overwhelm her, and ardently prayed that the wound might clofe her earth-ly campaign.

" Many were the adventures fhe paffed through : as fhe herfelf would often fay, volumes might be filled with them. Sometimes placed un-avoidably in circumftances in which fhe feared detection, fhe neverthelefs efcaped all fufpicion. The foldiers were in the habit of calling her " Mol-ly," in playful allufion to her want of

22

ing, we may judge, to the anguifh of her mind. Coming in view at length of the French encampment, near what was called *Cron Pond*, fhe fays, it was to her like being carried reluctant to the place of execution. They were conducted by the officer of the guards to an old hofpital, in which was a number of foldiers; whofe very looks, fhe fays, were enough to make a well man indifpofed, and the naufeous fmell, to infect the moft pure air. The French furgeon foon came; who, being informed of their circumftances, gave them two bottles of choice wine, and prepared to drefs their wounds. His mate, wafhing her head with rum, told her, he fuppofed it had not come to its feeling, as fhe did not flinch. Judge, my readers, whether this was not the cafe, as her other wound fo much affected her heart! She requefted the favor of more medicine than fhe needed for her head; and taking an opportunity, with a penknife and needle, fhe extracted the ball from her thigh; which, by that time, had doubt-lefs come to its feeling.

THEY never rightly knew how many they killed or wounded. They took nine prifoners and feven horfes, and killed a number of others on the fpot. Of their

a beard; but not one of them ever dreamed that the gallant youth fight-ing by their fide was in reality a fe-male." — [*Women of the Revolution*.]

Mrs. Ellet had never feen the "Fe-male Review," but received her infor-mation "from a lady who knew her perfonally, and had often liftened with thrilling intereft to the animated de-fcription given by herfelf of her ex-ploits and adventures." Yet fome of Mrs. Ellet's details are unreliable.

wounded was ROSE, STOCKBRIDGE, PLUMMER and the invincible FAIR. DISTON was killed.

AFTER fuffering almoft every pain, but death, with incredible fortitude; fhe fo far healed her wound unbeknown to any, that fhe again joined the army on the lines. But its imperfect cure, had it been known, would have been fufficient to exempt the moft hardy foldier from duty.

IN Auguft, on their march to the lines from *Collabarack*, fhe requefted to be left with a fick foldier, named RICHARD SNOW; moftly becaufe fhe was unable to do duty with the army, and partly out of compaffion for the poor object, who was fick." But the fortune of war to her proved adverfe. The fears and diftrefs, that here awaited her, were far greater than thofe, when with the army. The old Dutchman, whofe name was VANTASSEL, with whom fhe was left, was not only a tory and entertained the banditti, who plundered the Americans, but refufed them all kinds of fuccor. When fhe begged a ftraw bed for the expiring foldier, he virulently exulted—"*The floor is good enough for rebels.*" They were lodged in a dirty garret without windows; where the heat rendered it ftill more infupportable.

---

71 "About a fortnight after I rejoined my company, I obtained permiffion to ftay and nurfe a fick foldier, whofe name was Richard Snow, at a place called Collebarack. Opportunity was thus afforded not only for the exercife of humanity to a diftreffed comrade, but for the more fpeedy cure of my wound, which the duties of the camp would not allow to be perfectly healed." — [*MS. Memoir.*]
It never was perfectly healed.

ONE night, expecting to become a prey to the relent-
lefs cruelty of the rabble, fhe charged both their pieces,
refolving to facrifice the firft, who might offer to moleft.[72]
She likewife made faft a rope near an opening in the
garret, by which to make her efcape, in cafe they fhould
be too many. Thus, fhe continued conftant to him, till
almoft exhaufted for want of fleep and nourifhment. On
the tenth night, he expired in great agonies, but in the
exercife of his reafon, (of which he was before deprived)
and much refigned to the will of GOD; which may be a
confolation to his furviving relatives.

AFTER SNOW was dead, fhe rolled him in his blanket
and fat at the avenue.[73] She faw a party ride up to the
houfe, and the old churl go out to congratulate them.
They informed, the horfes they then had, with other
plunder, were taken from the Americans. Whilft the
houfe was again infefted with their ungodly career, it is
not in my power to defcribe her melancholy diftrefs in a
dark garret with a corpfe. A multitude of cats fwarmed
in the room; and it was with difficulty fhe difabled fome
with her cutlafs, and kept the reft from tearing the body
to pieces. At length, fhe heard footfteps on the ftairs.
Her heart fluttered; but her heroifm had not forfaken

[72] "The rabble" means the Tories, who reforted to the houfe, and were at the time in the lower part of the houfe, revelling in the fpoil they had taken from honeft people in the vicinity. "Both their pieces," — her gun and the fick foldier's.

[73] "After Snow was dead, I wrapped him in his blanket, and feated myfelf at the open window to inhale frefh air."

her. Haftening to the door, fhe put her hanger in a pofition to diflocate the limbs of any who fhould enter.
But the voice of a female, who fpoke to her in Englifh,
allayed her fear. It was VANTASSEL's daughter, who
feemed poffeffed of humanity, and who had before often
alleviated her diftrefs.

AT day-break, fhe left the garret; but finding the
outer doors bolted, fhe was returning, when fhe again
met the young female, who bid her good morning, and
faid—"If you pleafe, Sir, walk into my chamber." She
followed; and feating themfelves by a window, they re-
galed themfelves with a glafs of wine and a beautiful,
ferene air. After entreating her agreeable gueft not to
let the ill treatment fhe had received from her father
make her forfake the houfe, fhe bordered on fubjects that
might have enraptured the other fex.[74]—Summoned at
this inftant by her mother, they withdrew.

OUR HEROINE, with the affiftance of two others, buried
the dead; then fat out to join her company. She acquainted the Captain of the toryifm of VANTASSEL, of his
treatment of her, and thought it beft to furprife him.
The affair was fubmitted to her management. She frequented the houfe; and having learned that a gang was
to be there at fuch a time, fhe took command of a party

74 Inftead of the claufe, "fhe bordered on fubjects," &c., the MS. memoir has, "I replied that her father
would foon be obliged to leave his
houfe, and his country too, unlefs he
changed his courfe. She fpoke ftrongly againft her father's toryifm, from
which fhe herfelf had often fuffered."

and found them in their ufual reverie.[75]   Some thought
beft to rufh immediately upon them; but fhe deemed it
more prudent to wait till their intoxicated brains fhould
render them lefs capable of refiftance.   At midnight, fhe
unbolted the ftable doors, when they poffeffed themfelves
of the horfes; then rallied the houfe.   They came out
with confternation; which was increafed when they were
told, they were dead men, if they did not yield themfelves
prifoner of war.   They conveyed them to their company
as fuch.[76]   The Captain enquired, of the gallant Commander, the method of capturing them; which fhe detailed.   He gave her a bottle of good fpirits, and told her
to treat her men.   This done, fhe requefted, that the
prifoners might fare in like manner.   The Captain faid—
" Will you treat men, who would be glad to murder us?"
But fhe pleading the caufe of humanity, he gave her
another bottle.   Unlofing the hands of a fergeant, he
drank but in making them faft again, he acted on the
defenfive, and ftruck her to the ground.   She arofe, when
he made a fecond attempt; but fhe warded the blow.
His compeers chided him for his folly, as they had been
well ufed.   He vented many bitter oaths; alledging, fhe
had not only taken him prifoner, but had caufed his girl
(meaning VANTASSEL's daughter) to pay that attention to

75 For "reverie" read "revelry."
The meaning is, the tories were riot-
ing on the plunder they had taken.

76 Without fhedding any blood, our

heroine's party captured fifteen Tories and nine horfes, and brought
them fafely to camp.   The MS. memoir fpreads this affair over fix pages.

her, fhe once beftowed on him. He, however, received fifty ftripes on the naked back for his infolence; then was fent to Head Quarters, and after trial, to the Provoft, with the reft at Weft Point.

THE beginning of Autumn, fhe, with Lieut. BROWN and others, had a boifterous cruife down the Hudfon to Albany on bufinefs;[77] foon after, a fcouting tour into the Jerfies; and fhe was with the armies on the 19th of October in their grand Difplay at Virplank's Point.[78] I only inftance thefe, as parties of pleafure and a day of jubilee, when compared with the rougher events of war.[79]

WE come now to the firft of December, when fhe and a party were furprifed by a party of Dutch cavalry from an ambufcade and drove with impetuofity to Croton Ferry; where their only alternative was that of fording it, or of rifking their lives with the affailants: each of

[77] They could not go "*down* the Hudfon" from Weft Point to Albany.

[78] "About the middle of September, there was a grand difplay of the army at King's Ferry, on account of the return of Count Rochambeau from the South." —[*MS. Memoir.*] This review is noticed by Dr. Thacher in his "Military Journal." It was on the 14th of September, 1782. As ufual, the compiler of the MS. memoir borrows fome of Thacher's expreffions.

[79] On the former of thefe occafions, the fcouting-party, or raid, as it would now be called, went out to capture Tories, an employment in which our heroine delighted. She confidered them, as they really were, by far the worft enemies of the country. Never did a hunter in purfuit of game, with the pack in full cry, feel better than did fhe when in purfuit of Tories. She fays, "I loved to watch by thefe Tories, and to fteal away their dreams. And yet in no part of my military career have I been more expofed to danger. On this occafion we had little fuccefs, thefe freebooters having moftly taken refuge within the Britifh lines." This expedition was chiefly in New Jerfey.

which feemed to the laft degree dangerous. Without time for hefitation, compelling a Dutchman to pilot them on the bar, they entered the watery element; and, by the affiftance of that BEING, who is faid to have conducted the Ifraelites through the Red Sea, they reached the other fhore.[80]

THEY went to the houfe of the Widow HUNT; who, under pretentions of friendfhip, fent black *George* for re-frefhment.[81]   But our Heroine, more acquainted with the cunning of her fex, advifed them not to adhere to her fmoothnefs of fpeech. Accordingly, they went back to the ferry; and they can beft defcribe the wretchednefs of their fituation during a cold winter night. In the morn-ing, though the river was frozen, they determined to re-crofs it; left the enemy fhould drive them to a worfe extremity. Before they had two thirds croffed, the

---

[80] "In the fecond of thefe expedi-tions, about the 1ft of December," fays the MS. memoir, — though it could not have been later than early in November, — "we fell into an am-bufcade formed by the enemy's cav-alry. Endeavoring to efcape, we had no alternative but to ford Croton River, or rifk an engagement with treble our number. We chofe to ford the river; and, compelling a Dutch-man to conduct us to a place where the water was but breaft high, we reached the oppofite fhore in fafety." Our heroine's party were on foot.

[81] "We went to the houfe of a Widow Hunt, who proved to be a defperate female Tory. She fent her flave, black George, oftenfibly for re-frefhments, but really to give infor-mation to the enemy, the party whom we had juft efcaped. During that cold winter night, we were without fhelter, and my wound not yet per-fectly healed." They had juft forded the river. Of courfe, their clothes were drenched with the water, which froze upon them. "Before we had recroffed the river, a large body of the enemy appeared in purfuit," etc.

ftrength of our young FEMALE was fo exhaufted, that
the brifknefs of the ftream, which was in height to her
chin, carried her off the bar; when it was concluded, fhe
was for ever ingulphed in a watery tomb. As fhe rofe,
fummoning the laft exertions of nature, fhe got hold of a
ftring, which they buoyed to her; and thus, providentially,
regained the bar and fhore. Frozen and languid as they
then were, they reached a ftore; where not being well
ufed, they burft in the head of a brandy cafk, drank their
fill, gave a fhoe full to the negro of the widow, whom they
had before taken; then left him in a better fituation than
he faid, his miftrefs meant to have left them. She ren-
dezvoufed with her company at Pixhill Hollow.[82]

SOON after the army retired to Winter Quarters at
New Windfor, the clarion of war was again founded for a
reinforcement to affift Gen. SCHUYLER in fubduing the
Indians on the frontiers, on to Saratoga.[83] The officers
chofe to form their detachment of volunteers; as the
foldiers were worn down with the hardfhips of war.
Heavens! what will not refolution and perfeverance furmount, even in the *fair* fex!—Our Heroine offered her

[82] This fhould be, as in the MS. memoir, "Peekfkill Hollow." This was a noted military poft on the Hudfon in the Revolutionary War.

[83] According to Thacher's "Military Journal," the left wing of the army, under Gen. Heath, after a march from Verplanck's Point, reached the vicinity of New Windfor, on the weft of the Hudfon, where they were to erect log-huts for winter-quarters, on the 28th of October. Dr. Thacher makes no mention of this Indian expedition, though he is careful to note all paffing occurrences, and even the news from a diftance.

23

fervice; though an inflammation of her wound would
have deterred a veteran: it being an open fore a few days
before fhe croffed the river.[84]

[84] This winter expedition to the
Indian country, is, in the MS. memoir, expanded into twenty-eight
pages, which we will now materially
abridge.

Soon after the army retired to winter quarters, and therefore in November, 1782, a large detachment was
ordered to proceed to the head-waters
of the Hudfon, to reprefs the incurfions which the Indians were making
on the white fettlements. Our heroine, though not yet fully recovered
from her wound, volunteered to go.
They marched on the banks of the
Hudfon, and vifited Fort Edward,
Fort George, and Ticonderoga. At
Fort Edward they found Gen. Schuyler, on whom the compiler of the MS.
memoir beftows two pages of panegyric. Lake George, with the fcenery
around, alfo Ticonderoga and Crown
Point, are defcribed, occupying three
or four pages.

From Ticonderoga the party ftruck
off to the weft. The weather had
hitherto been fine, though cold, with
little or no fnow on the ground. But
now they encountered a fevere fnow-
ftorm, and marched through fnow a
foot deep; not "*three* feet deep," as
fays the "Female Review." Near the
place now known as Johnsburgh, in
Warren County, they had an encounter with a party of about a hundred
Indians, who had juft been murder-

ing white families, and burning their
houfes. Thefe Indians fought defpe-
rately, but were overpowered, and put
to flight.

"We came upon the Indians unex-
pectedly, at the diftance of a piftol-
fhot; and our firft fire dealt terrible
deftruction among them. Raifing
their horrid war-whoop, they returned
our fire. . . . Three of our party were
wounded, but not mortally. Fifteen
of the Indians were flain, and many
more were wounded. Numbers of
the enemy eluded our fhots, and made
their efcape into the woods. Obferving one man, light of foot, entering
the foreft, I happened to be foremoft
in purfuit of him. I had fcarcely
come up with him, when he cried for
quarter. My firft impulfe was to
bayonet him; but an inftant fympathy
turned away the pointed fteel. My
next thought was, that his imperfect Indian dialect was counterfeit.
Thrufting my hand into his bofom,
and making a wide rent in his inner
garment, I difcovered that he was the
child of white parents, while his face,
and his heart too, were as black as
thofe of any favage.

"The fhades of evening were now
fettling down about us. Returning
with our captive white Indian to the
general flaughter-ground, a fcene of
indefcribable horror prefented itfelf
to our view. The flames had levelled

THEIR marches were over the ruins of Indian barbarity. On their return, they flanked into parties, and took different routs through the wildernefs. She was in a party commanded by Capt. MILLS. Not far from Bradport, an

the houfe [of the man whom they faw fleeing for his life] nearly to the earth. The mother lay dead and horribly mangled a few feet from the threfhold. Two children were hung by their heels upon a tree," &c. " While this was going on, a fine little girl was difcovered by her piteous plaints. She had concealed herfelf under fome ftraw. She was brought forth, not only ftiff with the cold, but having a bad wound in the fhoulder from a tomahawk. At fight of her, the wretched father funk down upon the fnow, as if never again to rife, exhaufted by the lofs of blood from his own wound, as well as by the fcene that furrounded him. . . .

" We now retraced our courfe to Fort Edward, frequently tinging the fnow and ice with our own blood. Our fhoes were worn through, and our clothing torn by the thick undergrowth of the foreft."

Here two pages are devoted to the tragic ftory of Jane McCrea, murdered by the Indians, on the advance of Burgoyne's army, in Auguft, 1777. Six pages are then occupied with a brief *réfumé* of the Northern campaign of 1777, efpecially the battle of Bemis's Heights, on the 7th of October; taken from Thacher's " Military Journal" and other hiftories.

At Albany, the MS. memoir affirms that fhe was fent for by Gen. Schuyler to vifit him at his refidence, and complimented for her diftinguifhed bravery in the Indian expedition. Six or feven pages are given to this interview, and to the converfation which is faid to have there taken place. One of Gen. Schuyler's daughters, recently married to Col. Alex. Hamilton, is introduced as detailing to our heroine the friendly reception given by the family to Gens. Burgoyne, Philips, Reidefel, the Baronefs Reidefel, Lady Acland, and their children, after the furrender at Saratoga, including what was faid and done on that occafion. *Credat Judæus !*

" About the laft of January, 1783, we reached the winter-cantonments of the army on the Hudfon, having feen hard fervice, but without having loft a man. Scarcely had I taken a night's repofe in camp before the expreffions hero, champion, victor, applied to myfelf, ran currently through my regiment. I have fince thought it wonderful that I was not inflated with pride, which fometimes lifts one above himfelf into the airy region of fools." Not Deborah Sampfon, but Mr. Mann, the compiler of the MS. memoir, is refponfible for this language and the preceding ftatements.

Englifh fettlement, the fnow having fallen three feet deep, they faw a man fleeing for his life. On enquiry, he informed, that the Indians had furrounded his houfe, and were then in the heat of their butchery. Haftening with him to the place, they found the infernals had not finifhed their hellifh facrafices. The houfe was on fire, his wife mangled and lay bleeding on the threfhold. Two children were hung by their heels; one fcalped, and yet alive; the other dead, with a tamahawk in its brains. They took them.—Females, have fortitude. The dauntlefs of your fex thruft her hand into the bofom of one, and rent his vefture. The effect was the difcovery of his being of the complexion of an Englifhman, except where he was painted. They fent him to Head Quarters; but executed the reft on the fpot.

BEFORE they reached the army, their feet once more crimfoned the fnow—a token of their fufferings. But her name refounded with plaudits; which would have been enhanced, had the difcovery of her fex then taken place.

C H A P. IX.

She goes to live in a GENERAL OFFICER'S *family.—Mi*ſ*ɛɛ-
laneous incidents.—Marches with* 1500 *men for the ſup-
preſſion of a mutiny among the American ſoldiers at
Philadelphia.—Has a violent ſickneſs and is carried to
the hoſpital in this city.—*DISCOVERY *of* SEX.—*A young*
LADY *conceives an* ATTACHMENT *for our* BLOOMING SOL-
DIER.

IN the Spring of 1783, peace began to be the general
topic; and which was actually announced to Congreſs.
A building was erected; in which the officers held their
concerts. It would contain a brigade at a time for the
exerciſe of public worſhip. The timber was cut and
drawn together by the ſoldiers, and moſtly ſawn by hand.
Our Heroine worked againſt any hardy ſoldier, without
any advantage in her yoke. In its raiſing, a joiſt fell
and carried her from a conſiderable height to the ground;
but without doing any eſſential injury, except the diſlo-
cation of her noſe and ancle.[85]

ON the firſt of April, Gen. PATTERSON ſelected her for
his Waiter; as he had previouſly become acquainted with
her heroiſm and fidelity.[86] Ceſſation of hoſtilities was

[85] There is no reference in the MS.
memoir to any thing of this ſort.

[86] " Directly after our return to
headquarters, I found myſelf appointed waiter, or, as the more courtly
phraſe is, aide-de-camp, to my much-
eſteemed general, Patterſon, and taken
into his family. This was in conſe-

proclaimed on the 19th.[87] The honorary badge of diftinction, as eftablifhed by Gen. WASHINGTON, had been
conferred on her; but for what particular exploit, I cannot fay. Her bufinefs was here much lefs intenfe; and
fhe found a fuperior fchool for improvement.

THE General's attachment towards his new attendant

quence of the illnefs of Major Hafkell, who had ferved as his aide."

Dr. Thacher fpeaks of Major Haf-kell as being aide-de-camp to Gen. Patterfon, and fays he was a native of Rochefter, Mafs. It is not very probable that Robert Shurtliffe fhould have been taken from the ranks, or from the pofition of fergeant, which fhe is faid to have held, to be aide-de-camp to a general officer.

" I was furnifhed with a good horfe and fine equipments, and found my-felf furrounded with the comforts, and even the elegancies, of life. I no longer flept on a pallet of ftraw on the damp, cold ground, but on a good feather-bed. And here, I prefume, curiofity will be awake to inquire whether I always flept *alone;* and if not, with whom, and on what terms. I will tell the truth frankly, and chal-lenge contradiction. In the firft place, a foldier has not always his choice of lodgings or of bed-fellows. He often lies down in promifcuous repofe with his companions, without other parti-tion than his blanket, his knapfack, and his mufket.

" But, in Gen. Patterfon's family, my couch invited to foft, undifturbed re-

pofe, fuch as I actually enjoyed. My bed-companions were, fometimes one officer, and fometimes another. But no one was inferior to myfelf, either in rank or in virtuous principle, to fay the leaft and the worft of them. They as little fufpected my fex, as I fufpected them of a difpofition to vio-late its chaftity, had I been willing to expofe myfelf to them, and to act the wanton. If this explanation is not fatisfactory, if any ftill imagine that in my fituation nothing fhort of a con-tinued miracle could have kept me unpolluted, I muft content myfelf with the inward fatisfaction which confcious purity and virtue always afford, leaving them to ftruggle as they may with their doubts on the fubject."

There is reafon to believe that all the while fhe flept *alone.* '

[87] The Preliminary Treaty of Peace was figned at Paris, Nov. 30, 1782, but not publifhed by royal proclama-tion in London till Feb. 15, 1783. The ceffation of hoftilities was pro-claimed in the American camp, by order of Gen. Wafhington, on the eighth anniverfary of the battle of Lexington.

was daily increafing. Her martial deportment, blended with the milder graces and vivacity of her fex and youth, filled him with admiration and wonder. Anxious to avail himfelf of every advantage to infpire his troops with emulation in the caufe of their country; it is faid, perhaps juftly, that when he faw a delinquency or faint-heartednefs in his men, he often referred them to fome heroic achievement of his *fmockfaced boy*, or convinced them by an ocular example.[88]

KNOWING fhe had his commendations, fhe found new ftimulations for perfeverance. And fcarcely any injunctions would have been too fevere for her compliance. Hence it feems, he was led to conceive that fuch an affemblage of courage and refinement could exift but in the fuperior order of his fex; and that fuch a youth was highly calculated to fhine either in the fphere of war, or in the profeffion of a gentleman of tafte and philofophic refinement.

THUS, Females, whilft you fee the avidity of a maid in her teens confronting dangers and made a veteran example in *war*, you need only half the affiduity in your proper, *domeftic fphere*, to render your charms completely irrefiftible.

GENERAL orders were, every warm feafon, for the foldiers to go into the water, as well to exercife themfelves

[88] Here belongs the ftory related in the Appendix, refpecting her journey from Weft Point to "a place called the Clove."

in the art of fwimming, as to clean their bodies.[89]   Thefe
injunctions were fo directly in point, that her compliance
with them would unavoidably have been unbofoming the
delicate fecret.   To have pled indifpofition would have
been an argument againft her; as the cold bath might
have wrought her cure : and to have intimated cowardice,
would have entitled her to lefs lenity, than when before
in the Ferry.   So, after lying awake the firft night, fhe
concluded to be the firft to rife at roll-call.   Accordingly,
the regiment paraded and marched to the river.   She
was expert in undreffing with the reft.   After they were
moftly in the water, what fhould ravifh her ear but the
found of a fweet fountain, that percolated over a high
rock near the river's brink.   It was thickly enclofed with
the afpen and alder.   Thither fhe unnoticed retired.   And
whilft the Hudfon fwelled with the multitude of mafculine bodies, a beautiful rivulet anfwered every purpofe of
bathing a more delicate form.   Nor were there any old,
letcherous, fanctified Elders to peep through the ruftling
leaves to be inflamed with her charms.

. ONE more incident may amufe thofe ladies, who are
fond of angling.[90]—One day, fhe, with fome others, at the
ebb of tide, went to the Hudfon for this purpofe.   Near
the boat, fhe difcovered a beautiful azure rock, well
fituated for fifhing.   Too carelefs of her famed prede-

[89] This account is omitted in the
MS. memoir It is wholly improbable.

[90] This unlikely ftory is alfo omitted in the MS. memoir.

ceffor's difpofition, fhe difembarked from the boat to the rock. Soon after, they purpofely weighed anchor and left her furrounded with water. She continued not long, before, to her furprife, as well as the reft, the rock became a felf-moving vehicle, and fat out to overtake her company. Dreading the paffage, fhe leaped into the water and mire, and had many fevere ftruggles before fhe reached land. The rock proved a prodigious Tortoife. And left antiquity fhould not be cured of credulity and fuperftition, thereby enhance the prodigy to their generation—that a *female* was once a navigator on the back of a Tortoife, that he finally fwallowed her and fome time after, fpouted her alive on the fertile land;—it is only needful to mention, that they gaffed him, with much difficulty, towed *him* reluctant to the fhore, and foon after, on a day of feftival, ate him.

THIS Summer a detachment of 1500 men was ordered to march to Philadelphia for the fuppreffion of a mutiny among the American foldiers.[91] She did not go till four

---

[91] At the clofe of the war, it was found extremely difficult, and indeed impoffible, to pay off the foldiers of the Continental army. The United States were a nation; but there was no national government, — only a confederation. Congrefs did not poffefs the power of taxation; and no means exifted for raifing a revenue for national purpofes. The powers of government, fo far as any exifted, were held by the feveral States, which were flow to exercife them when they were likely to bear hard upon the people. Congrefs had reforted to loans; immenfe quantities of paper-money had been iffued during the war, but the Continental currency had depreciated rapidly, till, in the latter part of 1780, it became worthlefs, and ceafed to circulate. There were therefore no funds, at the clofe

days after the General left Weſt Point. She then rode
in company with four gentlemen, and had a richly variegated proſpect through the Jerſies and a part of Pennſylvania. In Goſhen they were invited to a ball; where ſhe
was pleaſed to ſee, eſpecially in the ladies, the brilliancy
and politeneſs of thoſe in New England. They were
here detained two days on account of Lieut. STONE, who
was confined for a duel with Capt. HITCHCOCK, who was
killed.[92] She found the troops encamped on a hill; from
which, they had a fine proſpect of the city and of the

of the war, to pay the troops. ✓ The
greater part of them bore the evil
with commendable patience, ſubmit-
ting to it as a matter of unavoidable
neceſſity. In many caſes, however,
there was diſcontent, and, in a few
caſes, as here, open mutiny.

A ſmall body of Pennſylvania
troops — Thacher ſays about eighty
— encamped at Lancaſter, in that
State, in the month of June, 1783,
clamored for their pay, roſe in revolt,
and marched to Philadelphia, ſixty-
ſeven miles diſtant, determined to
enforce their claim upon Congreſs
at the point of the bayonet. Arriving
in that city on the 29th of that month,
they proceeded to the barracks; and
being joined by two hundred troops
from Carolina, and obtaining artillery,
they marched, with drums beating,
to the State Houſe, where Congreſs
was then aſſembled. Placing guards
at every door, they ſent in a meſſage,
accompanied with a threat, that, if

their demands were not complied with
in twenty minutes, they would proceed to open violence.

The members of Congreſs ſucceeded, however, in making their eſcape,
and ſent information of the affair to
Gen. Waſhington, who immediately
ordered a detachment of troops on
whom he could rely, fifteen hundred
ſtrong, under the command of Major-
Gen. Robert Howe, to proceed to Philadelphia, and to ſuppreſs the mutiny.
This affair gave occaſion for our heroine to viſit Philadelphia. Happily,
the inſurgents ſubmitted at once.
Some of the ringleaders were tried
and ſentenced, two to ſuffer death,
and four to other puniſhment. But
Congreſs pardoned them all. Dr.
Thacher notices this affair. He ſays,
"On the 29th of June, about eighty
new-levy ſoldiers of the Pennſylvania
line marched to Philadelphia," &c.

92 The duel took place at Goſhen.
Very likely, it originated in that ball-

Allegany, which rifes majeftic over the intervening country. Here fhe had frequent occafion to vifit the city, fometimes on bufinefs, and often curiofity led her to view its magnificence. The gentility of her drefs and agreeable mien gained her accefs to company of both fexes of rank and elegance.

THE ftorm of war having fubfided, an agreeable profpect once more gleamed on the face of COLUMBIA. But fortune had more dangers and toils affigned her. An epidemic diforder raged in the city: and fhe was quickly felected a victim, and carried once more to the hofpital with all the horrible apprehenfions of her fituation.[93] Death itfelf could fcarcely have prefented a more gloomy profpect: and that feemed not far diftant; as multitudes were daily carried to the Potter's Field. She begged not to be left in the loathfome bunks of foldiers. Accordingly, fhe was lodged in a third loft, where were two other officers of the fame line, who foon died. Alone fhe was then left to condole her wretchednefs; except Doctor

room. "We left Hitchcock, who had been a good officer, dead upon the field, and Stone in prifon. This detained us two days."

[93] "A malignant fever was then raging in Philadelphia, particularly among the troops ftationed there and in the vicinity. I was foon feized with it. I fcarcely felt its fymptoms before I was carried to the hofpital.

All I diftinctly remember was the profpect of death, which feemed not far diftant. I was thrown into a loathfome bunk, out of which had juft been removed a corpfe for burial; foon after which, I became utterly infenfible." — [*MS. Memoir.*]

Would the authorities of the hofpital have treated in this manner an aide-de-camp of Gen. Patterfon?

Bana[94] and the Matron, Mrs. Parker, whofe folicitude fhe remembers with gratitude.

How poignantly muft refleçtion have here brought to her memory thofe foft and tranquil feafons, wherein fhe fo often deprived herfelf the midfummer's morning dream, to breathe with the lark the frefh incenfe of morning!— when with hafty fteps fhe brufhed the dews from vegetation, to meet the fun on the rifing grounds: by which, to catch frefh hints of CREATION, and to inhale thee, buxom HEALTH, from every opening flower! But fhe is now, not indeed, like Egyptian mummies, wrapped in fine linen and laid on beds of fpices, but on the naked floor, anticipating the Archer, Death, in all the frightful forms of his equipage.

BUT at length, fhe was deprived of the faculty of refleçtion. The Archer was about to execute his laft office. The inhuman fextons had drawn their allowance, and upon her vefture they were cafting lots. One JONES, the only Englifh nurfe, at that inftant coming in, fhe once more rallied the fmall remains of nature and gave figns of life. The fextons withdrew, and JONES informed the Matron fuch a one was yet alive; which fhe difcredited.[95] Doc-

---

[94] Dr. Binney, the furgeon of the hofpital, is here intended. Dr. Thacher mentions that he dined in Philadelphia, Sept. 9, 1782, with "Doçtor Binney of the hofpital."

[95] "It was not long before I came to fome degree of confcioufnefs, when I perceived preparations making for my burial. I heard the funeral-undertakers quarrelling about fome part of my clothing, which each of them wifhed to poffefs. One Jones, the only Englifh-fpeaking nurfe in the hofpital, coming in, I fucceeded, by

tor BANA at that inftant entered; and putting his hand in her bofom to feel her pulfe, was furprifed to find an inner waift-coat tightly compreffing her breafts. Ripping it in hafte, he was ftill more fhocked, not only on finding life, but the breafts and other tokens of a *female*.[96] Immediately fhe was removed into the Matron's own apartment; and from that time to her recovery, treated with all the care, that art and expenfe could beftow.[97]

an almoft fuperhuman effort, in convincing him that I was ftill alive. I well remember that he not only threatened thefe monfters, but ufed actual force to prevent their dragging me to the Potter's Field, the place of burial for ftrangers. The undertakers at length withdrew, when Jones informed the worthy matron, Mrs. Parker, that Robert Shurtliffe, a foldier in bunk No. —, who had been fuppofed to be dead, was actually alive. This fhe was inclined to doubt. It was faid that they came to afcertain the fact. But I knew it not; for I had funk once more into a ftate refembling death." — [*MS. Memoir.*]

96 "They had fcarcely retired a fecond time, when Dr. Binney, the furgeon, vifited the hofpital, to whom Jones made known the fact of my partial re-animation. He immediately came to my apartment, and called me by name. Though I diftinctly heard him, I could make no reply. He turned away for a moment to fome other patients. I thought he had left me again to the ravenous

undertakers. By a great effort, I made a kind of gurgling in my throat to call his attention to me. Never can I forget his elaftic ftep, and apparently deep emotion, as he fprang to my bed-fide. Thrufting his hand into my bofom to afcertain if there were motion at the heart, he was furprifed at finding an inner veft tightly compreffing my breafts, the inftant removal of which not only afcertained the fact of life, but difclofed the fact that I was a *woman!* He forced, by fome inftrument, a medicine into my ftomach, which greatly revived me, and caufed me to exhibit further figns of life." — [*Ibid.*]

97 This remarkable difcovery the benevolent furgeon imparted to none but Mrs. Parker, the matron of the hofpital, charging her to confine the knowledge of it to her own bofom. Our heroine was, after being conveyed to Mrs. Parker's apartment, nurfed with the greateft care. She now flowly recovered; and, as foon as fhe was able to ride, fhe was taken to Dr. Binney's houfe, and treated

THE amiable Phyſician had the prudence to conceal this important diſcovery from every breaſt but the Matron. From that time, the once more diſcovered *female* became a welcome gueſt in their families. And they recommended her to others, as an object worthy their attention and affection.—But there remains another event, perhaps, the moſt unparalleled of its kind, to be unfolded.

A YOUNG lady of the ſuburbs of Baltimore, beautiful in form, bleſt with a well cultivated mind, and a fortune, had often converſed with this illuſtrious *ſoldier*.[98] The gracefulneſs of her mien, mixed with her dignified, martial

with the moſt delicate attention. As her recovery proceeded, ſhe began to ſuſpect that a diſcovery had been made, to her moſt unwelcome. She could account in no other way for the tenderneſs with which ſhe was treated. Her kind friends, Mrs. Parker and Dr. Binney, were careful to conceal from her the knowledge they had acquired; but it was evident to her mind that they did not expect that ſhe would reſume her military attire.

"But in this," ſays Deborah, "they were miſtaken; and ſo was I miſtaken in the uſe which I preſumed would be made of the diſcovery of my ſex. Emaciated and pallid, I was introduced by the good Dr. Binney to his wife and daughters as a young and gallant ſoldier who had met in battle the enemies of our country, and had now riſen, as it were, from the bed of death. This introduction was ſufficient to commend me to their warmeſt ſympathies. In their company, I rambled through the ſtreets of the city, attended public exhibitions, ſailed upon the Delaware, and ſtrolled in the groves and flowery meads. The Doctor had no fears of the reſult. I was admitted as a gueſt in many wealthy families; ſtill known only as a Continental ſoldier."—[*Ib.*]

98 This love-ſtory is told in the MS. memoir with conſiderable variation. It is there ſaid that the young lady, the writer of the enſuing letter, was ſeventeen years of age, the daughter of wealthy parents in Baltimore, and now an orphan; that the acquaintance commenced in September, 1781, during the ſtay of the American army at Annapolis when on its way to Yorktown, and that they became mutually and tenderly attached. The letter in the MS. memoir is better written.

airs, enraptured her. At firſt, ſhe attempted to check the
impulſe, as the effect of a giddy paſſion; but at length,
ſuffered it to play about her heart unchided. Cupid, im-
patient, at length, urged his quiver too far, and wounded
the ſeat of love.—O Love! how powerful is your influence! how unlimited your domain! The gallant SOLO-
MON could not have compoſed three thouſand proverbs
and his madrigals to his love, without much of your conviviality. The illuminations of Venus were known in
thoſe days. And it was by her rays, the Preacher of love
ſo often ſtrolled with his Egyptian belles in his vineyard,
when the flowers appeared on the earth, the mandrakes
gave a good ſmell, and the time of the ſinging of birds
had come; when they reciprocated their love amidſt the
dews of dawn.

SUFFICIENT it is, that this love is preſerved, and that it
will remain incontrovertible. And happy it is, that it is
not only enjoyed by the prince of the inner pavillion. It
leaps upon the mountains; and, under the ſhadow of the
apple-tree, it is ſweet to the taſte. From the moſs-covered
cottage, it is purſued, even amidſt the thunders of war
and the diſtraction of elements. And the nymph of
Maryland was as much entitled to it, as the miſtreſs of
him, who had the careſſing of a thouſand. Hers was
ſentimental and eſtabliſhed: and ſhe was miſerable from
the thought, that it might not be interchangeable.

ON this account, the productions of her plantation

were no longer relifhed with pleafure. The mufic of her groves became diffonant, her grottos too folitary, and the rivulets purled but for her difcontent. From thefe fhe flew in fearch of him, whom her foul loved, among the buftling roar of the city. And the third morning after fhe was confined in the hofpital, a courier delivered her a letter and a handkerchief full of choice fruit. Inclofed was the fubftance of the following:

DEAR SIR,

FRAUGHT with the feelings of a friend, who is, doubtlefs, beyond your conception, interefted in your health and happinefs, I take liberty to addrefs you with a franknefs, which nothing but the pureft friendfhip and affeƈtion can palliate.—Know, then, that the charms I firft read in your vifage brought a paffion into my bofom, for which I could not account. If it was from the thing called LOVE, I was before moftly ignorant of it, and ftrove to ftifle the fugitive; though I confefs the indulgence was agreeable. But repeated interviews with you kindled it into a flame, I do not now blufh to own: and fhould it meet a generous return, I fhall not reproach myfelf for its indulgence.—I have long fought to hear of your apartment: And how painful is the news I this moment received, that you are fick, if alive, in the hofpital! Your complicated nerves will not admit of writing. But inform the bearer, if you are neceffitated for any thing, that can conduce to your comfort. If you recover, and think proper to enquire my name, I will give you an opportunity. But if death is to terminate your exiftence there, let your laft fenfes be im-

preffed with the reflection, that you die not without one more friend, whofe tears will bedew your funeral obfequies. —ADIEU.

SOME have been charmed, others furprifed by love in the dark, and from an unexpefted quarter; but *fhe* alone can conceive what effeft, what perturbation, fuch a declaration had on her mind; whofe neareft profpeft feemed that of her own diffolution. She humbly returned her gratitude, but happily was not in want of money; owing to a prize fhe in company had found in the Britifh lines, confifting of clothes, plate and coin.[99] In the evening fhe received a billet inclofing two guineas. The like favors were continued during her illnefs.[100] But fhe knew not in whofe bofom the paffion vibrated.—Her recovery muft make the next chapter eventful.

[99, 100] No ftatements like thefe appear in the MS. memoir.

C H A P. X.

Her critical fituation.—Commences a TOUR *towards the Ohio with fome Gentlemen.—Interview with her* LOVER. *—They meet a terrible* TEMPEST.—*She is left fick with the Indians.*

HEALTH having reanimated the fo much admired Virago, one might conclude fhe had bufinefs enough on hand: And, gracious Powers! what had fhe not on

25

her heart and mind? Sufpicious that a difcovery had been made during her illnefs, every zephyr became an ill-fated omen and every falutation, a mandate to fummon her to a retribution for her impofition on the mafculine character.

Such embarraffments foreboded the winding up of her drama. And fhe was doubtlefs careful to picture the event in the blackeft colours. A retrofpection of her life muft have brought, to her mind, a contraft, unknown to many and dreaded by all. But having ftood at helm during the feverity of the ftorm, fhe concluded, if a con-ceffion muft be extorted from her, it might appear lefs daftardly after a beautiful, ferene DAY had commenced: And that it mattered little, whether it fhould happen among the infatiable throng of the city, or the ruder few of the defolate heath.—Thus the lionefs, having pervaded every toil and danger, from the hounds and hunters, at length, cornered on all fides, difdaining their fury, yields herfelf a prey.

Doctor Bana was now waiting a convenient opportu-nity to divulge to her his fufpicion of her fex. He often found her dejected; and as he gueffed the caufe, intro-duced lively difcourfe. She had the happinefs to recom-mend herfelf much to the efteem of his difcreet and amiable daughters. And the Doctor was fond that fo promifing a *ftripling* fhould often gallant them into the city and country villages. The unruffled furface of a

fummer's fea was alfo often a witnefs to their paftimes.[101]
This rare fpecies of innocent recreation was, doubtlefs,
peculiarly gratifying to the Doctor; as his mind could
not be more at reft on his daughters' account. Nor need
they think themfelves chagrined, when it is known they
once had a *female* gallant; on the ftrength of whofe arm
and fword they would have depended in cafe of danger.

AFTER fhe had refumed her regimentals to rejoin the
troops, the Doctor, availing himfelf of a private confer-
ence, afked her, whether fhe had any particular confident
in the army? She faid, no; and trembling, would have
difclofed the fecret: but he, feeing her confufion, waved
the difcourfe. To divert her mind, he propofed her taking a tour towards the Ohio with Col. TUPPER[102] of Maffa-

[101] By "a fummer's fea," here, is
meant the River Delaware, on which
they fometimes enjoyed a fail. (See
note 97.) Mrs. Ellet here introduces
a love adventure between Deborah
and a niece of the doctor, which cor-
refponds with that between the former
and the Baltimore lady.

[102] Col. (afterwards Gen.) Benjamin
Tupper was born in Sharon, then a
part of Stoughton, Mafs., in 1738.
He was a private foldier in the "Old
French War," from 1755 to 1762.
He was in the military fervice of his
country during the whole Revolutionary War; firft as major, then as
colonel, of the Eleventh Maffachufetts Regiment. Very foon after the
war, he, with Gen. Rufus Putnam

and other officers of the Continental
army, united in a plan for the fettlement of what is now the State of
Ohio. The journey mentioned in the
text may have been connected with
this defign. In the fummer of 1785,
Gen. Tupper went as far as Pittf-
burgh, with the intention of making
a furvey of a portion of the lands in
that State, but was prevented by the
unfriendly fpirit of the Indian tribes
at that time. A furvey of feven ranges
of townfhips in Ohio was completed
in the fummer of 1786, under his direction. With two wagons, one for
his family, the other for their baggage,
he went all the way from Chefterfield,
Mafs., then his home, to Marietta,
Ohio, and, with others, commenced

chufetts, Meffrs. FORKSON and GRAHAM of Philadelphia; who were going, partly to contemplate the country and partly to difcover minerals. Knowing the mineral rods were peculiar to her, he faid, whilft the tour might be profitable, it might be a reftorative to her health, and an amufement to her mind.

SURPRISED to find this met her concurrence, he ufed fome arguments to diffuade her from it: But finding her unequivocal, he enjoined it upon her to vifit his houfe at her return; which fhe promifed. And about the laft of Auguft, they fet out from the *Conaftoga Waggon* and went, in the ftage, the firft day, to Baltimore, which is eighty miles.

NEXT day, as fhe was viewing the town, fhe received a billet requefting her company at fuch a place. Though confident fhe had before feen the hand writing, fhe could not conjecture what was commencing. Prompted by cu-riofity, fhe went; and being conducted into an elegant room, was ftruck with admiration, on finding alone, the amiable and all accomplifhed Mifs ———, of about feven-teen, whom fhe had long thought a confpicuous ornament to her fex. The lady expreffed furprife on feeing *him*, who, according to report, had died foon after fhe left the metropolis. An acquaintance being before eftablifhed,

the fettlement of that town in Auguft, 1788. He died in June, 1792. —[S. P. Hildreth's *Early Settlers of Ohio*.] It is not at all likely that Deborah Sampfon accompanied Col. Tupper on fuch an expedition.

mutual compliments paffed between the lovers. The young lady confeffed herfelf author of the anonymous letter.[103] And though uncertain of a conceffion—timorous as a young roe, yet pliant as the bending ozier, with the queen of love refident in her eye, fhe rehearfed her plaint of love with that unrefervednefs, which evinced the fincerity of her paffion and exaltednefs of foul. The foul is the emporium of love.—Their blufhes and palpitations were, doubtlefs, reciprocal; but, I judge, of a different nature. But while this liberal conceffion was the ftrongeft evidence, that fhe poffeffed love, without defire of proftitution, and friendfhip without diffimulation; let it be remembered, to her honor, that her effufions flowed with that affability, prudence and dignified grace, which muft have fired the breaft of an anchorite—inanimate nature itfelf muft have waked into life, and even the fuperftitious, cowled friar muft have revoked his eternal vows of celibacy, and have flown to the embraces of an object, exhibiting fo many charms in her eloquence of love.

THUS, ye delicate, who would be candidates for the fruition of this noble, this angelic paffion, it is refinement only, that renders your beauty amiable, and even unrefervednefs, in either fex, agreeable. The reverfe is only a happy circumftance between vice and virtue. While it there happily preys on every delicate fenfation, it renders

103 For the letter, fee page 192.

the idea of enjoyment loathfome, and even hurries delicacy herfelf into diftrefs.

HAD this unfortunate lover uttered herfelf in an uncouth, illiterate, unpolifhed manner, every word would
have loft its energy and all her charms become vapid on
the fenfes.—Or, had fhe affumed the attire—the cunning
of an harlot—the defperate fimplicity of a young wanton ;
had fhe begun her fubtle eloquence with a kifs ; and, with
the poifon of afps under her tongue, have reprefented her
bed of embroidery filled with perfume, and finally have
urged that the abfence of the good man gave them an
opportunity to riot in the extatic delights of love—while
our young fugitive would have needed fupernatural means
to have anfwered the demands of venerious appetition,
the fimple might have found fatiety in her feraglio : But
Virtue would have continued on her throne in fullen fad-
nefs.   But this was not the cafe.   Though fufpended between natural and artificial confufion—though ficknefs
had abated her acutenefs for the foft romances of love ;
fhe doubtlefs embraced the celeftial maid, and wifhing
herfelf miftrefs of her fuperior charms, could not but par-
ticipate in the genial warmth of a paffion fo irrefiftibly
managed.   Knowledge intermixed with beauty and refinement, enkindles a warmth of the pureft love ; and, like
the centre of the earth, commands the power of attraction.
She tarried in this fchool of animal philofophy the moft

of two days; then promifing to vifit her in her return, proceeded on her journey.[104]

FROM Baltimore, paffing Elk Ridge, they came to Alexandria in Virginia. Nine miles below, is Mount Vernon, the feat of the illuftrious WASHINGTON, which they vifited. It is fituated near a bend in the Potomak; where it is two miles wide. The area of the mount is 200 feet above the furface of the river. On either wing, is a thick grove of flowering trees. Parallel with them, are two fpacious gardens, adorned with ferpentine gravel walks, planted with weeping willows and fhady fhrubs. The manfion houfe is venerable and convenient. A lofty dome, 96 feet in length, fupported by eight pillars, has a pleafing effect when viewed from the water. This, with the affemblage of the green houfe, offices and fervant's halls, bears the refemblance of a rural village; efpecially

---

[104] Inftead of this rapfody, take the following, from the MS. memoir: "She received me with a dignified and yet familiar air. She apologized with infinite grace for overftepping the acknowledged bounds of female delicacy in making fuch an overture to a gentleman. She expreffed great pleafure and much furprife at feeing me alive; having been led to fuppofe, from an account that reached her not long before, that I had died in the hofpital. She confeffed the tender fentiments of her heart, which had led her to feek this interview. . . . What could I do, what could I fay, in fuch an exigency? How fhould I feel, on receiving fuch a declaration from fuch a heart? I could not act the hypocrite with fuch an artlefs girl; nor could I refufe the affection fo warmly proffered, and fo delicately expreffed. But I could not then difclofe to her the fecret I was fo anxious to conceal from all the world befide. In this ftate of embarraffment I continued the moft of two days, and finally compromifed the matter by promifing to call on her again on my return from the Weft."

as the grafs plats are interfperfed with little copfes, circu-
lar clumps and fingle trees. A fmall park on the margin
of the river, where the Englifh fallow deer and the
American wild deer are alternately feen through the
thickets by paffengers on the river, adds a romantic and
picturefque profpeĉt to the whole fcenery. Such are the
philofophic fhades, to which the late Commander of the
American Armies, and Prefident of the nation, has now
retired, from a tumultuous and bufy world.

THEIR next route was to the fouthweftern parts of Virginia.* Having travelled fome days, they came to a large
river; when the gentlemen and guide difputed, whether
it was the Monongahela, Yohogany, or the Ohio itfelf.[105]
They concluded to wait till the fog, which was very thick,
fhould be gone, that they might determine with more
precifion. But inftead of diffipating, it increafed, and
they heard thunder roll at a diftance. On a fudden, a
moft violent tempeft of wind and rain commenced, accompanied with fuch perpetual lightning and peals of
thunder, that all nature feemed in one combuftible con-
vulfion. The leeward fide of a fhelving rock illy fcreened
them from the ftorm, which continued to rage the moft

---

* I KNOW not whether it was in this tour, that fhe vifited the famous
Cafcade in Virginia, MADISON's Cave on the North fide of the Blue
Ridge, and the paffage of the Potomak through the fame ; which is one
of the moft auguft fcenes in nature.

105 This river proved to be the Shenandoah.

of the night. Happily they were preferved; though one
of their dogs became a victim to the electric fire. It is
faid, he was fo near their female companion, when killed,
that fhe could have reached him with a common ftaff.

NEXT day, the weather was calm. They difcharged
their pieces in order to clean them; the report of which
brought to their view fix of the natives in warlike array.
Many ceremonies were effected, before they could be convinced of friendfhip. When effected, they folicited the
guide to follow them; indicating by their rude noifes and
actions, they were much troubled. He refufing, their
Adventrefs laughed at his caution.[106] One of the Indians,
obferving this, ran to her, fired his arrow over her head,
took a wreath of wampum, twined it about her waift, and
bade her follow. She obeyed; though they checked her
prefumption. They conducted her to a cave; which,
fhe thinks, is as great a natural curiofity, as that of MAD-
ISON's. They complimented her to enter firft; which fhe
durft not refufe. They followed; and advancing nearly
to the centre, fell on their faces; and whilft the cave
echoed with their frightful yells and actions, our Adventrefs, as ufual, doubtlefs, thought of home. When they
rofe, they ran to the further part, dragged three dead In-

[106] " Obferving that he [the guide] hefitated, I ftepped forward with my gun, and offered to go in his place, at the fame time laughing at his ex-treme caution. My companions taxed me with prefumption and folly, but I was determined, then and always, not to be a coward."

26

dians out of the cave and laid their faces to the ground.
Then climbing a rock, they rolled down immenfe ftones;
then whooping, firft pointing to the fky, then to the ftones,
and then to the Indians; who were killed by the lightning
the preceding day. Having convinced them, fhe underftood it, and that the mate to a dog with her had fhared
the fame fate, they conducted her to her company. They
told her, they had defpaired of ever feeing her again;
concluding her fcalp was taken off, when they heard the
fhouting. She jocofely extolled them for their champion
courage, but not for their lenity; as they did not go to
her relief. They all then went to the cave and attended
their favage, funeral ceremonies.

THE Indians went with them up the river, which they
concluded to be one of the Kanhawas. But in this they
were miftaken; they being too much to the South. They
hired one of the tribe to pilot them[107] over the Allegany.
Paffing the Jumetta Creek and the Fork of the Pennfyl-
vania and Glade Roads, about 40 miles from the Jumetta,
they came to the foot of the Dry Ridge.[108]   Here they
found trees, whofe fruit refembled the nectarine; and, like
it, delicious to the tafte. Eating freely of it, till obferving
the Indian did not, they defifted. And happily fo; for it

[107] " Two of the Indians we hired
as guides over the next range of the
Alleghanies, which is more lofty and
majeftic than the Blue Ridge, the
range we had already paffed. There
are two Kenhawas."

[108] The Laurel Mountains, the weftern range of the Alleghanies.

came near proving mortal. Its firſt effect was fickneſs at the ſtomach. The defcendent of her, who is accufed of having been too heedleſs of the bewitching charm of cu-riofity, puked and bled at the nofe, till ſhe was unable to walk. The Indian was miffing; but foon came with a handful of roots, which, being bruifed and applied to her nofe and each fide of her neck, ſtopped the blood and ficknefs.

HENCE they vifited a tribe near a place, called Medfkar. She was here fo indifpofed, ſhe could not proceed on the journey. Her illnefs proved a relapfe of her fever.[109] The pilot interceded with the King for her to tarry with them till the return of her company; which, he faid, would be at the cloſe of one moon. Being convinced they were no fpies, nor invaders, he confented. He then ordered an Indian and his fquaw to doctor her; telling them, the *boy* would eat good, when fattened.[110]—She remarks, that their medicines always had a more fenfible effect, than thofe of common phyficians. Thus, in a ſhort time, ſhe recovered. But I ſhall not attempt to recount all her fufferings, efpecially by hunger, but a more intenfe torture of mind, during this barbarous fervitude.

HER aim was, never to difcover the leaſt cowardice, but always to laugh at their threats. A ſtriking inſtance of this ſhe exemplified at their coronation of a new King.

[109] It was a return of the fever ſhe had in Philadelphia. [110] This was faid to try her cour-age.

Her mafter, like a hell-hound, hooting her into the fquare, where were many kettles of water boiling, told her, he was going to have a flice of her for dinner. Being the only white man (a *girl!*) among them, fhe was inftantly furrounded by the infernals. She afked him if he ever ate Englifhmen? He anfwered, *good omfkuock!* She then told him, he muft keep her better, or fhe fhould never do to eat. Some underftood her; and giving a terrible fhout, firft told her to cut a notch in the great ftone kalendar, then putting her hands on the king's head, fhe joined the dance, and fared with the reft. Ladies at a civilized ball may be infenfible of this fcene.

THE reader keeps in view, I fuppofe, that all *female* courage is not jeoparded in this manner. I am perfectly enraptured with thofe females, who exhibit the moft refined fenfibility and fkill in their fweet *domeftic round*, and who can fhow a group of *well bred* boys and girls. But I muft aver, I am alfo happy, if this rare *female* has filled that vacuity, more or lefs in every one's bofom, by the execution of the worft propenfities: For, by fimilitude, we may anticipate, that one half of the world in future are to have lefs goads in their confciences, and the other, fafter accumulating a fund of more ufeful acquifition.

C H A P.   XI.

A hunting tour.—She kills her Indian companion.—Comes near perishing in the wildernefs.—Liberates an English Girl, condemned to be burnt.—Their return to Philadelphia.

AURORA had fcarcely purpled the Eaft after the coronation, before a large company, including our Adventrefs, fat out for hunting.[111] She quickly efpied a wild turkey on a high tree, which fhe killed. Then, with actions peculiar to Indians, they furrounded her to extol her being quick fighted and a good markfman. They encamped that night under an hickory; through which was a chafm cut fufficient for two to walk abreaft. In the morning they divided into parties. An old Indian, a boy and our Adventrefs compofed one. Elate with the beauty of the morning, the old Indian led off about the fun's rifing. Afcending a large hill, the dogs ftarted a buffalo, which fhe fhot before the Indian got fight. The boy was much elevated with her alertnefs: but the Indian difcovered much envy. He however craved the butchering; which fhe granted, referving the fkin to herfelf. Making a hearty meal of the buffalo, they travelled all day, without killing any more game, except three turkeys.

---

111 "Aurora now, fair daughter of the dawn, Sprinkled with rofy light the dewy lawn." — [*Pope's Iliad.*]

NIGHT having again drawn her fable curtains, they took
lodgings under a large fycamore: but fhe had an unufual
averfion to fleep; as fhe miftrufted the fame of the Indian. At length, fhe became fatisfied he had a fatal
defign on her life. Feigning herfelf afleep, fhe waited till
he had crawled within mufket reach of her; when, to her
furprife, fhe difcovered a hatchet in his hand. Without
hefitating, fhe leaped upon her feet, and fhot him through
the breaft, before he had time to beg quarters.

THE explofion of the gun awaked the boy; who, feeing
his countryman dead, rent his clothes, whooped and tore
the ground, like a mad bull; fearing he fhould fhare the
fame fate. She pacified him, by obferving, it was in defence of her own life fhe had killed him; and that, if he
would conduct well, and promife on his life to conceal it
from his countrymen, he fhould fare· well. He fwore
allegiance. And in the morning, they hoifted an old log
and left the barbarian under it.

BEHOLD now a young *female*, who might, doubtlefs,
have fhone confpicuous with others of her fex in their
domeftic fphere, reduced to the forlorn neceffity of roam-
ing in a defolate wildernefs; whofe only companion, except wild beafts, is an Indian boy; whofe only fuftenance
fuch as an uncultivated glebe affords; and whofe awful
profpect, that of perifhing at fo great a diftance from all
fuccors of humanity! To thofe, who maintain the doc-
trines of fatalifm, fhe is certainly a fubject of their greateft

fympathy. And even to thofe, who may be unwilling to adduce any other traits in her life, but wild, diffolute freaks of fancy, to be gratified at her option, fhe is rather an object of pity than contempt.

At night, almoft fpent with hunger and fatigue, they lay down to repofe. But they were immediately alarmed by voracious beafts of prey. Their only fafety, and that not fure, was to lodge themfelves in a high tree. The fires they had kindled gained their approach and en- creafed their howlings. The boy was fo frightened, he ran up the tree like a fquirrel. She followed, affifted, doubtlefs, by the fame thing. Though drowfy, they durft not fleep, left they fhould fall. With the ftrap of her fufee and handkerchief, fhe made herfelf faft to a limb and flept till day. It rained by fhowers the moft of the night. After fhe awoke, her fecond thought was of the boy. She fpoke to him; but he did not anfwer. Looking up at him, fhe was furprifed to fee him intently employed in difengaging his hair, which he had faithfully twined round the branches.

After defcending the tree and threfhing themfelves till they could walk, they fhaped their courfe for the Eaft; but God only knows which way they went. Towards night, they difcovered a huge precipice; but found it in- acceffible till they had travelled nearly four miles round it. Then afcending, they came to a rivulet of good water; and by it, took their abode during the night. In

the morning, they were at a ſtand, whether to defcend, or
attempt to reach its fummit. The poor boy wept bitter-
ly; which, ſhe fays, were the firſt tears ſhe ever faw an
Indian ſhed. They concluded on the latter; as their aſ-
cent might poffibly difcover fome profpect of efcape.
Paffing many ſharp ledges, they came to a fpot of *bear's
grafs*, on which ſhe reclined, thinking the period of her
life was haſtening with great rapidity, the following may
not be a rude ſketch of her reflections on this occaſion:

"WHERE am I! What have I been doing! Why did
I leave my native land, to grieve the breaſt of a parent,
who has, doubtlefs, ſhed floods of tears in my abfence,
and whofe cup of calamities feemed before but too full!
But here I am; where I think, human feet never before
trod. And though I have relatives, and perhaps, friends;
they can obtain no knowledge of me, not even to clofe
my eyes, when death ſhall have done its office, nor to
perform the laſt, fad demand of nature, which is to con-
fign the body to the duſt!—But ſtop! vain imagination!
There is a DEITY, from whom I cannot be hidden. It is
HE, who ſhapes my end.—My foul what thinkeſt thou of
immortality, of the world, into which thou art fo rapidly
haſtening! No words, no fagacity can difclofe my appre-
henſions. Every doubt wears the afpect of horror; and
would certainly overwhelm me, were it not for a few
gleams of hope which dart acrofs the tremendous gloom.
Happy, methinks I ſhould be, could I but utter even to

myfelf, the anguifh of my mind, thus fufpended between the extremes of infinite joy, or eternal mifery! It appears I have but juft now emerged from fleep! Oh, how have I employed my time! In what delirium has the thread of my life, thus far, been fpun! While the planets in their courfes, the fun and ftars in their fpheres have lent their refulgent beams—perhaps I have been lighted only to perdition!"

WHILE in this extacy, fhe availed herfelf of the opportunity to write to her female companion; and in it inclofed a letter to her mother, in hopes it might, by means of the boy, reach her.

DEAR MISS ——————,

PERHAPS you are the neareſt friend I have.—But a few hours muſt inevitably waft me to an infinite diſtance from all ſublunary enjoyments, and fix me in a ſtate of changeleſs retribution. Three years having made me the ſport of fortune—I am at length doomed to end my exiſtence in a dreary wilderneſs, unattended, except by an Indian boy. If you receive theſe lines, remember they come from one, who ſincerely loves you. But my amiable friend, forgive my imperfeĉtions, and forget you ever had affeĉtion for one ſo unworthy the name of

YOUR OWN SEX.

WHILE in this poſition, fhe heard the report of a gun. Starting about, fhe miffed the boy and her fufee. She could not recolleĉt whether he was with her when fhe fat

27

down, or not. But fummoning all her ftrength and refolution, fhe had nearly reached the fummit of the moun-
tain, when fhe met the boy. He told her he fired that
fhe might come to him; but as fhe did not, he concluded
fhe would do to eat, and was going to fill his belly with
good *omſknock.*[112] He feemed glad he had found fomething to relieve them. Giving her a fcrohon and four
grapes, he bid her follow him. Coming to an immenfe
rock, he crept through a fiffure; and, with much ado, fhe
after him. Here they found wild fcrohons, hops, gourds,
ground-nuts and beans. Though moftly rotten, they ate
fome of them, and were revived. Then, at a great diftance, opened to their view, a large river or lake, and
vaftly high mountains. Whilft they were contriving how
to get to the river, they heard the firing of fmall arms,
which they anfwered and had returns.

DESCENDING the precipice, they came to large rocks of
ifinglafs, and brooks of choice water. At its bafe, they
came up with a large company of Indians, who had been
to Detroit, to draw blankets and military ftores. But to
her furprife, who fhould make one of the company, but a
dejected young *female!* At once, fhe was anxious to
learn her hiftory; which fhe foon did at private inter-

---

[112] It is otherwife in the MS. memoir. " He faid he difcharged the
gun, that I might come to him; but,
as I did not, he concluded that I was
dead. Soon after, we found fome
ground-nuts," &c. Thefe adventures
in the wildernefs are related with greater fulnefs, and in far better language.

views.—She faid, fhe was taken from Cherry Valley—
had been fold many times, but expected to be fold no
more!—Tears prevented her proceeding.

In three days they arrived at the place from whence
fhe firft fat out on hunting. The old chief accufed her
for having run away after the Englifhmen : and it was the
boy, with the interpofition of Providence, faved her life.
She here quickly learned, that her unfortunate *fifter fuf-
ferer* was to be burnt, after they fhould have one court
and a *pawaw*, for letting fall a *papoos*, when travelling
with an intenfe load. At once fhe refolved to liberate
her, if any thing fhort of her own life would do it. Her
plan was thus concerted : She requefted to marry one of
their girls. They haughtily refufed ; but concluded, for fo
much, fhe might have the white girl. Begging her re-
prieve, till the return of her company, which happened
the next day, they all liberally contributed, and thus paid
her ranfom. The poor girl fainted at the news. But
hearing the conditions, fhe feemed fufpended in choice,
whether to fuffer an ignominious death, or be bought as
a booty to be ravifhed of her virgin purity:"[113]—For fhe
intimated that, among all the cruelties of thefe favages,
they had never intruded on her chaftity. Her intended
husband privately told her, the rites of the marriage bed
fhould be deferred, till the ceremony fhould be folemnized

---

[113] She regarded any marriage which
could take place under exifting circumftances as of no validity. The Indians had no marriage ceremonies.

in the land of civilization. At night a bear's fkin was fpread for their lodging; but, like a timorous bride, fleep was to her a ftranger. On their return to Philadelphia, they purchafed her a fuit of clothes; but fhe, unable to exprefs her gratitude, received them on her knees, and was, doubtlefs, glad to relinquifh her fham marriage, and to be fent to her uncle; who fhe faid, lived in James City."[114]

ARRIVED at Baltimore, fhe repaired to vifit her companion, who became much affected with her hiftory. She now thought it time to diveft herfelf of the mafk; at leaft to divert a paffion, which fhe feared had too much involved one of the choiceft of her fex. After thanking her for her generous efteem, and many evafive apologies— that fhe was but a ftripling foldier, and that had fhe inclinations, indigence would forbid her fettling in the world: The beautiful nymph replied, that, fooner than a conceffion fhould take place with the leaft reluctance, fhe would forfeit every enjoyment of connubial blifs: But, fhe added,

[114] "The next day, my company [Col. Tupper and the other gentlemen] fortunately reached the Indian camp, on their return home. The ftipulated ranfom being paid between us, we took the liberated girl to Baltimore in our party. There we procured for her a liberal fubfcription in apparel and money. Hence we fent her, with a heart overflowing with gratitude, to her parents, who, we were by accident informed, had removed, juft after the furrender of Cornwallis, to Williamsburg, in Virginia." If this unfortunate maid was taken, as is faid above, from Cherry Valley, fhe muft have been of New-England origin, and her parents would not at this time refide on the James River in Virginia. This story of the captive girl muft therefore be received with some diftruft.

if want of intereſt was the only obſtacle, ſhe was quickly
to come into the poſſeſſion of an ample fortune; and
finally intimated her deſire, that ſhe ſhould not leave
her.[115]

TOUCHED with ſuch a pathetic aſſemblage of love and
beauty, ſhe burſt into tears, and told her, ſhe would go to
the northward, ſettle her affairs, and in the enſuing ſpring,
if health ſhould permit, would return; when, if her perſon
could conduce to her happineſs, ſhe ſhould be richly en-

[115] "No ſooner had I returned to Baltimore than an irreſiſtible attraction drew me again into the preſence of the amiable Miſs P——. I went with the full determination to confeſs to her who and what I was. How ſhould I do this? I reſolved to prepare the way for ſuch a diſcloſure by endeavoring to weaken, without wounding, the paſſion in her breaſt. I told her I was but a ſtripling ſoldier; that I had few talents, and leſs wealth, to commend me to ſo much excellence, or even to repay her regard and the favors ſhe had already conferred on me. I told her, moreover, that I was about to rejoin the army, with a view to receive my diſcharge, and then to return to my relatives in Maſſachuſetts, and to that obſcurity from which I had emerged; but I found I had no power to diminiſh her regard for me.

"While taking her hand, as if to bid her a laſt adieu, I obſerved in her an indeſcribable delicacy ſtruggling for expreſſion, and mantling her fine features. Never can I forget the tender yet magnanimous look of diſappointment ſhe caſt on me, yet without the leaſt tincture of reſentment, when, ſtill holding her hand in mine, ſhe replied, that, ſooner than wring a reluctant conſent from me, ſhe would forego every claim to connubial happineſs. But the artleſs girl continued, if want of wealth on my part were the chief obſtacle, I might be relieved from all anxiety on that account, as ſhe was heireſs to an ample fortune; it being a legacy which ſhe was to poſſeſs on her marriage with a man whoſe worth ſhould be found in his perſon rather than in his outward eſtate. I longed to undeceive her. But the ſecret I had ſo long carefully guarded, I could not yet ſurrender. On parting, ſhe preſented me with ſix fine linen ſhirts, made with her own hands, an elegant watch, twenty-five Spaniſh dollars, and five guineas." — [MS. Memoir.]

titled to it.*¹¹⁶   Thus parted two lovers, more *fingular*, if not more *conftant*, than perhaps, ever diftinguifhed Columbia's foil.

THIS event, as it is unnatural, may be difputed. It is alfo rare, that the fame paffion fhould ever have brought a woman to bed with feven children at a birth: And I think *eight* would rather be miraculous than natural. But

* SHE has fince declared, fhe meant to have executed this refolution, had not fome traits of her life been publifhed in the intervening time; and that this *lady* fhould have been the firft to difclofe her fex. Before they parted, fhe made her a prefent of fix holland fhirts, twenty five guineas and an elegant filver watch. This fhe will not blufh to own, if alive; as it was out of the pureft regard for her own fex.

¹¹⁶ "It is no matter how I felt, or what I thought, faid, or did, on this occafion. I could not, if I would, defcribe either. I bade her adieu, and ftaggered to my lodging and to my bed. But, during the greater part of the night, my invocations to 'tired Nature's fweet reftorer' were as ufelefs as though 'balmy fleep' were never intended to refrefh the exhaufted body, or retrieve a bewildered intellect. At length the refolution with which I ftarted when I went to vifit my fair friend the day before — to difclofe to her the fecret of my fex — returned. I knew that this would be right: it was my indifpenfable duty. On refuming this intention, I fell into a fweet and tranquil flumber." And then fhe goes on to relate, with great delicacy of manner, and at much length, the interview that occurred at the lady's houfe that morning, in which the difclofure was fully made, and placed beyond all doubt by an actual infpection. The lady, as may well be fuppofed, was greatly aftonifhed: reafon, for a time, was wellnigh driven from the throne; but the final parting was fatisfactory on both fides.

"O Woman! thou bright ftar of love, whofe empire is beauty, virtue, refinement, the world were dark and chaotic without thee. Mifanthropy and groffnefs would characterize man if left alone; but in thy prefence his heart rifes to a pure and holy flame. Thy fmile is more powerful than the conqueror's fword. Thy fway is mightier than the monarch's fceptre. Thou bindeft man as with the fweet influences of a perennial fpring." —[*Ibid.*]

it is faid, that though perhaps the colouring is a little ex-
aggerated, that this is a fact that will admit of incontefti-
ble evidence. Nor need females think themfelves piqued
to acknowledge it; as no one denies, fhe was not an
agreeable object when mafqueraded; which, by the by, I
am forry to fay, is too often miftaken by that fex.

THUS, we have a remarkable inftance of the origin of
that fpecies of love, which renders the enjoyment of life
fatisfactory, and confummates the blifs of immortality.
The paffion entertained by the fexes towards each other
is, doubtlefs, from this fource; and will always be laudable, when managed with prudence. But I appeal to the
lady's own bofom, if, after difcovering her *fifter*, her
paffion had not fubfided into a calm, and have drooped,
like the rofe, or lilly, on its diflocated ftalk.—About the
third of November, they arrived at Philadelphia.[117]

[117] As Deborah Sampfon received
her difcharge from the army — fee in
the Introduction her petition to the
Legiflature of Maffachufetts — at Weft
Point, Oct. 25, 1783, here is an evident anachronifm in the text.

C H A P. XII.

DOCTOR BANA *gives her a letter to* Gen. PATTERSON, *then at West Point.—On her journey there, she is cast away on Staten's Island.—The letter discloses her* SEX *to the General.—Their* INTERVIEW.—*She obtains an honorable* DISCHARGE *and* RECOMMENDATIONS.—*Goes to her relations in Massachusetts.—Intrigues with her sex—censured.—Reassumes the* FEMALE ATTIRE *and* ECONOMY.

ELATED with her transition from a savage wilderness, to a land smiling with agriculture and civilization, her mind was once more illuminated with agreeable prospects. But a review of her situation cast an unfriendly group of objects in her way. A remembrance of the Doctor's queries and injunctions,[118] was but recognizing

---

[118] It does not appear what is meant by this. Dr. Binney had always treated her with the greatest delicacy and tenderness.

"On my return to the hospitable mansion of Dr. Binney, in Philadelphia, I told him I had called on him, not to tax his benevolence, which I had already largely experienced, but only to express my gratitude, and to bid him adieu, while hastening to rejoin the army preparatory to my discharge and my return home. Every lineament of his countenance beamed with tenderness and affection as he said, 'I shall insist on your staying with me at least twenty-four hours, as necessary to your rest and refreshment, and as much more time for the expression of the sympathy I feel for you.' Had I met at his house my father and mother, and all my relatives, I could not have felt more at home. The silence that was observed in reference to my sex created doubts in my mind whether the doctor was altogether satisfied with the discovery he had made ; and I trembled left I should be obliged to undergo another personal examination.

"When about to depart, the doctor, surrounded by his family, be-the neceffity of a garland of fig leaves to fcreen a pearl, that could glitter only without difguife.

On the day of her departure from Philadelphia, he entrufted her with the care of a letter to Gen. PATTERSON, then at Weft Point. Then taking an affectionate farewell of his family, fhe fat out for the place. She went in the ftage to Elizabeth Town, 15 miles from New York. The ftage boats being gone over, fhe, with about twelve others went on board the only one remaining. The fkipper was reluctant to accompany them; as it was late, rainy and a ftrong wind a head.—They quickly found the ftorm increafed; and they had not gone half their voyage, before they had the terrible profpect of the foundering of a boat with nineteen paffengers from South Amboy, bound to New York. Every one was loft. They heard their piteous cries, as the furges were clofing over their heads;

---

ftowed on me his parting counfels in a manner fo tender, that I muft have been from that moment a convert to virtue, had I previoufly been otherwife. In conclufion, he faid, ' Take a fhort prefcription as a token of my regard : Be careful of your health, and continue to be as difcreet in every thing as you have been true to the caufe of freedom ; then your country will have a wreath of undying fame for your brow. When you fhall have received your difcharge from the army, fend me a written fketch of your life.' This I partly promifed;

but, to my fhame, I confefs that I never fulfilled the promife.

" The doctor now put into my hand a large fealed letter, addreffed to Gen. Patterfon, faying, 'Fail not to deliver this : it contains a bequeft for you and for him.' He then, with his whole family, accompanied me to the ftage-office, where he had already engaged my paffage, and paid the expenfe of it from Philadelphia to Weft Point.

"About the 12th of October, I arrived at Elizabethtown, in New Jerfey." — [MS. Memoir.]

28

but could afford no relief. Nor was their own profpect much better. It was afked, whether it was poffible to fwim to Staten Ifland? It was unanimoufly negatived: but a few minutes put them to the defperate experiment. Being nearly in the centre of the channel, the current rapid, and the ftorm boifterous, the boat filled with water and funk under them. Though nothing but death now ftared them in the face; yet thofe exertions, which had before fnatched her from his jaws, we may fuppofe, were not here unemployed. She had on a large coat, which ferved to buoy her above the water; though fhe was often ingulphed in the furges. She was wafhed back twice, after reaching the foft fands. But, fortunately, clafping her arms on a bed of rufhes, fhe held till many waves had fpent their fury over her. Thus recruiting ftrength, and taking the advantage of the waves, fhe gained hard bottom and the fhore.

On the fhore, fhe found others in the fame wretched fituation, unable to ftand. She lay on her face all night. In the morning, the ftorm having abated, fhe heard Dr. VICKENS fay, " Bleffed be GOD, it is day; though I believe I am the only furvivor among you all!" Happily, they were all alive, except two; who unfortunately found a tomb in the watery element. They were foon taken up by a boat cruifing for that purpofe, and carried back to Elizabeth Town. Moft of her equipments, a trunk, including her journal, money, &c. was loft. Her watch and a morocco pocket-book, containing the letter, were faved."[119]

THE third day, fhe had a good paffage to New York;[120] from thence to Weft Point. Arrived at the General's quarters, fhe feemed like one fent from the dead; as they had concluded the Potter's Field had long been her home. Her next bufinefs was, to deliver the letter. Cruel tafk! Dreading the contents, fhe delayed it fome days.[121] At length, fhe refolved, her fidelity fhould triumph over every perturbation of mind in the delivery of the letter, and to apologize for her non-truft. Accordingly, finding him alone, fhe gave him the quivering treafure, made obeifance, turned upon heal and withdrew in hafte.[122]

PRECISELY an hour after, unattended, he fent for her to

[119] Mr. Wyatt, a contributor to "Graham's Magazine," fays the watch is ftill in the poffeffion of her defcendants. We have the authority of Rev. Mr. Pratt for faying that her canteen, preferved on this occafion, is now in the keeping of a relative of hers at Lakeville, Mafs.

[120] How could a Continental foldier, in full uniform, be allowed to vifit New York, when it was ftill occupied by the Britifh forces? The Britifh garrifon was not withdrawn till Nov. 25, 1783. She certainly did not fet foot in New-York City at this time.

[121] The MS. memoir fays fhe delivered it to him the next morning after her arrival, immediately after breakfaft.

[122] The MS. memoir contains the letter in full. The letter relates the circumftances of the difcovery, made by Dr. Binney in the hofpital at Philadelphia, of the fex of the young foldier; fpeaks very highly and tenderly of the individual; and dwells, at confiderable length, on the remarkable features of the cafe. It is expreffed with much delicacy and propriety, and is juft fuch a letter as might have been written by Dr. Binney, a man of benevolent feelings, to Gen. Patterfon; and it is certainly a creditable production.

his apartment. She fays—"*A re-entrance was harder than facing a cannonade.*" Being defired to feat herfelf, the General, calling her by name, thus gracefully ad-dreffed her :—" Since you have continued near three years in my fervice, always vigilant, vivacious, faithful, and, in many refpects, diftinguifhed yourfelf from your fellows.— I would only afk—Does that *martial attire*, which now glitters on your body, conceal a *female's form !*" The clofe of the fentence drew tears in his eyes, and fhe fainted. He ufed his efforts to recover her; which he effected. But an afpect of wildnefs was blended in her countenance. She proftrated herfelf at his feet, and begged her life! He fhook his head; but fhe remembers not his reply. Bidding her rife, he gave her the letter, which he continued to hold in his hand. Reafon having re-fumed its empire, fhe read it with emotions. It was in-terefting, pathetic and colored with the pencil of humanity. He again exclaimed—"*Can it be fo !*" Her heart could no longer harbor deception. Banifhing all fubterfuge, with as much refolution, as poffible, fhe confeffed herfelf —*a female.*[123]

---

[123] " Attempting to rife from my feat, in order to reply, I loft the con-trol both of body and mind, and had nearly fainted away. Recovering, I made out to fay, 'What will be my fate, fir, if I anfwer in the affirma-tive?'—'You have nothing to fear,' he replied. 'If you confirm the ftate-ments of this letter,'—ftill holding the letter of Dr. Binney in his hand, — 'you are not only fafe here, but en-titled to our warmeft refpect.'

"'Sir,' I faid, 'I am wholly in your power. God forbid that I fhould at-tempt to conceal what I fuppofe is now fully known. I AM A FEMALE !

ttt

He then enquired concerning her relations; but efpecially of her primeval inducements to occupy the *field* of *war!* She proceeded to give a fuccinct and true account; and concluded by afking, if her *life* would be fpared!— He told her, fhe might not only think herfelf fafe, while under his protection; but that her unrivalled achievements deferved ample compenfation—that he would

But, oh, fir, now that I am weak and helplefs, withdraw not your protection!'

"'Can it be fo?' he exclaimed, after a fhort paufe, as if ftill in doubt.

"'Sir,' faid I, 'I have no defire to deceive you. Procure for me, if you can, a female drefs,'—an elegant one, I knew, was in the houfe,—'and allow me a retired place and a half hour to prepare myfelf.'

"This was immediately complied with. ... I was completely equipped, from head to foot, in a lady's attire, within the appointed time. ... Affuming, for the time, fome of the modeft, bewitching feminine graces, I returned, and made my *entrée* to Gen. Patterfon.

"The effect was magical. Never before did I witnefs ecftafy fo complete in man. 'Remain as you are, a fhort time at leaft,' faid the general. 'This is truly theatrical. I will fummon Col. Jackfon, and fee if he knows you.'

"Col. Jackfon was called in, and I was introduced to him as Mifs Deborah Sampfon. 'She is from your own State, the cradle of Liberty; and

a fit perfon fhe is to rock it till the infant is full grown. Do you not recognize her?'

"'While I fhould be proud of an acquaintance with fuch a character, I have no recollection of this lady,' was the reply.

"The converfation then paffed to other topics. At length Gen. Patterfon afked if any information refpecting Robert Shurtliffe had been received. 'I fear,' faid Col. Jackfon, 'that gallant young foldier has fallen a facrifice to his devotion to liberty.'

"'But there are miracles now,— wonders, at leaft,'— faid the general. 'Our Revolution is full of them. But this young lady exceeds them all. Examine her clofely, and fee if you do not recognize Robert Shurtliffe!'

"Imagination may finifh the painting of this fcene. I will add, however, that in this coftume I was efcorted by thefe gentlemen over the tented ground, and amidft officers and foldiers, with whom, an hour before, I was as familiar as are the inmates of a family with one another; but none of them knew me."—[*MS. Memoir.*]

THE FEMALE

quickly obtain her difcharge, and fhe fhould be fafely
conducted to her friends.—But having had the tuition of
her as a *foldier*, he faid, he muft take liberty to give her
that advice, which he hoped would ornament the functions
of her life, when the mafculine garb fhould be laid afide
and fhe taken to the embraces of that fex fhe was then
perfonating.

IMMEDIATELY fhe had an apartment affigned to her own
ufe. And when the General mentioned the event to her
Colonel and other officers, they thought he played at ca-
jolery. Nor could they be reconciled to the fact, till it
was corroborated by her own words. She requefted, as a
pledge of her virtue, that ftrict enquiry fhould be made of
thofe, with whom fhe had been mefs-mate. This was
accordingly done.[124] And the effect was—a panic of furprife with every foldier. Groups of them now crowded
to behold a phenomenon, which before appeared a natural
object. But as accefs was inadmiffible, many turned in-

[124] "Having furnifhed the gentlemen with an account of my home,
my relatives, and the motives which
led me to affume the character of a
foldier, I requefted them to make the
ftricteft inquiry into my manner of
life fince I had been in the army.
This was accordingly done. The refult was a general furprife, and, on
the part of many, a total disbelief.
An apartment was now affigned for
my ufe, and garments for either fex
provided. But, in general, I preferred
my regimentals, becaufe that in them
I fhould be more fafe from infult and
annoyance. Many of the foldiers,
and many of my own fex, were defir-
ous to fatisfy themfelves as to the
truth of what they had heard ; but, of
courfe, it was impoffible to gratify
their curiofity."

Thus ends Mr. Mann's narrative of
the adventures of Deborah Sampfon,
in which, for the fake of greater force
and fpirit, the heroine herfelf is made
the fpeaker.

REVIEW. 223

fidels, and few had faith.—Her difcharge is from Gen.
KNOX; her recommendations from the Gens. PATTERSON
and SHEPARD.* [125]

BEING informed, her effects and diplomas were in readinefs, fhe payed her politeft refpects to the gentlemen,
who accompanied her to the place ; and wifhing an eter-

* SINCE, by misfortune, loft.

[125] The Definitive Treaty of Peace between Great Britain, France, Spain, and the United States, was figned at Paris, Sept. 3, 1783. A ftate of peace, however, had actually exifted in America from the 19th of April, in the fame year, when a formal proclamation of the ceffation of hoftilities was made in the army, by order of the Commander-in-Chief. Information of the Definitive Treaty having been received, the third day of November was affigned by Congrefs for disbanding the army of the United States. The city of New York was evacuated by the Britifh army, November 25.

On the 25th of October, at Weft Point, our heroine received an honorable difcharge from the fervice from the hand of Gen. Knox. Many teftimonials of faithful performance of duty, and of exemplary conduct in the army, were given to her, among others, from Generals Patterfon and Shepard, and Col. Jackfon, under whofe orders it had been her good fortune to ferve. Thefe papers may not have been preferved.

Mrs. Ellet and fome others have ftated that the commander of the company in which our heroine ferved, on being informed by Dr. Binney that Robert Shurtliffe was a female, fent the fair foldier with a letter to Gen. Wafhington, conveying information of the fact; that Wafhington then gave her a difcharge from the army, with a note containing fome words of advice, and a fum of money fufficient to bear her expenfes home. A lengthy detail of circumftances is given in connection with this ftatement. This account feems to be without any real foundation. In her petition to the Legiflature of Maffachufetts, Deborah fays fhe received her difcharge from Gen. Knox, as already ftated. Nor is it true, as ftated by Mrs. Ellet, that, during the adminiftration of Wafhington, Deborah received an invitation to vifit the feat of Government, and that, during her ftay, Congrefs paffed an act granting her a penfion, in addition to certain lands which fhe was to receive as a foldier. No penfion was granted her till Jan. 1, 1803, and then not by Act of Congrefs. See Introduction, pp. xvi. xviii. xix. xxiv.

nal FAREWELL to COLUMBIA'S CAUSE, turned her back on
the *Aceldama*, once more to re-echo the carols of peace
on her native plains.   In the evening, fhe embarked on
board a floop from Albany to New York: From thence,
in Capt. ALLEN's packet, fhe arrived at Providence.

THUS fhe made her exit from the tragic ftage.   But
how requifite was a parent's houfe—an afylum, from the
ebullitions of calumny, where to clofe the laft affecting
fcene of her complicated, woe-fraught revolution of her
fex!   With what eager fteps, would fhe have bent her
next courfe over the then congealed glebe—to give a
parent the agreeable furprife of beholding her long loft
child—to implore her forgivenefs of fo wide a breach of
duty, and to affume a courfe of life, which only could be
an ornament to her fex and extenuation of her crime!
The ties of confanguinity, of filial affection and of folemn
obligation, demanded this.   But being deprived of thefe
bleffings, fhe took a few ftrides to fome fequeftered hamlet
in Maffachufetts; where fhe found fome relations: and,
affuming the name of her youngeft brother, fhe paffed the
winter as a man of the world, and was not awkward in
the common bufinefs of a farmer.[126]   But, if I remember,

[126] About the 1ft of November,
1783, fhe arrived among her relatives
in Maffachufetts, after an abfence of a
year and fix months.   During this
period, her information refpecting
affairs at home had been very limited
and vague.   Not knowing in what
light fhe might be regarded by thofe
who had formerly known her, fhe did
not immediately difcover herfelf.   She
ftill wore her military coftume, and did
not go to Middleborough, where fhe

fhe has intimated—that nothing in the villa could have better occupied a greater vacuity, than the diadem—*edu-cation:* which, I fondly hope, fome guardian cherub has fince deigned to beftow.

BUT her correfpondence with her fifter fex!—Surely it muft have been that of fentiment, tafte, purity; as animal love, on her part, was out of the queftion. But I beg ex-cufe, if I happen not to fpecify every particular of this agreeable round of acquaintance. It may fuffice, merely, to fay, her uncle being a compaffionate man, often repre-hended her for her freedom with the girls of his villa; and them he plumply called fools, (a much hafher name than I can give them) for their violent prefumption with the young *Continental.* Sighing, he would fay—their unre-ferved imprudence would foon deteðt itfelf—a multitude of illegitimates!—Columbia would have bewailed the egregious event! Worfe, indeed, it might have been, had any one entered againft her—not a bill of *ejeðtment,*

---

had paffed moft of her life. She went to refide with her uncle in Stoughton, under the affumed name of Ephraim Sampfon, that of the younger of her two brothers, if we may truft the ftate-ment made in the text. But did not her uncle and his family *know* that the young foldier who fpent the winter with them was *not* Ephraim Sampfon? The fuppofition is incredible.

The uncle with whom our heroine fpent the winter was undoubtedly Mr.

Waters, the husband of her mother's fifter, Alice Bradford. Sharon was formerly a part of Stoughton. It was during this winter that fhe became acquainted with her future husband. It is faid he was determined to find out whether the new-comer was a man or not, and to fome attempt of this na-ture the next paragraph refers.

· She paffed the winter doing farm-work, and flirting with the girls of the neighborhood.

but a fyftem of *compulfion*, for having won of her a large
bet in a tranfport of blifs, after MORPHEUS had too fuddenly whirled away two thirds of the night—ftill refufing to
fatisfy the demand!—Blufh—blufh—rather lament, ye
delicate, when fo defperate an extremity is taken to hurl
any of your fifters into hymeneal blifs—wretchednefs.

To be plain, I am an enemy to intrigues of all kinds.
Our female adept had money; and at the worft could
have purchafed friends of our fex: But, methinks, thofe
who can claim the leaft pretenfion to feminine delicacy,
muft be won only, by the gentleman, who can affociate
the idea of *companion* without imbibing the principles of
libertinifm. Why did fhe not, after the crackling faggot
had rivalled the chirping of the cricket in the hearth,
caution thofe, who panted—not like the hunted hart, to
tafte the cooling rivulet—that the midnight watch might
not have regiftered the plighted vows of love! Having
feen the world, and, of courfe, become acquainted with
the female heart, and the too fatal avenues to it; why did
fhe not—after convincing them that fhe lacked not the
courage of a village HAMPDEN, preach to them the neceffity of the prudence and inftructions of fage URANIA?
That they might have difcovered their weakeft place, and
have fortified the citadel; left a different attack fhould
make a fatal inroad upon their reputation, and transfix a
deadly goad through their breafts! VENUS knows not
but fhe did: But they were all *females*.

SPRING having once more wafted its fragrance from the South, our Heroine leaped from the mafculine, to the feminine fphere.[127] Throwing off her martial attire, fhe

127 On the approach of fpring, Deborah refumed feminine apparel and employments.

On the 7th day of April, 1784, fhe became the wife of Benjamin Gannett, a refpectable and induftrious young farmer of Sharon.* They were married at his father's houfe in that town.

Her fubfequent hiftory muft of courfe have borne a fimilarity to thofe of moft of our countrywomen who

* The pedigree of Benjamin Gannett is as follows :—

I. MATTHEW GANNETT,[1] born in England, 1618, came early to this country, and fettled firft in Hingham. In January, 1651-2, he purchafed land in Scituate, an adjoining town, and removed to that place. He died in 1694, as we learn from his grave-ftone. He had feveral children, of whom Matthew[2] remained in Scituate, and Rehoboth removed to Morriftown, N.J., where he died without iffue.

II. Jofeph Gannett,[2] fon of Matthew;[1] continued to refide in Scituate, and died not long before his father. He married a widow Sharp.

III. Jofeph Gannett,[3] fon of the preceding, removed to Eaft Bridgewater about the year 1722. His brother Matthew[3] removed thither about the fame time. Jofeph[3] married Hannah Hayward, daughter of Dea. Jonathan Hayward, of Braintree. Their fon,

IV. Benjamin Gannett,[4] born 1728, married, 1750, Mary Copeland, daughter of Jonathan Copeland, of Bridgewater, and removed to Stoughton, the part afterwards Sharon.

V. Benjamin Gannett,[5] born 1753, was the hufband of Deborah Sampfon, the heroine of our ftory.

Benjamin Gannett,[4] born 1728, had a brother Jofeph,[4] born 1722, who was the father of Caleb Gannett,[5] who was a clergyman in Nova Scotia, afterwards tutor in Harvard College, and for many years fteward of that inftitution. Caleb

cheer and adorn the homes of New England. She lived to rear a family of reputable children. She had an only fon, Capt. Earl B. Gannett, and two daughters. There are grandfons, we believe, now living in Sharon.

She died at her home in Sharon, April 29, 1827, in the fixty-feventh year of her age. She fuftained to the end the character of a faithful and exemplary wife and mother, a kind neighbor and friend.

In ftature, Deborah Sampfon was five feet, feven inches. She was large and full around the waift. Her features were regular, but not beautiful. Her eyes were hazel, inclining to blue ; and were lively and penetrating. Her complexion was fair and clear ; her afpect was amiable and ferene, though fomewhat mafculine. Her limbs were well proportioned ; her movements were quick and vigorous ; and her pofition erect, as became a foldier. Her voice was agreeable ; her fpeech, deliberate and firm. The portrait at the beginning is from the old copper-plate ufed at

Gannett[5] married a daughter of Rev. Ezra Stiles, D.D., Prefident of Yale College. They were the parents of Rev. Ezra Stiles Gannett, D.D., of Bofton.

Jofeph Gannett,[3] who fettled in Eaft Bridgewater about 1722, had by a fecond wife, Hannah Brett, a fon Matthew,[4] born 1755, the father of Rev. Allen Gannett, late of Lynnfield, now of Bofton. —[Mitchell's Bridgewater.]

once more hid her form with the *diſhabille* of FLORA, re-

the iſſue of "The Female Review," ſeventy years ago. It was executed when the art of engraving was in its infancy in this country, and muſt not be ſuppoſed to do full juſtice to the ſubjeƈt.

In military attire, ladies conſidered her handſome. Several inſtances are recorded where they were deeply ſmitten by her good looks. Her delicate appearance, and particularly her having no beard, were often noticed. She was called the "ſmock-faced boy," and the like; but her ſex was never ſuſpeƈted.

The prominent traits of her character were courage, love of adventure, and perſeverance under difficulties. She was bold, enterpriſing, and fearleſs; ſhe had great ſelf-control, and a firm, reſolute will. As a ſoldier, ſhe exhibited great alertneſs, aƈtivity, fortitude, and valor. Her military life abounded with hardy and hazardous adventures, in all of which ſhe bore herſelf with the firmneſs, reſolution, and patient endurance which are often thought to belong excluſively to the ſtronger ſex. Where any dared to go, ſhe went; and not to follow merely, but to lead. She often volunteered on expeditions attended with ſpecial expoſure and hardſhip. It is ſaid that on ſcouting-parties ſhe would always ride forward a little nearer the enemy than any of her comrades ventured. On one occaſion, meeting the enemy ſuddenly in overwhelming force, it was neceſ-

ſary to abandon their horſes, and run acroſs a ſwamp for dear life. She then ſhowed herſelf to be as fleet as a gazelle, bounding through the ſwamp many rods ahead of her companions. It was thought that no man in the army could outrun her.

As we have already ſeen, ſhe went through two campaigns without the diſcovery of her ſex, and conſequently without the loſs of her virtue. This faƈt, which is perfeƈtly well eſtabliſhed, demonſtrates not only ſtriƈt moral principle, but the high qualities of firmneſs, reſolution, ſelf-control, and perſeverance. Such a caſe, perhaps, was never known before. It certainly ſtood alone in the Revolutionary war. She was never found in liquor,—a vice too common in all armies. It is well known that the Continental army, though compoſed in an unuſual degree of men of principle and virtue, contained many men of unſound charaƈter. No ſtain appears to have attached to the charaƈter of our heroine.

To gratify the curioſity of the multitude, ſhe once viſited Boſton; and in the theatre, clad in military attire, ſhe went through, at the word of a military officer, the manual exerciſe. Thoſe who witneſſed the performance ſaid that "ſhe would almoſt make the gun talk;" every time it came to the ground from her hand, the found was ſo ſignificant.

Her deportment was eminently ſoldier-like, and none were more expert in the drill than herſelf. Mr. Amos

commenced her former occupation ; and I know not, that

Sampſon, who is now living in Charleſtown at the age of nearly ſeventy-nine, told me that he witneſſed the ſcene, and that it occurred when he was an apprentice to the printing-buſineſs, and therefore between 1801 and 1808. He ſaid, moreover, that it was in the theatre, and not on the Common, as has been elſewhere repreſented.

It appears that the remarkable ſtory of Deborah Sampſon began to be bruited abroad very ſoon after her diſcharge from the army, before her marriage with Mr. Gannett, and even before her relinquiſhment of military coſtume. The Appendix will contain a notice of this ſingular caſe, as it was publiſhed in a New-York paper, and afterwards copied into ſome papers in Maſſachuſetts. The principal faƈts in her career were thus publiſhed to the world in a little more than two months after her diſcharge from the army. Theſe faƈts could only have been derived from the officers to whom the diſcloſure was originally made ; perhaps from Gen. Patterſon himſelf. The faƈts were ſo remarkable, that there was a ſtrong inducement to give them to the public. Their publication in Maſſachuſetts muſt have awakened inquiry reſpeƈting the heroine, and perhaps led the way to her diſcloſing the whole ſtory to the author of " The Female Review."

Immediately following the extraƈt to which we have juſt referred, is the

certificate of Col. Henry Jackſon, which further authenticates the caſe. A certified copy of it is on file in the office of the Secretary of the Commonwealth.

The following notice of Deborah Sampſon appeared in print ſeveral years before her death. It is taken from " The Dedham Regiſter " of December, 1820, and was copied into many of the papers of the day :—

" We were much gratified to learn, that, during the ſitting of the court in this town the paſt week, Mrs. Gannett, of Sharon, in this county, preſented for renewal her claims for ſervices rendered her country as a ſoldier in the Revolutionary army. The following brief ſketch, it is preſumed, will not be unintereſting : This extraordinary woman is now in the ſixty-ſecond year of her age : ſhe poſſeſſes a clear underſtanding, and a general knowledge of paſſing events ; is fluent in ſpeech, and delivers her ſentiments in correƈt language, with deliberate and meaſured accent ; is eaſy in her deportment, affable in her manners, robuſt and maſculine in her appearance. She was about eighteen years of age when our Revolutionary ſtruggle commenced. The patriotic ſentiments which inſpired the heroes of thoſe days, and urged them to battle, found their way to a female boſom. The news of the carnage which had taken place on the plains of Lexington had reached her dwelling ; the ſound of the cannon at the battle of

fhe found difficulty in its performance. Whether this

Bunker Hill had vibrated on her ears ; yet, inftead of diminifhing her ardor, it only ferved to increafe her enthufiafm in the facred caufe of liberty, in which fhe beheld her country engaged. She privately quitted her peaceful home and the habiliments of her fex, and appeared at the headquarters of the American army as a young man, anxious to join his efforts to thofe of his countrymen in their endeavors to oppofe the inroads and encroachments of the common enemy. She was received and enrolled in the army by the name of Robert Shurtliffe. For the fpace of three years, fhe performed the duties, and endured the hardfhips and fatigues of a foldier ; during which time, fhe gained the confidence of her officers by her expertnefs and precifion in the manual exercife, and by her exemplary conduct. She was a volunteer in feveral hazardous enterprifes, and was twice wounded by mufket-balls. So well did fhe contrive to conceal her fex, that her companions in arms had' not the leaft fufpicion that the "blooming foldier" fighting by their fide was a female ; till at length a fevere wound, which fhe received in battle, and which had well-nigh clofed her earthly career, occafioned the difcovery. On her recovery, fhe quitted the army, and became intimate in the families of Gen. Wafhington and other diftinguifhed officers of the Revolution. A few years afterwards, fhe was

married to her prefent husband, and is now the mother of feveral children. Of thefe facts there can be no doubt. There are many living witneffes in this county, who recognized her on her appearance at court, and were ready to atteft to her fervices. We often hear of fuch heroines in other countries ; but this is an inftance in our own country, and within the circle of our acquaintance."

It will be obferved that the foregoing account confirms and authenticates the general ftatements made in this volume. There are fome errors of detail, which might eafily creep into an account like this, where perfect accuracy was not demanded. The ftatement that Mrs. Gannett ferved *three years* as a foldier, originated, no doubt, from the fact that fhe *enlifted* for three years, though her actual length of fervice was much lefs.

Under date of June 25, 1859, Rev. Stillman Pratt, of Middleborough, who had become interefted in her hiftory, writes : —

"In my recent vifit to Sharon, I fpent fome time at the refidence and by the grave of Mrs. Deborah Gannett, formerly Deborah Sampfon. The houfe was built by Mrs. Gannett, her husband, and his only fon, about fifty years ago, with brick ends, the refidue of wood. It is two ftories high. The weftern portion is literally embowered with willow-trees, one of which was fet out by Deborah her-was done voluntarily, or compulfively, is to me an enig-

felf, and now meafures twelve feet in circumference, and almoft conftitutes a grove of itfelf. The eaftern portion is covered by a woodbine, which extends over the roof, and climbs to the top of the chimney. Rofe-bufhes and other flowering fhrubs are interfperfed with perennial plants. The barn ftands directly back of the houfe; in the rear of which rifes a fugar-loaf mound, of peculiar afpect, extending back towards a denfe foreft.

"The farm confifts of a hundred acres of land, with every poffible variety of foil. The mowing lands are irrigated by artificial ftreams of water, branching off in all directions, and difcharging themfelves into a fmall river below. In the hedges, and along the walls, are rafpberry and barberry bufhes; while fruit and fhade trees are promifcuoufly mingled through the fields.

"One mile fouth of this refidence is located the old cemetery. On the tenth row from the entrance are three plain flate-ftone flabs, commemorative of the laft refting-place of Mr. and Mrs. Gannett, and of Capt. Earl B. Gannett, their only fon."

A friend of the publifhers of this volume has lately vifited the fpot, and has enabled them to furnifh the reprefentation of thefe funeral monuments, which will be found on the following leaf.

After Mrs. Gannett's death, the following notice appeared in "Niles's Weekly Regifter," vol. xxxii., p. 217, Baltimore, May 26, 1827 : —

"A FEMALE VETERAN.—The Dedham Regifter ftates that Mrs. Deborah Gannett, wife of Mr. Benjamin Gannett, of Sharon, Mafs., died on the 19th [29th] ult. She enlifted as a volunteer in the American army of the Revolution, in the Maffachufetts corps, having the drefs and appearance of a foldier. She continued in the fervice until the end of the war, three years, fuftaining an unfullied character, and performing the duties of a foldier with more than ordinary alertnefs and courage, having been twice dangeroufly wounded; though fhe preferved her fex undifcovered. At the disbanding of the army, fhe received an honorable difcharge, and returned to her relatives in Maffachufetts, ftill in her regimentals. When her cafe was made known to the government of that State, her full wages were paid, and a confiderable bounty added. Congrefs allowed her a penfion, which fhe regularly received. Soon after fhe refumed the fphere of her own fex, fhe was married to Mr. Gannett, an induftrious, refpectable farmer. She has borne and reared him a reputable family of children; and to the clofe of life fhe has merited the character of an amiable wife, a tender mother, a kind and exemplary neighbor, and a friend of her country.

"Mr. H. Mann, of Dedham, publifhed a memoir of her life fome time

ma.   But fhe continues a phenomenon among the revolutions of her fex.

fince, of which the whole edition, 1500 copies, has been entirely fold. Another edition may be foon expected, enlarged and improved, which will probably meet a rapid fale."

This obituary notice was undoubtedly written by Mr. Mann himfelf; who, if not the editor, was, I believe, a principal contributor to the "Dedham Regifter" at that time. Some of the expreffions in this obituary notice, ufed in fumming up her character, are identical with fome which are employed for the fame purpofe in the MS. memoir, from which I have fo often quoted. And this very MS. memoir, now in my poffeffion, is, beyond queftion, the document referred to in the laft fentence quoted above from "The Regifter."

The publifhers of the prefent edition having determined to iffue an exact reprint of "The Female Review," it was a matter of neceffity to reproduce every fentence and every expreffion, however faulty in point of tafte, and objectionable in refpect of moral fentiment. There are many paffages, there are entire paragraphs, which the prefent editor would gladly have omitted. Many expreffions are awkward and ungainly, and do not truly reprefent the author's own meaning. For the infertion of fuch paffages, the editor muft not be held refponfible. To have attempted any thing in the way of counteraction would have been worfe than ufelefs.

The editor is of opinion that Deborah Sampfon was worthy of an abler biographer than fhe found in the original compiler, and that her adventures, which were certainly very remarkable, were worthy of being related in far better ftyle.   J. A. V.

BOSTON, July, 1866.

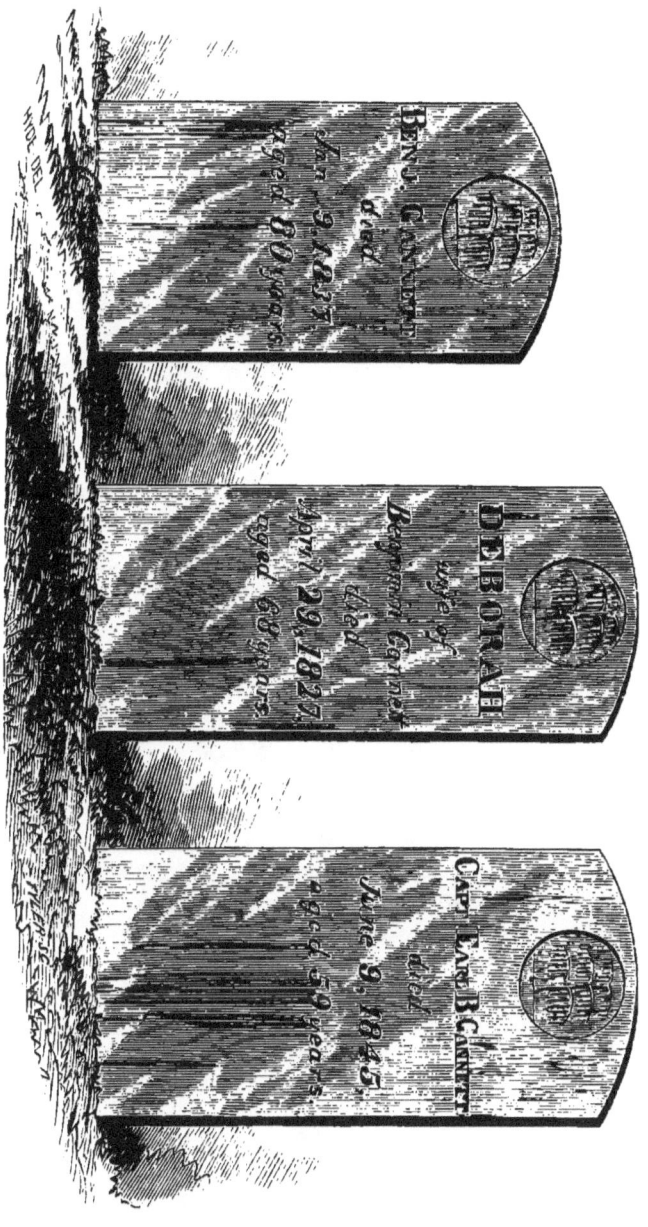

APPENDIX.

CONTAINING—CHARACTERISTIC TRAITS *and* REFLECTIONS,
with REMARKS *on* DOMESTIC EDUCATION *and* ECONOMY.

AFTER deliniating the life of a perſon, it ſeems natural to recapitulate, in a cloſer aſſemblage, the
leading features of his charaƈter.

·PERHAPS, a ſpirit of enterprize, perſeverance and com-
petition was never more diſtinguiſhable in a female, than
in Miſs SÁMPSON. And whilſt we are ſurpriſed that ſhe
left her own tranquil ſphere for the moſt perilous—the
field of *war*, we muſt acknowledge, it is, at leaſt, a cir-
cumſtantial link in the chain of our illuſtrious revolution.
She never would accept a promotion while in the army;
though it is ſaid, ſhe was urged to take a Lieutenant's
commiſſion.

I WILL here give an inſtance of her dread of rivalſhip.
It was ſoon after ſhe inliſted.—Having been reluƈtantly
drawn into a ring of wreſtling, ſhe was worſted; though
it is ſaid, ſhe flung a number. But the idea of a competi-
tor deprived her of ſleep the whole night.—Let this be a
memento to Columbia's daughters; that they may be-
ware of too violent ſcuffles with our ſex. We are athletic, haughty and unconquerable. Beſides, your diſlo-
cated limbs are a piteous ſight!—And it ſeems this was a
warning to her: For it was noted by the ſoldiers, that

fhe never wreftled, nor fuffered any one to twine his arms about her fhoulders; as was their cuftom when walking.

AND left her courage has not been fufficiently demon-ftrated, I will adduce one more inftance, that muft fur-pafs all doubt.—In 1782, fhe was fent from Weft Point, · on bufinefs, to a place called the *Clove*, back of the high hills of Santee. She rode Capt. PHELON's horfe. On her return, juft at the clofe of twilight, fhe was fur-prifed by two ruffians, who rufhed haftily from a thicket, feized her horfe's bridle, and demanded her money, or her life. She was armed with a brace of piftols and a hanger. Looking at the one, who held the horfe, fhe faid, " *J. B——, I think I know you; and this moment you become a dead man, if you perfift in your demand!* " Hearing a piftol cock at the fame time, his compeer fled; and he begged quarters and forgivenefs; which fhe granted, on condition of a folemn promife, ever to defift from fo defperate an action.

IT is, perhaps, fufficiently authenticated, that fhe pre-ferved her chaftity, by a rare affiduity to conceal her fex. Females can beft conceive inconveniences to which fhe was fubject. But as I know not, that fhe ever gratified any one with the wondrous eclairciffement, I can only fay, perhaps, what more have heard, than experienced— " *Want prompts the wit, and firft gave birth to arts.*" If it be true, and if—" A moment of concealment is a mo-ment of humiliation;" as an anonymous writer of her fex obferves, fhe has humility enough to bow to the fhrine of modefty, and to appear without difguife, from top to toe.

SINCE writing thefe fheets, I have been pained for a few, efpecially *females*, who feem *unwilling* to believe, that a *female* went through three campaigns, without the difcovery of her fex; and confequently, the lofs of virgin purity.*

WE hear but little of an open proftitute in the army, or elfe where—of COLLIN and DOLLY, the milk maid, in their evening fauntering to the meadow.   Then why fhould any be fo fcrupulous of her, becaufe fhe did not go in the profeffed charaƈter of a foldier's trull!   Though it is faid, fhe was an uncommonly modeft foldier; yet, like you, I am ready to aver, fhe has made a breach in female delicacy.   But bring forth her fallacious pretenfions to virtue; and I am bound, as a moralift, to record them—as vices, to be guarded againft.   I have only to defire this clafs of my readers to think as favorable as poffible of our fex; but, on all accounts, to cherifh the lovely fugitive—*virtue*, in their own.   For, too much fufpicion of another's, argues, too ftrongly, a want of the fame charming ornament in themfelves; unlefs they are old maids, or bachelors.

I SHALL here make a fmall digreffion.—As our Heroine was walking the ftreets in Philadelphia, in a beautiful, ferene evening, fhe was ravifhed by the fweet, penfive notes of a *piano-forté*.   Looking up at a third loft

---

* " SHE *had no beard*," is an objeƈtion, to which, I know not, that this clafs of readers can be reconciled.—A chaplain, fince known in Maffachufetts, was once at Gen. Patterfon's quarters.   In the prefence of his fmockfaced attendant, he took occafion to compliment the General—" I admire your fare ; but nothing more, than your very polite attendant ; who appears to poffefs the graceful aƈtivity and bloom of a girl."

fhe difcovered a young female, who feemed every way expreffive of the mufic fhe made. She often after lift-ened to the fame founds; and was as often furprifed, that a figh fhould be blended with fuch exquifite harmony and beauty.—Of this female, I will tranfmit to my readers the following pathetic hiftory.

FATIMA was the eldeft of three daughters; whofe par-ents had acquired an ample fortune, and refided in a part of the United States, where nature fheds her bleffings in profufe abundance. But, unhappily, their conduct to-wards them was diftinguifhed, like that of others, whofe fondnefs fo infinitely exceeds their prudence. They were not, however, deficient in many external accomplifhments. Early was FATIMA taught to fpeak prettily, rather than properly; to admire what is brilliant, inftead of what is folid; to ftudy drefs and pink alamode; to be active at her toilet, and much there; to dance charmingly at a ball, or farcical entertainment; to form hafty and mifcel-laneous connexions; to fhow a beautiful face, and figh for admiration;—in fhort, to be amufed, rather than inftruct-ed; but at laft—to difcover an ill accomplifhed mind! This is beauty in a maze. Such occupations filled up her juvenile years. Her nobleft proficiencies were mufic, drawing, &c. but an injudicious choice of books exclu-ded their influence, if they had any, from her mind. Thus we may conclude her courfe of education led her to fet the greateft eftimate on this external new kind of creature; whilft her internal fource—her immortal part, remained, as in a fog, or like a gem in a tube of adamant.

NATURE had been lavifh in the formation of FATIMA. And on her firft appearance, one muft have been ftrong-

ly impreffed in her favor. But what fays the fequel?—
The invigorating influence of Venus had fcarcely warmed
her bofom, when, towards the clofe of a beautiful, foft
day, in her rural excurfion, fhe firft beheld PHILANDER;
who had become a gleaner in her father's fields. A mutual impulfe of paffions, till then unfelt, fired their bofoms: For PHILANDER was much indebted to nature for a
polifhed form; and fomething uncommonly attracting in
his looks, feemed to veil the neglect of his mind. Unfortunate youth! His parents were poor: and to add to
his mifery, they had deprived him of their only, and yet
moft important, legacy—I mean, the cultivation of his
mind. Had not this been his lot, he might have made
himfelf rich and FATIMA happy.

AFTER this, FATIMA's chief delight was—to walk in
the fields, to fee her father's flock, and to liften to the
pipe of PHILANDER. Repeated interviews brought them
more acquainted with each other. Each attempted to
fteal the luftre of the eye and the crimfon blufh; which
a too warm conftitution could ill conceal. At length, an
unreferved familiarity took place. Both had been taught
to *love;* and both had miffed PLATO's and URANIA's fyftem, which fhould have taught them—*how.* FATIMA
durft not let her parents know, that a peafant poffeffed
her virginal love. She, therefore, under pretence of re-
galing herfelf in the garden, often referved the keys,
that fecured its avenues: and whilft the dew diftilled its
penfive fweets, the fequeftered alcove, or embowered
grafs plat, too often witneffed their lambent amours.

ONE night—a night that muft ever remain horrible to
their remembrance, and which fhould be obliterated from

the annals of time—FATIMA fat at the window of her apartment, to behold, rather than contemplate, the beauties of
the evening. The hamlet was at reft, when fhe difcovered PHILANDER paffing in the ftreet. Her *difhabille* too
plainly difclofed her charms, when fhe haftened with the
fatal key to the garden gate; where PHILANDER had juft
arrived. The maffy door having grated upon its hinges,
they walked a number of times through the bowling-
green, till at length, almoft imperceptibly, they found
themfelves at the door, that led to FATIMA's apartment.
—The clock ftruck twelve, when they tip-toed through
a number of windings, till they arrived at the chamber;
which, till then, had been an afylum for the virginity of
FATIMA.

It is needlefs to paint the fcenes, that fucceeded. A
taper, fhe had left burning on her fcrutoire, with the rays
of the moon, reflected a dim light on the rich furniture
of the room, and on the alcove; in which lay, for the laft
time, the tranquil FATIMA! But this light, feeble as it
was, difclofed to PHILANDER a thoufand new charms in.
the fafcinating fpectacle of fo much love and beauty.· Sen-
fuality took the lead of every reafoning faculty; and both
became inftrumental to their own deftruction. PHILAN-
DER became a total flave to his paffions. He could no
longer revere the temple of chaftity. He longed to erect
his fatal triumph on the ruins of credulous virtue. He
faw nothing but what ferved to inflame his paffions. His
eyes rioted in forbidden delights. And his warm embraces kindled new fires in the bofom of this beauteous
maid.—The night was filent as death: not a zephyr was

heard to ruſtle in the leaves below—but HEAVEN was a recording witneſs to their criminal pleaſures!

THE loſt FATIMA beheld her brutal raviſher with horror and diſtraction. But from that fatal moment, his enthuſiaſtic love cooled; and he ſhunned her private receſſes and public haunts. FATIMA, to avoid the indignation of her parents, eloped from them. Her eyes were opened! Many were her wearisome ſteps to find an aſylum from that guilt, which, through her parents' neglect, ſhe incurred on herſelf. In vain did ſhe lament, that ſome piteous cherub had not preſerved her to a more propitious fate—that ſhe had not been doomed to a cloiſtered convent, to have made an eternal vow of celibacy, to have proſtrated herſelf to wooden ſtatues, to have kiſſed the feet of monks and to have pined away her life in ſolitude!—Thus ſhe continues to mourn the loſs of that happineſs, ſhe loſt through neglect of education.

FATIMA was in her *female* attire—our Heroine was a *ſoldier*. And I ſhould ſacrifice many tender feelings to prefer, to my FAIR readers—the ſituation of either.

I CONFESS, I might juſtly be thought a monſter to the female ſex, were I willing to ſuggeſt, that her original motive was the company of the venal ſycophant, the plotting knave, the diſguſting, ugly debauchee: or that her turning volunteer in Columbia's cauſe, was a meditated plot againſt her own ſex. Oh! this would be too cruel.—Cuſtom is the dupe of fancy: nor can we ſcarcely conceive what may not be reliſhed, till the fugitive has worn out every ſhift. But let us remember, though it conſtitutes our eſteem and reverence, it does not, always, our prudence and propriety. A high cut robe, for in-

31

stance, though it may agreeably feast the imagination, may not prove the most prudent garb for every fair object, who wears it. But in the asylum of female protection, may I not be thought their meanest votary, should not a humble ejaculation prevent every robe-wearer from being led

"O'er infant innocence—to hang and weep,
Murder'd by ruffian hands—when smiling in its sleep!"

It need not be asked, whether a proper union of the sexes is recommendable and just. Nature claims this as her primogenial and indissoluble bond: And national custom establishes the mode. But to mention the intercourse of our Heroine with her sex, would, like others more dangerous, require an apology I know not how to make. It must be supposed, she acted more from necessity, than a voluntary impulse of passion; and no doubt, succeeded beyond her expectations, or desires. Harmless thing! An useful veteran in war!—An inoffensive companion in love! These are certainly requisites, if not virtues. They are always the soldier's glory; but too seldom his boast. Had she been capacitated and inclined to prey, like a vulture, on the innocence of her sex; vice might have hurried vice, and taste have created appetition. Thus, she would have been less entitled to the clemency of the public. For individual crimes bring on public nuisances and calamities: And debauchery is one of the first. But incapacity, which seldom begets desire, must render her, in this respect, unimpeachable.

Remember, females, I am your advocate; and, like you, would pay my devoirs to the Goddess of love. Admit that you conceived an attachment for a *female foldier*. What is the harm? She acted in the department of that fex, whofe embraces you naturally feek. From a like circumftance, we are liable to the fame impulfe. Love is the ruling dictate of the foul.—But viewing VENUS in all her influential charms—did fhe gain too great an afcendancy over that virtue, which fhould guard the receptacle of your love? Did the dazzling enchantrefs, after fafcinating you in her wilds, inhumanly leave you in a fituation—ready to yield the pride and ornament of your fex —your white robed innocence, a facrifice to lawlefs luft and criminal pleafure!—I congratulate the fair object, whoever fhe was, and rejoice with her moft fincerely, that fhe happily miftook the *ferocity* of the *lion*, for the *harmleffnefs* of the *lamb!* You have thus, wonderfully, efcaped the fatal rock, on which fo many of both fexes (it wounds me to repeat it!) have made fhipwreck of this ineftimable prize. You have thus preferved inviolate, your coronet of glory, your emblematic diadem of innocence, friendfhip, love, and beauty—the pride of your fex—the defpair and envy of the diffolute incendiary! This is your virginity—that chaftity which is fuch an additional ornament to beauty.

THE fun, with all his eclat, which has fo often gone down on your innocence, fhall continue to rife with increafing beauty, and give you frefh fatisfaction and delight. Taunt, invective and calumny may ftorm; and, tho' you may dread, you may defy, their rage.—But what will be a ftill greater fource of comfort, old reflection fhall not awfully ftare you in the face on your bridal day: nor remorfe fteal an imperceptible courfe into your bofoms; nor, as with the fcorpion's dagger, wound your tendereft place. Inftead of a girdle of thorns, the amaranthine wreath fhall encircle you, and the banners of friendfhip, love and tranquillity fhall ever hover over you. Whilft others, guilty of a breach in this emblem of paradife, may efcape with impunity the deferved lafh of afperfion from a chafte husband, (for there may be chafte men as well as chafte women) you fhall be prefented to your partner of life, an object uncontaminated from the hands of your CREATOR. And next to the GIVER of all good, he fhall extatically hold you in his embraces, and efteem you as the object of his fupreme affections.

As the pure and brilliant dew-drop on the rofe and lilly gathers their fragrance; as the furface of the limpid ftream outfpreads its azure flow for curious inveftigation: So, fhall your words and actions be received by all who are round about you. Your children, as coming from an unpolluted fource, fhall rife up and call you bleffed. And whilft the dupe and rude in thought fhall deign to bow at your fhrine, your worth fhall daily be enhanced in your husband's eftimation. He fhall not forget to heap encomiums on your merit, when he fits among the primogeniture of the land. A mutual exchange and increafe of affection will be perpetuated to you, through a long feries of fatisfactory enjoyments—even till fecond childifhnefs fteals upon you, and till time itfelf diffolves your earthly compact, and feals you in the duft. Heaven, the refidentiary manfion of blifs, for the faithful and pure, will, at laft, condefcend to crown you with a rich reward for your fervices, for your integrity and virtue.—FEMALES, ADIEU!

COLUMBIA demands our review.—To ftretch the memory

to the momentous EPOCH, when the optics of fage COLUM-
BUS, firft lighted on the American fhores, and to trace the
mazy clue of her annals, from a favage wildernefs to the
prefent period, when fhe ftands confeffed, a new *ftar*
among the nations of the earth—an elyfian field of beauty,
muft feaft the intellectual fyftem with every idea, perhaps
of pain and pleafure. When we remember the fweat of
the brow in the culture of her once ftubborn glebe, our
encounters with the tomahawk, and with the more formidable weapons of death in our late revolution ; the breaft
muft be callous to fenfation, that does not own the privileges and felicity, to which we are now exalted, have been
bought at a rate, dear enough to be inftructive.

WE have moulded a conftitutional government, at our
option. It alfo guarantees to us the privilege of making
amendments : and under its continued aufpices, what
good may we not anticipate ? Scarcely three hundred
years have rolled away, fince America was a folitary haunt
for favages and beafts. But behold, now, under the foftering hands of induftry and economy, how fhe fmiles ;
even from the magnificence of the city, paffing the pleafant country villas, to the mofs-covered cot! The fun of
fcience is gleaming on her remoteft corners; and his
penetrating rays are faft illuminating the whole empire of
reafon.—Hail, then, thou happy, radiant SOURCE of beauty!
—Our progrefs has, indeed, been rapid : Heaven grant it
may be lafting.

O *war*, thou worft of fcourges ! Whilft we hear of thy
depredations, which are now laying Europe in blood and
afhes—indeed, Columbia, we think of you ! And is there
any, who are ignorant of the honors of war, and thirft for

the gratification? Let fuch be cautious of their propenfities. You have heard, I fuppofe, that an Emperor,
Cardinal, or a gracious, fable-headed Pope, has iffued an
edict, laying claim to a certain territory, to which, no
body ever miftrufted he was entitled. But the nation has
turned infidels to his *creed;* and though he is a man of
infult, he is not to be infulted.—He collects his forces,
and marches to glory; kills millions, gains his conqueft,
renews his quarrels and puts others to the fword. His
men are called *veterans!* What are ours called?—A
youth, a female, a young nymph may tell.

AND muft the fcourge of war again caft a gloom over
COLUMBIA's beauteous furface? Muft infernal furies, from
diftant regions, confpire her ruin? Shall her own SONS,
forgetful of that happinefs they have purchafed fo dearly,
unmindful of an infinite variety of alluring objects, that
furround them, grow wanton in luxury and indolence,
and thirft, like tygers, to imbrue their hands in the blood
of any of the human race? GOD forbid! For in that
day, the beaft fhall again retire to his lair; the bird fhall
clap its well fledged wing, and bear itfelf acrofs the ocean;
(HEAVEN grant it there may have a chance to land!)
and the fifh fhall lie in torpitude, or refufe the angler's
bait—but all, looking up to that fublime and exalted
creature, MAN, bewail the time he had rule given over
them!

BUT, COLUMBIA, this muft never be faid of your progeny.
It has been neceffary they fhould encounter the *bitters*—
the *calamities* of *war.* It now remains, that they *tafte* and
long preferve the *fweets of profperity.* The fylvan bard
fhall compofe for YOU, his canzonets and roundelays: And

the minftrel fhall rehearfe them to his tranquil audience, in your filent, green-wood fhade. From the city, the failor fhall quit your beauteous fhores with reluctance and with a figh. And while old ocean is heaving his barque from his home, as your leffening turrets bluely fade to his view; he fhall climb the maft—and while he is fnatching a fond review, reflection fhall feaft his memory with every pleafurable and penfive fenfation. And though feparated from his natal clime by oceans, climes and nations; his choiceft hopes and wifhes fhall dwell in his native land.

It remains, to authenticate the facts afferted.—The following firft appeared in a New York paper, from which it was copied in others, in Maffachufetts.

NEW YORK, *January* 10, 1784.

AN extraordinary inftance of *virtue* in a FEMALE SOL-DIER, has occurred, lately in the *American army*, in the Maffachufetts line, viz. a lively, comely young nymph, nine-teen years of age, dreffed in man's apparel, has been dif-covered; and what redounds to her honor, fhe has ferved in the character of a foldier for nearly *three* years, undif-covered. During this time, fhe difplayed much alertnefs, chaftity and valor: having been in feveral engagements, and received two wounds—a fmall fhot remaining in her to this day.—She was a remarkable, vigilant foldier on her poft; always gained the applaufe of her officers—was never found in liquor, and always kept company with the moft temperate and upright foldiers.—For feveral months, this Gallantrefs ferved, with credit, in a General Officer's

family.   A violent illnefs, when the troops were at Philadelphia, led to the difcovery of her fex.   She has fince
been honorably difcharged from the Army, with a reward,* and fent to her connexions; who, it appears, live
to the Eaftward of Bofton, at a place, called *Meduncook*.

THE caufe of her perfonating a man, it is faid, proceeded from the rigor of her parents, who exerted their
prerogative to induce her marriage with a young gentleman, againft whom, fhe had conceived a great antipathy;
together with her being a remarkable heroine and warmly
attached to the caufe of her country: In the fervice of
which, it muft be acknowledged, fhe gained reputation;
and, no doubt, will be noticed in the hiftory of our grand
revolution.—She paffed by the name of ROBERT SHURT-
LIEFF, while in the army, and was borne on the rolls as
fuch.—For particular reafons, her name is witheld: But
the facts, above mentioned, are unqueftionable and unblemifhed.

BOSTON, *Auguft* 1, 1786.

To all whom it may concern.

THESE may certify, that ROBERT SHURTLIEFF was a
Soldier in my *Regiment*, in the *Continental Army*, for the
town of Uxbridge in the Commonwealth of Maffachufetts,
and was inlifted for the term of *three years*—that he had
the confidence of his Officers, did his duty, as a faithful
and good *Soldier*, and was honorably difcharged the
Army of the United States.

HENRY JACKSON, *late Col.*
in the American Army.

* THIS fhe has not received. — EDITOR. [*H. Mann.*]

RESOLVE *of the* GENERAL COURT—*January* 20, 1792.

ON the petition of DEBORAH GANNET, praying compenfation for fervices performed in the late Army of the United States:

WHEREAS it appears to this Court, that the faid DEBORAH GANNET inlifted under the name of ROBERT SHURTLIEFF, in Capt. WEBB's company in the fourth Maffachufetts regiment, on *May* 21, 1782, and did actually perform the duties of a *foldier*, in the late Army of the United States, to the 23 day of October, 1783; for which, fhe has received no compenfation. And whereas it further appears, that the faid DEBORAH exhibited an extraordinary inftance of *female heroifm*, by difcharging the duties of a faithful, gallant *foldier;* and at the fame time, preferved the virtue and *chaftity* of her *fex*, unfufpected and unblemifhed, and was difcharged from the fervice, with a fair and honorable *character*.

THEREFORE, *refolved*, that the Treafurer of this Commonwealth be, and hereby is directed to iffue his note, to faid DEBORAH, for the fum of *thirty four pounds*, bearing intereft from *October* 23, 1783.

———

As it is nothing ftrange, that any girl fhould be married, and have children; it is not to be expected, that one, diftinguifhed, like Mifs SAMPSON, fhould efcape. The greateft diftinction lies in the qualification for this important bufinefs. And, perhaps, the greateft requifite for EDUCATION is—complete union with the parties, both in theory and practice. This is remarkably verified in the

32

party spirits that bring on wars and public calamities. They extend to the remote fire fide.

IT is hear-fay, that Mrs. GANNET refufes her husband the rites of the marriage bed. She muft, then, condefcend to fmile upon him in the filent alcove, or grafs plat; as fhe has a child, that has fcarcely left its cradle. It is poffible, fhe experiences, not only corporal but mental inabilities; and in mercy to her generation, would keep it in non-exiftence.—But this is not the part of a biographer. I am forry to learn, this is moftly female complaint; and not authentic: For her neareft neighbors affert, there is a mutual harmony fubfifting between her and her companion; which, by the bye, is generally the reverfe with thofe deprived of this hymenial blifs. All who are acquainted with her, muft acknowledge her complaifant and humane difpofitions. And while fhe difcovers a tafte for an elegant ftile of living; fhe exhibits, perhaps, an unufual degree of contentment, with an honeft farmer, and three endearing children, confined to a homely cot, and a hard-earned little farm.

SHE is fometimes employed in a fchool in her neighborhood. And her firft maxim of the government of children is *implicit obedience.* I cannot learn, fhe has the leaft wifh to ufurp the prerogatives of our fex. For, fhe has often faid, that nothing appears more beautiful in the *domeftic round,* than when the husband takes the lead, with difcretion, and is followed by his confort, with an amiable acquiefcence. She is, however, of opinion, that thofe women, who threaten their children with, "*I will tell your father*"—of a crime, they fhould correct, is infufing into them a fpirit of triumph, they fhould never know.

The cultivation of humanity and good nature is the grand bufinefs of education. And fhe has feen the ill effects of fighting, enough, to know the neceffity of fparing clubs and cuffs at home. The fame good temper, we would form in our offspring, fhould be exhibited in ourfelves. We fhould neither ufe our children as ftrangers; nor as the mere tools of fanciful fport. All tampering and loofe words with them, are, like playing, careleffly, with the lion or tiger, who will take advantage of our folly.—In fhort, inftructions fhould be infufed, as the dew diftils; and difcipline, neither rigid, nor tyrannic, fhould reft, like a ftable pillar.

How great—how facred are our obligations to our off-fpring! Females, who are the vehicles, by which they are brought into the world, cannot confider, too ferioufly, the fubject. Let it not be delayed, then, till that love, which coalefces the fexes, produces an object for experiment. Form a pre-affection for the fweet *innocent*, while in embryo—that it may be cherifhed, with prudence, when brought to view. And may *we* never have it to lament—that while any females contemplate, with abhorrence, a *female*, who voluntarily engages in the *field* of *battle—they* forget to recoil at the idea of coming off victorious from *battles*, fought by their own domeftic—*fire-fides!* We have now feen the diftinction of one *female*. May it ftimulate others to fhine—in the way, that VIRTUE prefcribes.

THE END.

LIST *of such* SUBSCRIBERS' NAMES *for this Work, as were returned to the Printers, previoufly to its coming from the Prefs.*

A

REV. David Avery, *Wrentham.*
Col. Philip Ammidon, *Mendon.*
Mr. Benjamin Allen, *R. I. College.*
    Armand Auboyneau,   *Do.*
    Jafon Abbot, *Boylfton.*
    Oliver Adams, *Milford.*
    John Whitefield Adams, *Medfield.*
    John Wickliffe Adams,   *Do.*
    Charles Aldrich, *Mendon.*
    Ahaz Allen,   *Do.*
    Seth Allen, *Sharon.*

B.

Mofes Bullen, Efq. *Medfield.*
Maj. Noah Butterworth, *Wrentham.*
Capt. Eli Bates, *Bellingham.*
Doct. Thomas Bucklin, *Hopkinton.*
Mr. Nicholas Bowen, Merchant, *Providence.*
    George Benfon, Do.   *Do.*
    Liberty Bates, *R. I. College.*
    John Baldwin,   *Do.*
    Lemuel Le Bararon, *Do.*
    Allen Bourn, *Do.*
    Horatio G. Brown, *Do.*

Mr. Jofeph Brown, *Byfield.*
Jafon Babcock, *Dedham.*
Eli Blake, *Wrentham.*
Ifaac Bennett, *Do.*
David Blake, *Do.*
Henry S. Bemis, *Stoughton.*
George Boyd, *Bofton.*
Amos Boyden, *Medfield.*
Baruch Bullard, *Uxbridge.*
Ebenezer Bugbee, *Roxbury.*

C

Mr. Nathan Cary, *R. I. College.*
Judah A. Mc. Clellen, *Do.*
Gaius Conant, *Do.*
Jofeph B. Cook, *Do.*
Afa Cheney, *Milford.*
Ichabod Corbett, *Do.*
Luther Cobb, *Bellingham.*
John Cobb, *Wrentham.*
Jofeph Cleavland, *Do.*
Jofeph Cleale, *Byfield.*
Jabez Chickering, jun. *Dedham.*
Winflow Corbett, *Mendon.*
George Crane, *Stoughton.*
Jofeph Curtis, *Roxbury.*
Calvin Curtis, *Sharon.*

D

Capt. Ifaac Doggett, *Dedham.*
Lieut. Samuel Day, *Wrentham.*
Mr. Andrew Dexter, jun. *R. I. College.*

Mr. Paul Dodge, *R. I. College.*
James Dupee, *Walpole.*
Jofeph Daniels, Merchant, *Franklin.*
John Dummer, *Byfield.*

E

Capt. Amos Ellis, *Bellingham.*
Mr. Samuel Ervin, *R. I. College.*
James Ervin, *Do.*
John Ellis, *Dedham.*
Aaron Ellis, *Walpole.*
Afa Ellis, jun. *Brookfield.*
Ebenezer Eftee, *Milford.*
Samuel Elliot, *Byfield.*

F

Hon. Timothy Farrar, *New Ipfwich.*
Amariah Froft, Efq. *Milford.*
Lieut. Samuel Fuller, *Walpole.*
Mr. Theodore D. Fofter, *R. I. College.*
Drury Fairbanks, *Do.*
Ebenezer Fales, *Walpole.*
Suel Fales, *Do.*
Shubael Fales, *Do.*
Elijah Fifher, *Sharon.*
Ebenezer Fofter, *Wrentham.*
William B. Fifher, *Do.*

G

Rev. Thomas Gray, *Roxbury.*
David S. Grenough, Efq. *Do.*
Mr. William Green, *R. I. College.*

Mr. Franklin Green, *R. I. College.*
Ifaac Greenwood, *Providence.*
Otis Greene, *Mendon.*
Jofeph Gay, *Wrentham.*
Ephraim Grove, *Bridgewater.*
John Green, *Medway.*
Mifs Sufanna Gay, *Wrentham.*

H

Alexander Hodgdon, Efq. *Dedham.*
Maj. Samuel Hartfhorn, *Walpole.*
Mr. John P. Hitchcock, *R. I. College.*
Wafhington Hathaway, *Do.*
Samuel Hayward, *Milford.*
Nathan Hawes, *Wrentham.*
David Hartwell, *Stoughton.*

I

Mr. Thomas P. Ives, Merchant, *Providence.*
James Jones, *Byfield.*
Phinehas Johnfon, *R. I. College.*
Jeffe Joflin, *Thompfon.*

K

Mr. Richard King, *Byfield.*
Afa Kingsbury, *Franklin.*
Ambrofe Keith, *Northbridge.*

L

Mr. Grant Learned, *Bofton.*
Laban Lewis, *Stoughton.*
Mifs Alice Leavens, *Walpole.*

M

Col. Timothy Mann, *Walpole.*
Sabin Mann, *Medfield.*
Capt. Daniel Morfe, *Brookfield.*
Mr. William P. Maxwell, *R. I. College.*
Elias Mann, *Northampton.*
Windfor Mainard, *Mendon.*
Paul Moody, *Byfield.*
John Meffinger, jun. *Wrentham.*
David Moores, *Byfield.*
Lewis Miller, *Dedham.*

N

Mr. John Nelfon, Merchant, *Milford.*

O

Mr. Nathaniel G. Olney, *R. I. College.*
Mifs Hannah Orne, *Bofton.*

P

Doctor Elias Parkman, *Milford,* 6 *Copies.*
Capt. Abijah Pond, *Wrentham.*
Deac. Jacob Pond, *Do.*
Mr. Eleazar Perry, Merchant, *Hopkinton.*
Samuel Penniman, *Milford.*
Jofiah Penniman, *Mendon.*
Baruch Penniman, *Do.*
Abiel Pettee, *Dedham,*
Adam Ward Partridge, *Chefterfield.*

R

Benjamin Randall, Efq. *Sharon.*

33

John M. Roberts, A. B. *R. I. College.*
Mr. John Rogers, Merchant, *Cumberland.*
James Reed, *Stoughton.*

S

Seth Smith, jun. Efq. *Norton,* 6 *Copies.*
Ebenezer Seaver, Efq. *Roxbury.*
Capt. John Soule, *Middleborough,* 6 *Copies.*
Mr. John Sabin, *R. I. College.*
    John Simmons, *Do.*
    William H. Sabin, *Do.*
    Jonas Smith, *Rutland.*
    Afa Smith, *Brookfield.*
    Lebbeus Smith, *Medfield.*
    Samuel Smith, jun. *Walpole.*
    John Shepard, *Foxborough.*
    David Southworth, *Ward.*
    Oliver Shepard, *Stoughton.*
    Gordon Strobridge, *Northfield,* (*Ver.)*
Mifs Lucinda Smith, *Norton.*

T

Doft. Ezra Thayer, *Swanzey,* (*N. H.)*
    Daniel Thurber, *Mendon.*
Mr. Alvan Tobey, *R. I. College.*
    James Tallmadge, jun. *Do.*
    James Thompfon, *Do.*
    Allen Tillinghaft, Merchant, *Wrentham.*
    Aaron Thomas, *Boylfton.*

U

Mr. Alvan Underwood, *R. I. College.*
    Jonathan Upham, *Stoughton.*

W

Rev. William Williams, *Wrentham*.
Mr. Edmund T. Waring, *R. I. College*.
Conrade Webb, *Do*.
William H. Williams, *Do*.
———— Witherſpoon, *Do*.
Nathaniel Willis, *Boſton*.
Joſeph Ware, *Medway*.
Obed Wheelock, *Milford*.
Abner Wight, *Do*.
Moſes Woodman, *Byfield*.
Miſs Hannah Wight, *Foxborough*.

ERRATA.

PAGE 37. line 23. after I, read *ſhould*. and for *highly* r. *meanly.*—
P. 47. l. 10. for 1756 read 1656.—P. 43. laſt line, for 1796 r. 1797.—
P. 76, l. 13. after revenue, r. *in America*.

The following were returned too late to be inserted in order.

CAPT. JOHN BLISS, *Springfield.*
Lieut. Samuel Bolter, *Northampton.*
Mr. John Breck, Merchant, *Do.*
Mrs. Sarah Chandler, *Boston.*
Jonathan Dwight, Att. at Law, *Springfield.*
Benjamin A. Edwards, Q. M. *Northampton.*
Mr. William Ely, *Springfield.*
 Daniel Fay, *Westbury.*
Jonathan Grout, Att. at Law, *Belcherstown.*
Ebenezer Hunt, jun. M. D. *Northampton.*
Mr. David Hunt, Merchant, *Do.*
 Jacob Hunt, *Do.*
 William Hutchens, *Do.*
 John W. Hooker, *Springfield.*
 James Ingols, *Northampton.*
 Samuel King, jun. *Do.*
Levi Lyman, Esq. *Do.*
Maj. Samuel Lyman, *Do.*
Daniel Lombard, Merchant, *Springfield.*
Lieut. Moses Parsons, jun. *Northampton.*
Mr. Seth Pomeroy, *Do.*
 Nathaniel Patten, *Hartford.*
Doct. George Rogers, *Northampton.*
Solomon Stoddard, Esq. *Do.*
Mr. Nathan Stores, *Do.*
 Levi Shepard, Merchant, *Do.*
 Charles Steele, *Boston.*
 Caleb Smith, *Hadley.*
 Jacob Wicker, *Northampton.*

INDEX.

INDEX.

P.

Patterson, Gen., 133, 181, 217, 219; Deborah's sex disclosed to him, 219–221 ; probably disclosed it to others, 229.
Pension office, documents from, xv., xvii.
Penthesilea, xxxi.
Pomeroy, Gen. Seth, a volunteer at Bunker Hill, 90.
Pratt, Rev. Stillman, xv., 124 ; visits the residence and grave of Mrs. Deborah Gannett, 230.
Prescott, Col. William, commands at Bunker Hill, 89.
Putnam, Gen. Israel, at Bunker Hill, 90.

R.

Report of a committee of Congress respecting Deborah Sampson, xx.
Resolve of Legislature of Massachusetts respecting Deborah Sampson, xxiv., 249.
Revival of religion in Middleborough, 101, 102.
Rhoades, Benjamin, xxii.
Robinson, Rev. John, of Leyden, 45, 46.
Rochambeau, Count, 144.

S.

Sampson, Abraham, 45 ; Ephraim, 51, 225 ; Henry, 45 ; Isaac, 46 ; Jonathan, 46, 50.
SAMPSON, DEBORAH, her story in brief, x., xi. When did she enlist ? xv., xviii., xxi., xxiii., xxv., xxix., 136. Applies for a pension, xv., xvi. Obtains a pension, xvii., xix. A

34

pension granted to her heirs, xviii., xix. Report of the committee on Pensions relative to her case, xx.–xxiii. Her petition to the Legislature of Massachusetts, xxiii. Resolve of the Legislature, xxiv. Action of the church in Middleborough on her case, xxviii. Her autograph, xxiv. Her character, xxxii., 113, 228–231. Her pedigree, 45–48. Her childhood, 52–59. Her home in childhood, 59. Her thirst for knowledge, 55, 60. Her slight opportunities, 56–59. Her early training, 59, 61. Her interest in public affairs, 76–78, 94, 109, 117. Her remarkable dream, 79–84. Her girlhood, 99. Teaches school, 100, 250. Becomes interested in religion, and joins the church, 102. Is excommunicated, xxviii. Dissatisfied with home employments, 111. Desires to travel, 113. Resolves to see the world, 114. A daydreamer, ib. First assumption of male attire, 114, 115. Visits a fortune-teller, 115. Secretly prepares for her departure, 116. Resolves to enlist as a soldier, 117. Unrequited affection of a young man for her, 121. First enlistment as a soldier, 124. Resumes female apparel, ib. Her irresolution, 125. Final departure in male attire, 126. Fears discovery and pursuit, 127. Partial engagement as one of the crew of a privateer, 128. FINAL ENLISTMENT, 129, 130. Arrives at West Point, 131, 136. Her military equipments, 133. · First en-